DOG LAW

Legal thrillers by Michael Monhollon

Criminal Intent

Trial by Ambush (Robing Starling #1)

Juggling Evidence (Robing Starling #2)

Dog Law (Robin Starling #3)

Laughing Heirs (Robin Starling #4)

Guilty Knowledge

A Robin Starling Legal Thriller
Volume 3

DOG LAW

Michael Monhollon

Reflection Publishing
Abilene, Texas

ISBN: 0971214247
ISBN-13: 978-0971214248

In memory of Sadie, who greeted each day with joy

It is the judges that make the common law. Do you know how they make it? Just as a man makes laws for his dog. When your dog does anything you want to break him of, you wait till he does it, and then beat him for it. This is the way you make laws for your dog: and this is the way the judges make law for you and me. They won't tell a man beforehand what it is he *should not do*—they won't so much as allow of his being told: they lie by till he has done something which they say he should not *have done*, and then they hang him for it.

Jeremy Bentham, 'Truth versus
Ashhurst' (1792).

Chapter 1

When I viewed Natalie Stevens through the small window of reinforced glass, she was sitting in the middle of a bench that was bolted to one wall, her shoulders slumped, her clasped hands between her knees. She was wearing faded jeans and a flannel shirt, and her light brown hair was pulled back in a long ponytail.

"That your client?" asked the deputy sheriff who had walked me in.

"I guess so." I'd been told Natalie was a college student just home for Christmas break, and this girl looked the part.

The deputy opened the door for me. The cell had a cement floor and cinderblock walls painted the color of pond scum. As I entered, Natalie looked up at me, then down at the floor again. She had a pretty face with a complexion that was flawless but for a dusting of pinpoint freckles on her cheekbones and across the bridge of her nose. I was encouraged. Probably the case would never go to a jury—this might be the case where I learned to negotiate a plea bargain—but I had to believe that good looks were not a bad attribute for a client accused of a felony.

As the door thumped shut behind me, I went and sat on the bench next to her, setting my briefcase on the floor by my feet and, next to it, the drawstring bag containing the sneakers I had worn to walk across downtown Richmond, draping my coat over both. Natalie's jeans had a hole in one leg, and I was wearing a wool-blend dress, so I could see three of our four knees.

"I'm Robin Starling," I said, turning my head to look at her. "Your lawyer, if you want me."

She nodded, mouth pursing slightly, but her eyes stayed on the floor. "They said they would appoint one for me."

"You're Natalie Stevens, I take it."

She took a breath, nodded. "You got that right." She gave the floor a smile that showed a dimple in the cheek nearest me, but a tear dropped from her face to spot the floor.

"I'm not court appointed though."

Her head whipped toward me, her eyes lighting. "Daddy's back? He hired you?"

"No. Your stepmother. Chloe."

She deflated, her eyes losing their focus as she turned her head away. "Chloe," she said.

"She gave me a ten thousand dollar retainer, said to spare no expense."

"To do what? Make sure I get the chair?"

"You're charged with manslaughter, not first degree murder."

"Distinction noted."

"Besides which, in Virginia the default option is death by lethal injection. A person has to choose the electric chair."

"Well, I'll try to find something to be glad about there."

"You've read *Pollyanna*."

She looked startled. "I guess I have. It was on my grandmother's shelves when I was growing up."

"Actually, my understanding is that I'm supposed to represent you to the best of my ability," I said.

"Ah. The best of your ability."

"It's what I've got."

"Yes. It is."

"What's that supposed to mean?" I asked.

"Chloe hired you. There had to be a kicker."

"She was acting for your father, or so she said."

"I haven't been able to get hold of him. Not that I've had a lot of opportunity."

"He's lost his cell phone. That's what Chloe said, anyway."

"That's encouraging."

"You want to tell me about it?"

"Not really."

"Would it help if I told you something about myself?"

"No."

"I went to law school at the University of Virginia," I said. "Graduated in the top ten percent of my class. Before that I was an English major at Washington & Lee, where I played basketball. My senior year we went to the Final Four."

She looked at me with what I took to be a spark of interest. "I'm a freshman at Longwood. I play soccer."

"That's Division I, isn't it? You JV?"

"Varsity."

"Very impressive, especially for a freshman. How'd you do this season?"

"Second round of the playoffs."

"Well, that's not bad."

For a while, neither of us said anything.

"If it helps, I didn't like your stepmom much," I said.

"It's because you're not a man."

"That's probably true. With her in the room, a lot of the men I know would have trouble keeping the slobber off their chins."

It earned me a snort, so I pressed my advantage: "I on the other hand, while I had to acknowledge that she was the most attractive woman in the room, was able to keep my salivary glands under control."

One side of her mouth quirked upward, which I thought was a major achievement on my part given that she was sitting in a jail cell. Her eyes cut toward me and away. "I don't know what you're talking about. You're stunning," she told the floor. She glanced at me again, and I cocked an eyebrow at her. "Okay, striking," she said.

"I'm tall."

"Yes, you are that." She sighed.

"When was it the police told you they were getting you a lawyer?"

"The first time was right there in the house. They asked my name, if that was my Lexus in the garage, if I'd been driving it last night."

"What did you tell them?"

"Natalie Stevens. Yes, it was my Lexus. Why did they want to know?"

"What did they tell you?"

"That I had the right to remain silent, I had the right to an attorney, all that stuff."

"And then what?"

"They asked me if I understood those rights. I said yes. Then they asked me again if I'd been driving the Lexus."

"And you said…"

She shook her head. "I didn't have anything to say that would do me any good, so I remained silent."

"That's good."

She looked at me with eyes that were suddenly bloodshot. "It is?"

"You look like a pampered little coed who spends her evenings reading romance novels by the fire, but you play Division I soccer and you can keep your mouth shut in police custody. That makes you one in a million."

Tears welled in her eyes, and she turned them back to the floor. I could hear her breathing.

"They say I killed some man down on the Southside sometime after midnight yesterday," she said in a low voice. "That I ran right over him and left him for…dead." Her voice hitched on the last word, and she broke off.

"But you didn't," I said.

"Would you believe me if I said I didn't?"

"I wouldn't disbelieve you."

"What does that mean?"

"I'd take your statement under advisement: Natalie is accused of felony hit-and-run, but she denies it. I need to get more facts."

"They showed me a picture. The police. His head was crushed, and most of his face…"

"It's all right," I said when it became clear she wasn't going to finish the sentence, though of course it wasn't all right. "Was this supposed to have happened last night, sometime this morning?"

She nodded.

"How did you happen to be driving around the Southside in the middle of the night? Can you tell me?"

She raised her shoulders slowly, then dropped them. "I wouldn't have said I was. I would have said I was home in bed before midnight, that I'd been at a party, but I was feeling sick."

"Why not say it?"

"Somebody saw me, evidently."

"Somebody who knew you?"

She shook her head. "I don't think so, but they got the license number of my car."

"And you don't remember any of it." She took a breath, blew it out through pursed lips.

"I was at a party, like I said. I had a couple of drinks."

Uh oh, I thought. "Two drinks?"

"Maybe one-and-a-half. I didn't finish the second one."

"What were you drinking? Mason jars of white lightning?"

"Beer. They had a keg, red plastic cups."

She was eighteen or nineteen and couldn't have bought the beer herself.

"The police give you a breathalyzer?"

"They took a blood sample."

"When did you stop drinking last night?"

She shrugged. "Ten, ten-thirty? Before eleven."

"That'll be all right then."

"Like I said, I started feeling sick."

"Nausea? Headache?"

"Weird, disconnected. I'd be in one room talking to someone, then I'd be in another room talking to someone else, and I couldn't remember anything in between. It was like I was hopping from one point in time to another, not living in the moments in between."

"'Billy Pilgrim has come unstuck in time,'" I said, making a literary allusion of my own.

"What?"

"It's a novel. Kurt Vonnegut."

"Oh." Evidently, she hadn't read Vonnegut. Her Eleanor Porter reference was a fluke.

"Where was this party?" I asked.

"An apartment out in Short Pump. A couple of guy friends from high school live there."

I frowned. Short Pump was in the far West End. I wondered where on the Southside this accident had occurred. "What high school?" I asked.

"St. Catherine's."

"I thought that was an all-girl school."

"The guys went to St. Christopher's. Both schools are Episcopal and have a lot of combined classes once you get to high school."

"Do you remember driving home from the party?"

"I think so. I remember being sick, that strange, disconnected feeling, and wanting to go home. I remember..." Her voice faded until it was barely audible. "...being in the car, a traffic light turning yellow, then red, as I jerked to a stop. I remember some street signs. I know I shouldn't have been driving, but I don't remember hitting anyone."

"And don't remember crossing the James River to the Southside."

She shook her head.

"You were just kind of bouncing along the timeline all the way home."

"The only thing I remember after I got home was brushing my teeth. When all the pounding on the door woke me up, I was in my clothes, kind of rolled up in the comforter on top of the bed. Evidently, I didn't even crawl in."

"Who were these guys who were hosting the party?"

"I told you. A couple of guys from…"

"Their names," I said.

"Oh." She gave them to me. I got out a legal pad and jotted them down, along with the name of the apartment complex and the name of the street it was on.

"How long did you sleep after you got home?" I asked.

"Till nearly one o'clock this afternoon. That's when the police showed up."

I'd appeared with a defendant before a magistrate once before, and the appearance on that occasion had been conducted in her office, her sitting behind her desk and looking up at us. This time a deputy sheriff led us to a little courtroom and stood facing us at the corner of the bench, right hand over his left, looking ready to leap to the defense of the magistrate should we rush the bench.

"Is this Natalie Stevens?" the woman sitting above us asked. She wore glasses with square, black plastic frames.

"Yes, your honor," I said. "I'm Robin Starling. I'll be representing her."

"Is that right, Ms. Stevens?"

Natalie cleared her throat. "Yes, ma'am."

The magistrate looked as if she would say something about the honorific, but she let it go. "You've seen the complaint?" she asked me.

"No, your honor."

She held up some papers. As I went forward to take them from her, the deputy sheriff stiffened, but didn't try to repel me. As I returned to my place beside my client, the magistrate said, "She's charged with felony hit-and run."

I glanced through the complaint as she read it to us. Someone named Kim Beecher had called 911 to report a hit-and-run at 1:34 a.m. Monday morning and had given police a license plate number. The number had led them to a residence in Wyndham, where they had found a Lexus CT 200 parked in an open garage. It had the license plate they were looking for. The left headlight was broken and a substance that appeared to be blood was on one of the remaining lens fragments and on the bumper below it. A woman who identified herself as Natalie Stevens opened the door in response to their knock. She had admitted to owning the Lexus in the garage.

The magistrate finished reading the complaint and asked Natalie if she would like to enter a plea.

"Not guilty."

I could barely hear her from where I stood beside her, but the magistrate seemed satisfied.

"I'm going to admit you to bail."

"Your honor," I said. "Given that Natalie is an A-student at Longwood College and has no criminal history, it might be more appropriate to release her on her own recognizance."

She eyed me over the tops of her glasses. "You think so."

"Her father owns a business here in town." Mark Stevens and his brother were partners in Stevens Imports, something I'd picked up from Natalie's stepmother when she hired me. "There's no chance she'll fail to appear."

"No, chance at all, you think?"

"Well, there's a chance she'll be hit by a meteor and all this will be moot, but it's not a chance we need to worry about."

Her mouth twitched. I think I almost persuaded her, but when she spoke finally, she said, "I'll set bail at seventy-five thousand dollars. We'll all sleep better." She picked up her gavel and cracked it on the bench, and the hearing was over.

They put us in a room with a long plastic folding table and two metal chairs. "I'll get a matron," the deputy sheriff said as he left us. Neither of us sat down.

"What happens now?" Natalie asked me.

"I think they're going to bring you an orange jumpsuit and transport you to the city jail. I need to get hold of your stepmother to talk about making bail."

"She'll be delighted at the thought of me in jailhouse orange."

"There's not a lot of love lost between the two of you, is there?"

"Not a lot, no."

"I really didn't notice any animosity on her part this morning," I said in Chloe's defense. "She did overdo the sweetness a bit."

"She always does. It's to cover up the underlying animosity."

"She wrote me a ten-thousand-dollar check. If we can keep her overdoing the sweetness thing, we should have you home before the end of the day. Tomorrow at the latest."

She crossed to one of the metal folding chairs and dropped into it, causing the legs to scrape back along the floor. "I'll survive."

"Sure you will. You're a tough girl."

Her lip curled at me.

"Aren't you?"

"I guess we'll see."

Chapter 2

The Ironfronts, an office building with an iron façade painted white, dated from 1866, the year after the fire set by the retreating Confederate Army razed downtown Richmond. I was cold from my hike across downtown Richmond from the John Marshall Courthouse, so I took the stairs to the second floor and pushed through the double doors into the Executive Suites. The receptionist was a woman about my age with a mass of brown curls and a nose that could have served as the handle for a good-sized tea kettle.

"Hi, Robin," she said. "Back from court?" She handed me a pink square of paper with a phone message. I'd missed a call from Mark Stevens, Natalie's father.

"He didn't leave a message?"

"Just that he'd call back. He said he'd be out of pocket, so he didn't leave a number."

Great. The man in the world I most wanted to talk to. "Thanks, Carly." I crossed the reception area toward the archway in the wall of exposed brick. Halfway there I turned back.

"Carly? That woman who came to see me this morning?"

"Your first client." Carly beamed at me, a friendly, upbeat expression that made her look simple-minded.

"Yes. What did she say when she came in? Did she ask for me specifically?"

"Not specifically, no. She asked if we had any lawyers here in the Executive Suites, and I told her about you." Her smile, which had faltered a bit at my question, brightened again to full wattage.

"Thank you," I said. "Why not Dave, though?" Dave was the lawyer down the hall from me, six months on his own after six years with the commonwealth attorney's office. I, on the other hand, had been in the Executive Suites for two weeks.

"Well, I did," Carly admitted. "She said it was a criminal case, so I mentioned Dave and all his experience as an assistant D.A., and then I told her about you."

"And she chose me."

"She sure did."

"Well, thank you again."

I went through the archway into a small secretarial area that as yet boasted no secretary. It did have a water cooler, my one extravagance, and I got myself a drink in a paper cone. Three offices opened off the secretarial area, the one on the far left still vacant. Brooke Marshall's door was closed, so I went into my office on the right, a narrow room that ended in a rough wall of exposed brick. The wall needed a big, framed picture of a landscape to compensate for the lack of a window, but I hadn't gotten to it yet. I went around my desk, set my briefcase and the drawstring bag with my heels against the wall at the end of it, and sat in the faux-leather chair I had purchased at Costco the week before.

Chloe Stevens had sat in one of the client chairs facing me, the one on the left. She declined water, declined coffee, which I would have had to get from the Executive Suites' kitchen, and kept her coat on, an embroidered jacket that was almost as long as her dress. She did take off her sunglasses upon entering the windowless office, and, as she folded them, she sat in the client chair and crossed her legs. As short as her dress was, she had to cross them to keep from being indecent.

"I'm here about my stepdaughter Natalie," she said, her chin tucked and her expression wide-eyed and serious. "She was arrested for felony hit-and-run a short time ago." She had a rich, throaty voice that would have sounded seductive in other circumstances.

"A short time ago today?" I asked.

She looked at her watch, which hung loosely on her wrist like a bracelet. "About ninety minutes ago," she said. "A little less."

"You're working fast."

"She is my stepdaughter, and my husband is out of the country, so there's only me."

"You want me to represent her?"

"Yes. Money is no object. I'm prepared to write you a check for ten thousand dollars—unless that isn't enough."

"It should be enough. I charge by the hour. Your money starts off in a trust account: It's your money, but I'll be holding it to pay legal fees and expenses. Each week, I'll take out whatever I've earned and what I've had to spend on Natalie's account. You did say Natalie?"

"Natalie Stevens, yes. I'm Chloe Stevens."

"And I'm Robin Starling," I said again. "Can you tell me where the hit-and-run occurred?"

"Not exactly." She lifted her hands to smooth her long, dark hair in front of her shoulders. She was wearing a pale, silk blouse, open at the throat to show a pearl necklace. "It was somewhere on the Southside."

"Inside the city limits?"

"I don't know. I assume so."

I didn't ask her on what basis she assumed it. "What else can you tell me? Natalie hit somebody. Was the person on foot or in another vehicle?"

"On foot, I think. One headlight of her car was broken, and there was blood."

"Blood on the front of her car?"

Chloe nodded solemnly, and rubbed her hands on her bare thighs, nicely tanned even in winter.

"Do you know who she hit? Was it a man or a woman?"

"Man, I think. I don't know. I don't think they've identified him. The tires went over his head, tore most of his face off, I understand. Of course, Natalie was pretty hysterical." Chloe, clearly, was not.

"Who told you this? Natalie? The police?"

She shook her head. "Natalie called from the police station. It took me some time to get her father on the phone—he's out of the country—then I came here."

There was something off about Chloe Stevens, as beautiful as she was. "How are you handling it?" I asked.

"I'm not the one who's in jail." A smile touched her mouth, giving it just a hint of frost, then it was gone.

"Where did they arrest her, do you know?"

"At our house, in Wyndam." She gave me the address, and I wrote it on my legal pad. I went ahead and asked her for her phone number while I was at it, and she gave me a landline and a cell.

"Were you home?" I asked.

She shook her head, her eyes still a bit too wide. I was having trouble getting a read on Chloe Stevens, but I got her to write me a check. Then I got her up and got her out of my office so I could get to work. Her jacket and the dress beneath it clung to her body so that I could see her hips move as she went out through the glass doors to the elevator.

"Who is Mrs. Onassis?" a voice said at my elbow, and I started. It was Brooke Marshall, in the doorway of her office.

"A client," I said. "Stepmother of a client, actually."

"She could start a fire."

I glanced at her, grinned. Outside the glass doors the elevator opened, and Chloe Stevens stepped onto it. She had her sunglasses on again, and her eyes were opaque. "How old would you say she is?" I asked.

"A woman like that, could be anywhere from twenty-five to forty."

"You'd assume near the upper end of that range, wouldn't you?"

"I'm catty enough that I'd like to," Brooke said.

Now that I had met Natalie at the police station and walked her through her presentation before the magistrate, it was time to talk to Chloe again. I took a breath, then leaned over to get my legal pad out of my briefcase. Chloe Stevens' phone numbers were on the first page. I dialed the landline first.

"Yes," Chloe said in her throaty voice.

"Hello, Ms. Stevens. It's Robin Starling."

"Hello, Ms. Starling."

"I'm calling with an update. I've met with Natalie, and she's okay with me representing her. We've appeared before a magistrate, and bail's been set at seventy-five thousand dollars."

"Seventy-five thousand dollars!" She didn't sound shocked, more like she was rolling it around on her tongue because it was delicious.

"She's going to be in the Richmond City Jail until you can raise the money. Would you like me to contact a bail bondsman for you? If you'd like a recommendation, I'd go with Ricky Anderson, the Club-footed Tornado."

"The what?" She gave a little laugh.

"It's how he bills himself. He used to be a professional wrestler, but he's older now and largely gone to fat. I've dealt with him before though and found him to be very professional."

"Oh, I can manage seventy-five thousand on my own, I think."

"You'll need a certified check from your bank. If you'd like to bring me the check, I'd be happy to take care of it for you. If you want to do it yourself, you should call the jail first, just so you'll know which door to go in and who to ask for."

"Well, I want to thank you, Ms. Starling. You've been a wonder."

"I'd just need the funds to work with."

"I understand."

As I put down the phone, I bumped my computer mouse, and the monitor came on, displaying the game of Spider Solitaire I'd been in the middle of when Chloe Stevens showed up with her ten-thousand-dollar check. I saw a move, put my hand to the mouse to make it.

"You're back." Brooke Marshall was in my doorway.

"Your door was closed," I said. "I thought you had someone with you."

"I had work to do. Carly likes to stand at the door and talk."

"Yes, she does like to do that. You, on the other hand, like to come in and sit," I said as Brooke came in and dropped into the client chair Chloe Stevens had occupied a couple of hours before.

"Sorry. Am I interrupting something?"

I turned my monitor around so she could see it. She laughed and pushed her thick, pale red hair behind one ear. "Maybe you'll have less time for that now," she said. "Congratulations on the new client. I am surprised you got her, though."

"Thank you for the vote of confidence."

"I was coming back from the restroom when she was talking to Carly. You should have heard the build-up Carly gave Dave. You'd have thought he was Johnnie Cochrane." The lawyer who defended O.J. and won his acquittal.

"What did she say about me?" I asked.

"That you were new here and really, really nice, but she understood you'd been fired from your last job for being—" She dropped her voice to a conspiratorial whisper. "—something of a loose cannon." The drop in volume was a habit of speech Carly had when she was delivering the goods on someone.

"And after those introductions, Chloe chose me over Dave. Interesting. Disconcerting, even."

"She said her daughter would be more comfortable with a lady lawyer."

I shook my head. Lady lawyer was a phrase I'd be happy to go the rest of my life and never hear again. "Natalie—that's the daughter—stepdaughter actually—thought I must be incompetent if Chloe had hired me to defend her. Didn't seem to think Chloe had her best interests at heart."

"You do wonder why she'd be lawyer-shopping in an executive suite."

"Yes. I imagine that, like me, even like Dave from the D.A.'s office who's only been on his own six months, lawyers in executive suites aren't often well established. So Chloe showed up at one, chatted up the receptionist, and chose the least likely candidate available."

"That pretty clever really, if she wants to submarine her stepdaughter without being too obvious about it."

"Yes, Natalie's father is out of the country and seems to be out of pocket at the moment, but of course he'll be back. I may have scared her though. I recommended a bail bondsman and even told her what he looks like. Shows I've been around the block a few times."

"You have been around the block. Twice."

"Getting to be an old-timer."

"Does it bother you that she thought you'd be a lightweight?"

"Not at all. I'm a blonde female just a few months over thirty-one. I get that kind of thing all the time. What bothered me is that Chloe didn't seem to have those kinds of smarts. Street smarts, but not any understanding of commercial arrangements."

"What kind of street smarts do you think she has?"

"She's evidently the second wife of a wealthy businessman. She's used her looks to set herself up pretty well in life. Seemed to be trying to use her looks on me, too. Stroked her hair as she talked, crossed her legs, rubbed her thighs a couple of times."

Brooke's eyebrows had climbed her forehead.

"Fortunately, I'm immune," I said.

I hung around another hour waiting for Chloe to call back with instructions, or, alternatively, just to drop in with a nice, fat cashier's check. I didn't waste the afternoon completely. I finished my game of spider solitaire with a win—my stats were now above sixty percent—and started another one. I got on Facebook and Instagram and downloaded pictures of everyone I could think of onto my phone: Natalie Stevens, her father Mark, and even her mother-in-law Chloe, who looked pretty spiffy clad all in black leather, the jacket open halfway to her navel, leaning up against a low-slung sports car of (to me) indeterminate make.

When I hadn't heard from her by four o'clock, I decided to head for home so I could go by the police station on the way. I found Detective Jordan behind a door that had Homicide Division stenciled on the pebbled glass in the door. No one responded to a knock, so I opened the door and found an office with eight desks in it. Only three of them were occupied, two on the left side and Jordan's in the back right corner. He was typing on a keyboard, his eyes squinted and his shoulders hunched as he jabbed at it. He looked fit and healthy, an improvement over the last time I'd seen him.

I went past the other two cops, drawing no more than a glance from each, and sat on the corner of his desk. His eyes cut to my knees, then worked their way up to my face. He pushed his chair back, one roller screeching on the dingy linoleum.

"Robin Starling," he said.

"Detective Jordan. I see biker moustaches are still in style."

"And will be as long as Hulk Hogan and I are around to keep them in fashion. What brings you down into the bowels of the police station?"

"We're on the fourth floor," I said. "Hardly the bowels of the station."

"I was speaking figuratively. Don't tell me you've got another murder case. I don't think I can survive another one."

"Sort of. It's felony hit-and-run, but the victim died."

He grimaced and shook his head. "I haven't got one of those at the moment. What gives? I thought criminal defense was just a sideline with you."

"I got fired, had to open my own office. I'm in the Ironfronts over on Main Street."

"And you've decided to specialize in criminal law?"

"I've decided to specialize in anything that comes in the door. You know, mortgage to pay and all that."

"So what do you want?"

"I think I want to talk to someone named Tom McClane. That's the name on the complaint anyway."

Jordan pointed to a desk two in front of his. "Well, that's his desk, but he's not in it."

"No, I can see that."

"Anything else I can do for you?"

"I expected you to sound more helpful after I saved your life."

"You mean after you got me shot?"

I sighed. "Sorry about that."

"Me, too. My wife and kids weren't too crazy about it either."

"How about you fill me in on some police-station protocol?"

He looked at me doubtfully, and I gave him a smile. "Please?"

A voice from the direction of the door said, "Whoa. What gives?"

I turned toward it and saw Ray Hernandez, Jordan's partner. The two other cops in the room seemed to have stopped what they were doing, and I wondered how long they had been watching me try to wheedle information out of Jordan.

"Hello, Ray," I said.

He ignored me and spoke to Jordan. "What's this skinny b…barrister doing here?"

"Nice save," Jordan said.

"No, it's not," I objected. "Forget the b-word. You don't call a woman skinny. Lean, maybe. Slender. Skinny has negative connotations."

"Tell me she's not on one of our cases," Hernandez said to Jordan.

"You make me sound like a hand grenade in a foxhole," I said.

"Since we haven't caught a case of vehicular homicide in the past week, I'm thinking not," Jordan said. "She's somebody else's problem this time."

"This is outrageous," I protested.

"She came by to ask about police station protocol."

"She did?" Hernandez had come to a stop at the next desk. He was not a tall man—shorter than I was—but he was big through the shoulders. He had a broad face, a big nose, and heavy cheekbones. "That's different," he said. He swung the desk chair around, its wheels spinning, and sat. "What does she want to know?"

That sounded promising, but I said, "You gonna address any of your comments to me, or you just going to talk to Jordan?"

He grinned at me. "We'll see."

"Better," I said.

"So what do you want to know?"

"If I want to see a police file, can I just ask to look at it, or do I have to go through the process of filing my discovery motions and all that?"

"We talking an active case?"

"Sure. It's my hit-and-run." I pulled a manila folder out of the side pocket of my briefcase. "She's just been presented before the magistrate. I've got a copy of the complaint, but that's it."

Jordan took the folder from me and flipped it open to glance at the document inside. It consisted of two-and-a-half sheets of single-spaced type. "This just happened yesterday. A complaint may be all there is at this point."

"My client says they showed her a photograph of the victim—who isn't identified here, by the way."

"May not know yet," Hernandez said.

Jordan added, "A lot of it's going to be up to Tom McClane, since it's his case. The law says that investigative information 'may but need not be disclosed.'"

"So what constitutes investigative information?"

Jordan shrugged. "You know the answer to that. It's whatever a judge says it is."

I nodded. "So what kind of guy is McClane? Is he a stickler for the rules, or is he a sweetie like you guys?"

Hernandez was grinning. "I don't think anyone would call McClane a sweetie."

Jordan said, "I don't think I've ever heard anyone call us sweeties either."

Chapter 3

I got on the Downtown Expressway, intending to take it up to I-64, but on impulse took the left fork onto the Powhite Parkway. As I went over the James River, I increased my chances of an accident fourfold by punching an address on Everglades Drive into my Google Maps. According to the complaint, Everglades was where the witness to the hit-and-run lived.

I was there in less than ten minutes. Kim Beecher lived in a cracker-box house just a stone's throw from the intersection of two highways. There were no driveways and no car in front of the house. I caught a glimpse in my rearview mirror of a car pulling to the curb behind me and turned to look over my shoulder. Brooke Marshall got out and came forward wearing a milk-chocolate leather jacket that looked good with her red skirt.

"What are you doing here?" I asked as my window slid down.

"Following you. You pulled onto the Downtown Expressway right in front of me. When you took the

Powhite, I thought I'd tag along and see what you were up to."

"I came to look at the crime scene." I got out of my car, reached back in to get my own jacket.

"What's there to see?"

We scanned the pavement for bloodstains or anything else of interest, but there wasn't anything we could make out.

"Maybe we parked on top of it," Brooke suggested.

"Let's back up."

We each backed up about twenty-five feet, which put us next to a tall chain-link fence with weeds growing up through the asphalt on the other side. It looked like the parking lot of a business that faced the Midlothian Turnpike. I had to get of my car to see enough of the sign to realize it was a gentlemen's club.

"Nice neighborhood," Brooke said, noticing it.

"Good to know there's always work for a couple of nice-looking girls."

She shivered, and not just from the breeze that was blowing a Styrofoam takeout carton along the street behind us. "Let's take a closer look at the pavement."

A man had come out of Kim Beecher's house and was standing on his lawn of weeds and hard-packed earth, his arms crossed over his chest against the cold. His hair was cut, and his face was clean-shaven, though he was beginning to show some five-o'clock shadow. He was wearing dark slacks and a white dress-shirt open at the collar.

"Kim Beecher?" I asked as we approached.

"Yes, who am I talking to?" He looked about my age or maybe a couple of years younger, say late-twenties.

"I'm Robin Starling, a lawyer representing Natalie Stevens. This is my sidekick, Tonto."

"I thought you were my sidekick," Brooke said, looking at me.

"Live and learn."

Kim Beecher was looking perplexed.

"I'm sorry," I said. "Her name's not really Tonto. It's Brooke Marshall. She's a friend of mine." I held out a hand, and he unfolded his arms to take it. "We wanted to take a look at the crime scene."

He held out a hand in invitation. He wasn't wearing a wedding ring, which I thought might help us to get along.

"There doesn't seem to be much to see," I said.

"No, there's not. It happened right here." He walked us two paces to the other side of the road. "This is where the car was…" Another step. "…and here was the body, right behind it."

"Behind it? So the car went completely over the body?"

"Seems to have. Both sets of tires, maybe. But I didn't see it happen."

It went a long way toward explaining the crushed head and the lacerated face, I thought. "What did you see?"

"I saw this woman getting out of the car and walking back toward the body."

"You actually saw her getting out?"

He caught his lip in his teeth and reflected a moment. "I guess not," he said. "I saw her walking with the open car door behind her."

"What was she wearing?"

"Slacks. Short fur coat."

That was a surprise. "Heels?" I asked.

He shook his head. "I don't know."

"Did she walk like this?" I held out my hands out as I walked a few steps away from him. I was still wearing my heels from my visit to the police station, so my gait was slightly unsteady on the tar-and-chip surface of the road. "Or like this." I gestured to Brooke, who walked a few steps in her flats.

He was back to chewing his lip, so we turned and walked back toward him as he studied us. I felt like we were auditioning for the stage at the nearby gentlemen's club.

"More like you," he said, tilting his head in my direction.

"Okay. We have a woman wearing a fur and heels. How old was she?"

He shrugged. "There's just the one streetlight." He pointed. "It makes for some stark shadows."

"Could she have been sixty? An older woman?"

"Oh, no. No more than forty at the outside."

"You can't always tell from a distance. A well-dressed woman, make-up, slender figure...Was this woman slender?"

He nodded. "Medium build."

"So she looked like me?"

He hesitated. "Not so tall and..." He hesitated again. "...stretched out."

I tried to absorb the blow without flinching. First skinny, now stretched out.

"More like her." He pointed, and we both looked at Brooke.

"Could it have been her?" I said.

Brooke said, "Hey!"

He nodded thoughtfully. "I think so. She's the right height, the right build."

That was unfortunate, since Brooke and Natalie Stevens had pretty much the same build.

"But she could have been ten, fifteen years older," I said.

He moved his head uncomfortably. "Could have been," he conceded, "but she moved well—gracefully if you know what I mean."

Gracefully like a twenty-year-old soccer-player was what I was afraid he meant.

"Let's go at it the other way," I said. "Brooke here is thirty years old…"

"Hey!" Brooke said again.

"Could the woman you saw have been very much younger?"

He moved his head again. "Could have been," he said finally. "I would have said about the same age, though."

"Put her in heels and a short fur, and you could be looking at the woman you saw?"

Brooke stamped her foot. "You cut that out."

Beecher was nodding.

"Do you have an alibi for two a.m. this morning?" I asked Brooke. "Live-in boyfriend? One-night stand?"

"You know I don't." She sounded almost tearful, and I felt a pang of guilt over framing her for felony manslaughter.

"It couldn't have been her because of the hair," Beecher said. "I'd have noticed the red hair, I think, even in the streetlight."

"Ah. What color hair did this woman have?"

"Darker. Beyond that, I couldn't say."

"So it couldn't have been me either."

"No, but it's not just because the hair…"

"I know, don't say it. I'm too tall and stretched out."

"I'm sorry. I didn't mean…"

"You don't know how long those words are going to haunt me," I said.

"Look. Would you like to come inside? I can show you where I was standing."

I looked at Brooke, who gave me an almost imperceptible shrug. "Sure," I said.

We went inside, and Beecher offered us something to eat, drink, smoke, or chew.

"That's not very specific," I said. "I don't know whether to ask for a highball or a piece of gum."

"It can't be a highball," Beecher said. "I don't drink."

"So we're down to eat, smoke, or chew, unless you don't smoke either."

He smiled a little weakly, turned to his picture window. "I was standing here when I saw the woman," he said. "At first I didn't realize it was a body on the road. I thought it was a bundle of some kind, clothes or something."

"How did you come to be looking out the window just then? Did you hear an impact? A scream maybe?"

"I couldn't sleep. I was just standing at the plate-glass window, having a cookie and a glass of milk, and I noticed the woman."

A cookie and a glass of milk. "Were you a boy scout?"

"Are you still a boy scout?" Brooke asked.

"I was for a couple of years. I made it to First Class, I think."

Not an Eagle Scout. "How about the car?" I asked. "What can you tell us about it?"

"I got the license plate. It was lit up with a little bulb above the bracket."

"Do you remember the number?"

"GBX something. One-one-something. The car itself was a light colored sedan, white maybe, small to medium-sized."

"You could see the license plate from here?" I was doubtful.

"Well, no. I saw the woman. She walked back and squatted down next to this..." He hesitated. "...this thing in the road. Then she stood up and started back to her car, so I started out through the front door to see if I could help."

"Did she see you?"

"I don't think so. She didn't change her pace or anything. Never looked in my direction. It was when I got onto the porch that the bundle of clothes took on more of a human shape, so I yanked the cell phone out of the pocket of my robe as I ran toward the street and dialed 9-1-1. The car was moving by that time, already two or three houses away. I read off the license number to the dispatcher."

"You could see the plate clearly?"

"All but the last digit. It was a six or an eight, I think."

"It couldn't have been a four?" I asked, not because I thought it might have been, but just to test his recollection.

"I suppose it could have been a four."

"It must have been pretty ghastly," Brooke said.

Beecher turned to her. "It was. You should have seen the guy's face—well, his lack of a face, I should say. And the shape of his head. His skull looked like it had been crushed. The car must have hit him with incredible force, then dragged him, then the tires must have gone right over his head."

"Maybe that's what woke you up," Brooke said, not quite managing to suppress a shudder.

He shook his head. "I'd been awake awhile."

I said, "But you didn't hear the impact—no squeal of brakes, no thump or anything."

He looked thoughtful. "No. I didn't."

"Have they had you in for a lineup?"

"Tomorrow."

Tom McClane was working his case. "Shown you any photographs of anyone?"

He nodded. "Yes, but I don't know if it was her."

"Just the one photograph?"

"Well, several photographs. Just one woman, though. Girl, actually. She couldn't have been over eighteen."

Nineteen, I thought. If the police had shown him Natalie's picture, she was going to look familiar to him when he saw her in the line-up. They'd increased their chances of an identification and probably on purpose.

"I wonder if you'd take a look at one of my pictures," I said.

He shrugged. "Sure."

I got out my phone and opened my photos app. When I'd found the picture of Chloe Stevens in her motorcycle leather, I handed the phone to Beecher. Beside him, Brooke peered at it, too.

"She's hot," Beecher said.

"You can drool if you need to, but try not to get any on my phone."

His laugh sounded a bit defensive.

"Is this the woman the police showed you a picture of?" I knew it wasn't, of course.

"No. This woman has a more polished look, and I think she's older. She could be thirty, or close to it."

She was more likely forty, I thought, though I had seen her up close and in decent lighting.

"Forget the pictures the police showed you," I said. "Think about the woman you saw last night. Could this have been her?"

"I don't know. It's just the one streetlight, like I said. Her features were in shadow, and I never got a look at her head on."

At least he was honest. "It couldn't have been Brooke because of her hair," I said. "It couldn't have been me because of my height. Is there anything about this woman's appearance that rules her out, that lets you say, no, it couldn't have been her?"

"Nooo," he said slowly. "No, I don't think there is."

"So she's a possibility."

He nodded.

"And the girl the police showed you is a possibility."

"Is she your client?"

I nodded. "I wonder if you'd be willing to give me a call after the lineup. Let me know how it went."

"Sure," he said. "What's your number?"

I smiled and gave him one of my newly printed business cards. I'd had them a week. "Her name's Natalie Stevens," I said, wanting to personalize her a little. "She's a college student at Longwood, plays varsity soccer."

"Really. I used to date a girl who went to Longwood."

"Oh? You didn't go there yourself, I take it."

"No. University of Richmond."

"What do you do now?"

"I'm an accountant with a firm downtown." He held up a hand. "I know what you're thinking. What am I doing in a little two-bedroom house in this neighborhood?"

"You have some very nice pieces of furniture," Brooke said, looking around.

"Thanks. I got them when one of our clients was liquidating. We all picked up a few nice pieces."

"So why this house and this neighborhood?" I asked.

He smiled, showing even teeth. "Tax-deductible rent. I'm saving my money. When I get married, I'll be able to afford a place that's really nice."

"So you're engaged," Brooke said.

"Not yet. Not even dating anyone in particular. Just planning for the future. You know, like everyone."

When we were on the street again, and by ourselves, I said to Brooke, "How about you? Are you planning for the future?"

She gave me a look as she opened the door of her car.

"Maybe a future with a handsome young accountant who's been saving his money?" I suggested.

"You're the one who gave him your number," she said primly. She swung into her car and closed the door.

She had a point. I went to my own car and stood looking around for a moment. I could see five homes, two of which needed painting and a third that was boarded up. In addition to the gentlemen's club with its chain-link fence and part of a neon sign showing through the bare-limbed trees, I could see a Jiffy Lube and, far down the street, something that looked like it might be the back-end of a motel.

It was possible to take thriftiness a good deal too far, I thought, and got into my own car, a VW Beetle, and drove away.

Chapter 4

Brooke had roomed with me through the summer and early fall, but she had her own place now. I got home to an empty house, set my purse and briefcase on the floor just inside the door from the garage, and dropped my keys on the kitchen counter. Undoing the belt on my coat, I shrugged out of it and tossed it over the back of a chair. Then I dug in the refrigerator for the opened bottle of zinfandel, filled a coffee mug halfway and carried it into the living room, kicking off my shoes en route to the recliner.

A little wine at the end of the day was a new habit for me, one I had acquired while Brooke was living with me. When she was here, we used stemware, but alone I found a coffee mug more stable and less inclined to spill. The TV screen in front of me was blank, but I made no move to turn it on. I didn't have anything good recorded—I'd watched the new *Duck Dynasty* and the new *Big Bang Theory* over the weekend—and the news almost invariably informed me about aggravating events and government policies I couldn't do anything about.

Idle ruminations about Natalie Stevens, my first case as a solo practitioner, led me to the conclusion that I needed more facts upon which to ruminate. Most importantly, I'd like to know the identity of the hit-and-run victim. I couldn't imagine, in this digital age, that his identity would remain unknown for very long, but I should probably do more than wait for it to surface. I had a client, evidently a client who could pay, and I should make the most of my resources.

When my wine was half gone, I gathered my shoes and went back to the bedroom to change into sweatpants and a T-shirt. I washed my face to remove what little makeup I wore, then padded barefoot into the kitchen.

Making supper was not a big production. I dumped some mixed greens from a bag into a soup bowl, hand-shredded some deli-sliced turkey onto it, then sprinkled on some balsamic vinegar and a little pumpkin seed oil, dark and fragrant. I carried my salad into the living room and sat with one leg curled under me to eat it. I did turn on the TV then and found a romantic comedy starring Matthew McConaughey in progress on one of the movie channels.

When I finished my salad, I paused the movie and carried my bowl back into the kitchen to wash it. I had the rest of my evening before me, and the house seemed empty. A couple of days a week, I stopped off at the Y on my way home to shoot some hoops. Now that I was living alone again, maybe I ought to up it to three days a week.

I went back to my movie, though, and watched for about thirty minutes before I paused it to go put on running shoes and a hoodie. Though I generally waited longer after I ate to run, I was feeling restless.

The doorbell rang as I was pulling open the door, and a man jumped so violently he nearly fell backwards off the stoop. "You scared the hell out of me," he said, recovering his balance. It was Paul Soldano, a man I'd been seeing sporadically for the past couple of months.

"Sorry. I was going for a run. What's that?" A head had popped out of his jacket like a birthing alien, but I recognized it even as I flinched. "Is that a puppy?"

As if in confirmation, the puppy gave me a yap of greeting. Paul lifted it out, and its tail was going. I put a hand on the puppy's head, and it twisted its neck to lick my forearm.

"He's beautiful."

"He's a chocolate lab, has AKC papers and everything."

"Where did you get a full-blooded lab?"

Paul beamed at me. "Parking lot of Walmart. I had to pass an interview to get him, too."

I stepped back to let them in, closing the door behind them. "Who interviewed you?"

"The whole family: first a little girl, then her big brother, then Dad." He pushed the little brown puppy into my arms, and it wriggled against me, soft and warm from Paul's jacket. "The final and toughest, though, was Mom."

"What kind of questions did they ask?"

"Oh, you know. How big is your yard, how much time do you have to spend with it, would it be an outside dog or an inside dog."

I laughed, stroking the dog. "How did you pass that interview? You live in an apartment and work all day."

"I probably cheated a little. I described your yard."

My eyes narrowed against the possibility that he was broaching the idea of moving in with me, which wasn't going to happen.

"My fence is just chain-link," I said. "That's not going to hold this guy when he's full grown."

I sat on the couch with the dog, and it twisted to look into my face with amber eyes.

"We've got time. He's just eight-weeks old. Eyes are already turning, though. The little girl told me two weeks ago they were blue."

"When you say we've got time…"

"To train him. I really see him as mostly an inside dog, though."

"Well, sure. You haven't got a yard." The puppy had its neck extended, and seemed to be smelling my breath and memorizing the scent.

"And my apartment doesn't allow pets."

I picked up the dog and turned him toward Paul, its front legs sticking straight out, back legs dangling. "Then what's the idea of this little guy?"

"I thought he could stay here. Actually, I kind of got him for you."

"What do you mean, kind of?" I set the dog on the floor, where it sat to look up at me.

"I guess I mean I'm equivocating in hopes of avoiding an explosion."

The dog toddled toward the French doors, where he stopped, nose pressed against the dark glass, evidently looking at his reflection. He yipped, and his tail wagged.

I got up and turned on the outside light, and the tail stopped for a moment, then began wagging harder than ever.

"I can't have a dog," I said. "I'm gone all day."

"But you run every day. You'll have a running buddy, and he'll get plenty of exercise."

I looked at him. "Is that what this is about?"

"What?" His round face, beneath his dark, wavy hair, was open and disingenuous.

"I ask you to run with me, and so you go find a dog to stand in for you?"

"Look out!"

I looked down. The puppy, looking out at the grass and the pine trees, had squatted and begun to pee.

Paul was already there, scooping him up and holding him upside down so that the pee went up in a tiny fountain. I fumbled with the lock on the French door and wrenched it open, and Paul ran out and put the puppy in the grass. It was too late. The puppy evidently was done, its bladder empty. It looked up at us and wagged its tail.

"I picked up a crate at Walmart. It's probably a good idea to let him sleep in that, if you want to housetrain him. Of course, one of us will have to get up every few hours to let him out."

"One of us?" I had my arms crossed over my chest and my hands tucked into my armpits for warmth.

"I can sleep on the couch the next couple of nights till he settles in."

"No, you can't."

"If you don't want to get up, I mean."

"What I really don't want is this puppy." I felt something and looked down. The puppy had its front paws on my foot and was looking up at me. When I made eye contact, he wagged his tail.

I sighed. "What's his name?"

"Anything you want. The kids called him Brown Dog, I think because he was the only chocolate in the litter, but he hasn't learned it yet. I was thinking maybe Deacon."

I bent and scooped the dog off the grass, holding him so that he faced me with his legs dangling. He looked at me with what might have been reproach.

"Deacon's a big name for such a little guy," I said.

"He'll grow. The momma was there with the puppies, and she was pretty big. They said the daddy weighed a hundred twenty pounds."

"A hundred twenty! That's huge for a lab."

"So he'll grow into the name."

I tucked Deacon under my arm and carried him back inside. "Grab some paper towels and see what you can blot up from the carpet," I said. "Then go get the crate. I'll take him into the kitchen and sponge him off."

I never did get my run in. Paul stayed until eleven, and when he left the puppy stayed with me, along with his crate, a leash and collar, and a small bag of kibble. The crate was about the size of a deep desk drawer, so he was going to grow out of it in a matter of weeks. I put it on the floor next to my bed.

As I got ready for bed, Deacon followed me from the closet to the bathroom, from the bathroom to the hall to turn out a light, from the hall to my bed, moving a bit unsteadily on his short legs. I held open the door of his crate and nodded at it.

"Bedtime," I said, but he only looked at me. "Bedtime," I said again, scooping him up and putting him in his crate. He wasn't able to turn around fast enough to keep me from withdrawing my hand and shutting the wire-door, but he yapped his objections.

"Bedtime," I said, and got into bed.

He whined. I knew the best thing to do was let him whine himself out, which I expected him to do fairly promptly. After five minutes, though, I got up and cleared off my bedside table, putting the clock, cell phone, and water bottle on the floor. His crate was a little too long for the table, but not by much.

"There," I said. "You can look at me."

He looked.

I got into bed and turned onto my side so I could look at him, too. He hesitated, then lay down and put his head on his paws.

"Bedtime," I murmured to him, and his tail thumped softly in reply.

Chapter 5

For breakfast Deacon had kibble, and I had oatmeal. "I still say Deacon is a mighty big name from such a little dog," I told him as he ate. His tail wagged, but he continued to gobble his kibble as if it were filet mignon.

When we'd finished breakfast and I was dressed and ready to go, I still hadn't decided what I was going to do with him. There were three choices as I saw it: put down some newspapers and leave him in the garage, leave him in the house inside in his crate, or leave him in the back yard. In the garage he could get into mischief. There was no telling what he would chew up, and he might eat something he shouldn't.

His whining had wakened me shortly before three. I'd carried him outside and stood hugging myself against the cold while he nosed around and, eventually, peed. Evidently, he'd already developed an aversion to peeing in his crate, which was good. Equally evident, his bladder was still too small to last him the night—or all day, which was not so good.

That left the back yard. I took him out and watched him run around a bit, then, when he wasn't looking, slipped back into the house. I sighed, hating to leave him. This was why I shouldn't have a dog. But I did, at least for now, and I had done the best I could for him.

Forgoing the interstate, I took West Broad Street into town so I could stop by the Stevens house, where Natalie had been arrested. Her stepmother Chloe should be there, alone now until Mark Stevens returned from parts unknown.

It was a big house on a one-acre lot: dark red brick, wood shingles on the gables, one story in some places and two stories in others. "*The House of Seven Gables*," I murmured to myself, shivering in the early morning cold. I hadn't counted them, but I thought the architect might have beaten Nathaniel Hawthorne by a gable or two. I glanced at my watch as I walked up the sidewalk, thinking that it might be early in the day for a wealthy woman who didn't have a job or a family to get up for. On the other hand, what reason could such a woman have for staying up late?

I rang the bell, which gave me a simple ding-dong, no chimes. No one answered, so I rang again. And waited again. It was cold enough that I could see my breath. I went back down the sidewalk a little way so I could look through the arched window above the door. A bit of staircase was visible, and the railing of a second-floor hallway. No lights on that I could make out in the daylight, though, and no Chloe.

Well, I was a lawyer and was supposed to be obnoxious. I stepped back onto the stoop and began pressing the doorbell repeatedly: ding-dong-ding-dong-ding-dong… I kept it up for thirty seconds or so and stepped back again to look through the window.

No light had come on that I could tell. No one was at the rail, looking out. So. Chloe was a sound sleeper, or she was lying in her bed with her pillow clutched around her head—I pictured her in a mauve satin teddy—cursing the inconsiderate moron who was pumping her doorbell. Or she wasn't home.

I moved off the sidewalk onto a plush lawn that looked professionally maintained, moving along the shrubbery that lined the house, but the window treatments foiled any hope I had of seeing inside. At the end of the house I came to a pair of double-wide garage doors, both closed. A gate that consisted of iron scrollwork was set in the brick wall that enclosed the back yard. Peering through it, I could see a deck, some patio furniture, and a whole lot of trees. It was a nice place, really, the sort of place I might consider acquiring, should there come a day when I was representing millionaire playboys accused of murdering their wives.

Since I was taking the slow road into town already, I stopped by the office of Rodney Burns, the man I was beginning to think of as my detective. He occupied an office on the backside of a strip shopping center that was nearly half vacant. When I got there, I drove around the end of the strip, avoiding the potholes that spotted the cracked asphalt. As always, the Venetian blinds inside Rodney's plate glass window hung slightly askew, the ends of the blinds bent here and there. I opened my car door, and a cold wind jerked it from me so hard it bounced back at me. Goose bumps appeared instantly on my bare legs.

I got out, shifting my briefcase to the hand that clutched my dress so I could slam the car door, then putting my other hand on top of my head to keep my hair from blowing away. When I let go of my hair to yank open the glass door into the office, the wind pulled it straight out like a flag, but at least it stayed with me. Inside, other than a short counter and a sink with some cabinets over it, the outer office was vacant except for a couple of client chairs and a modular computer desk and chair that held no computer and at which a secretary never sat. I let go of my dress and used both hands to brush my hair back from my face as I looked around the office. Actually, there was something at one end of the computer desk. It looked like…

"Seen my new coffee pot?" Rodney asked me, poking his head out of the cluttered inner office. "It's a Cuisinart."

"I see it. It looks nice." I shrugged out of my coat and draped it over the empty wing of the computer desk.

"I just made a fresh pot. Would you like a cup?"

I moved my head equivocally. "Sure."

He disappeared back inside the inner office, calling, "It's Krispy Kreme. I used to stop every day on my way to work, but now I can buy their ground coffee by the pound."

I followed Rodney to the doorway, blinked, then spotted him squatting at the end of his desk to shift a stack of files from in front of a cabinet. "It smells good," I offered as he got the cabinet door open and extracted a gold mug with a VCU ram on it. He stood, holding the mug high like an athletic trophy he'd just won. On his way back past his desk, he snagged another mug, this one with a picture of Edgar Allan Poe on it and stained brown inside with old coffee. "Now I can have coffee any time of day I want, and I don't have to go anywhere to get it."

He handed me the VCU mug with the air of one conferring an award. I took it in the same spirit, inclining my head in acknowledgment of the honor. He poured, but stopped in mid-pour with a stricken look.

"I didn't ask if you took cream or sugar."

"Black is fine."

He took a breath. "Because I don't have cream or sugar. I'll have to get some. I don't have any on hand because I don't use it myself."

"Why spoil a good cup of coffee?" I said.

He smiled. When he had finished pouring the coffee, we sat in the client chairs in the outer office and looked at each other over the steaming mugs. The overhead fluorescents glinted off the slightly oily comb-overs that stretched across his narrow head. A little moustache emphasized the smallness of his mouth and added to an ineffectual look that I believed to be entirely misleading.

"He invented the detective story," Rodney said.

I blinked at him.

"I noticed you looking at my mug. Poe's fictional detective was Auguste Dupin. 'Murders in the Rue Morgue,' 1841."

"Oh. Sure. Woman's body stuffed up the chimney. I don't think I've read it since junior high, didn't realize it was the first detective story." Probably not the time to mention I was an English major in college. I held up my own mug. "Did you go to VCU?"

He nodded, birdlike. "For a year. Then I dropped out to start my agency."

As I sipped my coffee, my gaze strayed to the mangled blinds.

"So what brings you to the West End?" he asked me.

I lived in the West End, of course, but I worked downtown, so I took his meaning.

"Well, I've got a case…"

"Already! And you've just been on your own…"

"A week and a half. I've become a grand master at spider solitaire, but it is nice to have something productive to do." I told him about it, leaning over to extract the complaint from my briefcase. "See what you can find out. In addition to some general background on the Stevens family—you can probably get something on the internet—I'd like to know the name of the victim, what the police got from examining Natalie's Lexus, anything you can get. This morning I'm going to stop by the station in hopes of talking to the officer in charge of the case. I'll let you know what I find out."

"If anything."

"Well, that's why I came to you. Backup." I stood up and put my mug on the computer desk. "This is good coffee."

He nodded complacently, then as I was leaving said, "Ms. Starling."

I stopped with my hand on the door. "Robin," I told him.

"Robin. Another agency has given me some work recently. It's tedious, and it doesn't pay very well—searching records and collecting documents. Still, it does pay something, and I'm going to set it aside for this."

I gave him a grin. "I got a big retainer," I said. "I'm good for it."

He looked relieved. "I hated to ask, but I know you're not with the big firm anymore."

"Understood. We all have to pay our bills." As I opened the door, a cold wind hit me right in the face and rustled papers all the way back in Rodney's inner office.

Once I found a space in the parking garage of the police station, I grabbed my briefcase—actually a leather portfolio that looked like a flat, oversized purse—and got out. The parking garage was cold, but I wanted to look as professional as possible inside the police station, so I stripped out of my coat and hustled without it for the door.

There were three men in the homicide division. One of them looked in my direction, and I said, "Tom McClane?"

He jerked his head in the direction of two men sitting in the back talking about college basketball. I approached, and one of the men looked up at me. He was wearing chinos, a white shirt, and what looked like a clip-on tie, his shield hooked to his belt.

"Tom McClane?"

He inclined his head in the other man's direction.

McClane was the clothes-horse. He was wearing a tweed jacket and a knit tie of the sort I hadn't seen in a decade. He also wore a vest with lapels, which was something I hadn't seen since the 1800s.

"Help you?" he said.

"I'm Robin Starling. I'm representing Natalie Stevens in the hit-and-run case."

McClane took his feet off his desk. "The vehicular homicide."

"Well, yes."

The other man stood, jerked his chin at McClane and headed for the door. McClane stayed in his seat. "That tells me who you are," he said. "It doesn't tell me what you want."

"What I want is to see the file."

He let out a bark of laughter. "And people in hell," he began, and I nodded.

"Want a glass of ice water," I finished.

It got me another bark of laughter. I got the idea he barked at a lot of things that weren't funny.

I said, "I can get it all through discovery, I know, but at the moment it's 'investigative information that may but need not be disclosed.' I'm hoping we can work with the 'may' part."

He nodded his square head, which seemed all the squarer because of his salt-and-pepper flat-top. "I bet you are," he said.

I waited.

He rolled his head on his shoulders, either loosening himself up for a prize fight or thinking. He cut his eyes upward, looking at me over the tops of his black-framed glasses. "I'll get the file," he said, pushed back his chair a couple of feet, and stood up.

I blinked down at the top of his head and the scalp showing through the flat-top. Standing he was only five-seven or eight, several inches shorter than I was. He'd seemed much larger sitting down. He went to a row of filing cabinets, opened a drawer, and pawed through it while whistling tunelessly through his teeth. He jerked out a manila folder with an air of decisiveness and came back to his desk.

"You can pull over that chair," he said, indicating the next desk.

I pulled the chair over and sat down. McClane squared the folder on the desk in front of him, shot his cuffs, and opened the folder. His face spasmed immediately.

"Oh, hell," he said.

He turned the eight-by-ten photograph toward me, and I flinched. It was a close-up of gore, not immediately recognizable as a head because the shape wasn't right.

"That's his face," McClane said. "It looks like the tires spun against it as the car went over him. Peeled it right off."

I felt my gorge rising.

He lifted the photograph and several more under it and pushed them over to me. "You want to spend some time with them?"

I shook my head. "Do we know who he is yet?"

"Not yet. Haven't heard back from iafis yet. Probably today."

"Iafis?"

"Integrated, automated, ah, fingerprint…It's the FBI database."

"And that will tell you who the victim is if he has a criminal record?"

"It may help identify him even if he doesn't. There're a lot more civil records in the system than criminal, millions of them—firearms purchases in Maryland and a few other states, not Virginia, employment background checks for certain kinds of jobs, and so on. You're a lawyer. Didn't you get fingerprinted when you got your license?"

I nodded. "Right here in this building."

"So you're in the system."

"Let's hope this one doesn't come back as me."

He gave me a look. "Funny," he said gravely.

"Well." I shrugged in self-deprecation.

He pushed the photographs to one side with stubby fingers. A class ring with a red stone dominated his right hand. There was an indentation on the ring finger of his left hand where another ring had recently been, probably a wedding band.

"I assume you've got a copy of the complaint," he said.

"Yes. Is there an autopsy report?"

He pushed at the papers. "Not yet. Got a copy of the 9-1-1 call."

"From Kim Beecher?"

"You know Kim Beecher?"

"The name was in the complaint."

"Ah." He pushed the transcript toward me, and I picked it up, scanning past the date and time, the name of the dispatcher, Kim Beecher's name and phone number, and other preliminaries.

Dispatcher: 9-1-1. How can I help you?

Caller: License plate GBX 118. I think. The last digit could be a six.

Dispatcher: Can I help you?

Caller: I'm on Everglades Drive. Someone's been hit. I think you'd better send an ambulance.

Dispatcher: What is your address?

Caller: 1610 Everglades, just north of the Midlothian Turnpike. You'd better hurry. I think it's bad.

Dispatcher: You say a person was hit by a car?

Caller: Yes. I'm going back to him now. It's a man. He's...oh crap.

Dispatcher: Is he alive?

Caller: No. I don't know. I don't see how he could be.

Dispatcher: Is the car there? Is the driver injured?

Caller: The car just drove away. It was a little one. I read you the license plate.

Dispatcher: GBX 118 or 116.

Caller: Yes. Is an ambulance on its way? This is bad.

Dispatcher: Yes, an ambulance is in route.

Caller: The body must have caught on her bumper and gotten dragged a good way. His head...

Dispatcher: What was that? Are you all right?

Caller: Sorry. I just threw up.

Dispatcher: You said 'her.' Did you see the driver?

Caller: Yes. When I got to my window, she was out of her car, walking back toward what looked like a bundle of clothes. There's a streetlight just a couple of houses down, but it casts a lot of shadows, and I really couldn't see that well. This woman bent over him, bent over the clothes, and I think she had a flashlight. At least, I think I saw a light just for a few seconds. Then the light went out, and the woman went back to her car. I'm going back to my porch. I can't stand this.

Dispatcher: Can you describe the woman you saw?

Caller: I don't know. Young, I think. Well dressed. I think I hear the ambulance. Yes, it's coming. Thank the Lord.

I flipped the page, but the last page was blank. There wasn't anything else.

"Have you interviewed him?" I asked.

"Yes. I've typed up my notes, just haven't printed them yet to put them in the file."

"Can I see them?"

McClane shook his head. "I don't think so, not yet. I haven't done my proof-reading."

"Will you email me a copy when they're ready?"

"You don't want a lot, do you?"

"Just whatever I can get."

"Well, you're looking at it. Right now, this is all there is."

I closed the folder and held it out to him. "Don't think I don't appreciate it," I said.

"You ought to. It's not every attorney who can waltz in here and flip through an open police file."

I raised my eyebrows. "Why me then?"

The corner of his mouth twitched. "Jordan's told us about you. I was actually looking forward to meeting you."

Unfortunately, I could imagine all too well the stories Jordan might have told.

"Well, it's good to meet you." I held out a hand, and he took it with a calloused, short-fingered hand that felt like sandpaper.

"It's very good to meet you," he said. He let go of my hand before I had to take it away from him, but only just.

"Thanks again," I said. I picked up my portfolio and turned toward the door.

"Starling."

I turned back.

"Maybe we can do lunch sometime. Coffee."

I hesitated. "How about some coffee right now?"

He looked surprised. "Okay."

"Maybe we can stop by the impound lot and look at my client's car on the way."

It was his turn to hesitate. "It's not exactly on the way."

"My car's here. I'll drive."

His gaze swept downward all the way to my shoes, then came back to my face. "Sure, why not?" he said. "I'll drive, though. It's just a few blocks."

Evidently, long legs are good for more than getting a person from here to there. I felt a little sick, but I smiled and showed him my dimple.

"I'll get my coat," he said.

Chapter 6

McClane's coat was a cashmere topcoat, and it was hanging on a rack near the door. His car evidently belonged to the city; it was a dark Impala with a whipcord antenna, a police radio under the dash, and a backseat full of trash. We got in, and he turned to look at me with bright eyes and a half-smile that said, "Yeah, baby. I'm Batman."

He put the car in reverse, then twisted to brace his hand on the back of my seat so he could steer the car out of its parking space. The suspension squealed as he started forward. Was he masterful or a bit crazy? The jury was out.

The impound lot was in a warehouse district north of Broad Street. We hit all the traffic lights, so, close as the lot was, it took us ten minutes to get there. More time for small talk. Yippee.

McClane pulled up to the security shed at the gate and flashed his badge. Natalie's car, a white Lexus, was about halfway back on the right between a late model BMW and an eighties-era pickup. We got out. McClane looked comfortable with both hands in the pockets of his topcoat, and the wind left his flat-top undisturbed. For my part, I was holding onto my skirt with one hand while my hair whipped around my face like the hair of a Medusa. I deeply regretted having left my coat in my car.

"Broken headlight, see?" McClane said.

I bent to look at it. "Is that blood?"

"Appears to be. I haven't heard back from forensics yet. All this just happened yesterday, you know. You're really on the ball."

It's what came of having only one case to work on. "It's this or Spider Solitaire," I said. The only damage to the car that I could see was the broken headlight. "Not all of the glass fragments are here. Were they recovered at the scene?"

"I don't think so. Probably fell out on her way home."

"Huh." I peered through the tinted windows. "Can we look inside?"

"Uh, no. I didn't bring the key."

I straightened. "Okay. I'm done here."

"Coffee then?"

I'd forgotten about the quid pro quo. "Sure," I said brightly.

There was a Starbucks not far away. (Is a Starbucks ever far away?) But he took me to the Krispy Kreme on Broad, probably the same one where Rodney Burns got his coffee. We sat on stools at the counter and watched doughnuts being fried and moved along on a conveyer belt.

The waitress put down our coffee, which served in ceramic mugs.

"Doughnut?" McClane said.

I shook my head. "Just the coffee."

59

McClane ordered a glazed and a chocolate-covered. "I work out, so I eat what I want," he said as he poured cream into his coffee from a little metal jug. He held up the jug as evidence.

I shook my head again, pulled my coffee closer.

"You like your coffee like your men?"

I tried not to groan. He went on to tell me all about the workouts that let him eat whatever he wanted. They involved one-arm barbell lifts, running with a backpack full of rocks, moving a tractor tire back and forth across his back yard…Maybe I should have been taking notes, but I lost track. I did get to feel his bicep, which I suppose was the highlight of the longest coffee date I could ever remember. At last he took me back to the police station, laughing and talking and rolling his shoulders all the way, and he stopped behind my car.

"This was really fun," he said.

"It really was."

"We'll have to do it again sometime."

I smiled at him and tilted my head in equivocation—an unfortunate gesture in that he seemed to think I was being coquettish. He reached over and patted my forearm with one of his blunt-fingered hands.

"See you," I said. I got out of the car and went to mine. He waited, watching me, and I tried not to hurry as I opened the door and tossed my briefcase across. I glanced back at him just before I got in, and he winked at me.

It's good to have friends, but sometimes I think there are too many people in my life who are way too familiar with me. I got to the Ironfronts, nodded at

Carly, who was on the phone, and went back to my office, where, lo and behold, a man was sitting at my desk looking at my computer monitor—not just any man, but one John Parker, with whom I had worked at the law firm of Northcutt, Hambrick and Larsen. I'd also had a rocky romantic relationship with him, which hardly made his presumption any more palatable.

"How did you get in here?" I demanded from the doorway.

"The door was open."

Brooke Marshall came out of her office next to mine. "I'm sorry. I unlocked them both when I came in. I didn't think…"

I finished the sentence for her. "…about some man waltzing in and taking a seat as calm as you please at the desk where I might have any number of confidential materials."

"I didn't hear him come in," Brooke said meekly. John Parker turned the computer monitor toward us to show my most recent game of spider solitaire, still in progress.

"You seem to have gotten stuck," he said. "I was backing up, trying to work your way out of your difficulties. For the sake of security, you really ought to log off your computer before you go home in the evenings. You can always save your game, you know."

Rolling my eyes, I put my purse and briefcase on the floor next to the desk and shrugged out of my coat.

"Carly tells me you've got a case," John said.

"Does she now?" I hung my coat over the hook on the back of my door and opened the door wide again. Carly was there, just behind Brooke.

"John Parker's here," she announced. "He said he knew the way."

"He certainly seems to," I said.

"I told him the good news about your first big case. I guess I shouldn't talk about those things. It's just so exciting. And he told me how you two used to, you know…" She tapped the ends of her index fingers together.

I turned, throwing up a hand, and dropped into one of the client chairs. Brooke took the other one, and Carly remained standing in the doorway.

"You could really use another chair in here," Carly said. "I could squeeze in another one for you, if you want."

The phone rang, and we all looked at it through a second ring before I stood and gestured for John to get out of my chair.

"Maybe it's another case," Carly said.

I maneuvered past John to get around my desk, then paused with my hand on the phone to observe all their expectant faces.

"Maybe it's something highly confidential," I said.

Carly pursed her lips and raised her eyebrows as she turned away.

"We're family," Brooke said. "Oh, okay. Come on, John."

I picked up the phone as they went through the door.

"Robin Starling," I said.

"Hello, Ms. Starling, Mark Stevens here."

I sat and grabbed a pen. "Hello, Mr. Stevens. I saw your daughter yesterday."

"That, of course, is what I'm calling you about. How is she holding up?"

"Surprisingly well. Being in custody is hard on her, but she's a tough kid."

"Are you going to be able to help her?"

"Bail is set at seventy-five thousand dollars. I'm waiting to hear from Chloe."

"I mean long-term. Can you get the charges dismissed, or get her acquitted or whatever?"

Or whatever. "Dismissed, no. Acquitted, I can do my best, though when you go to court the outcome is never certain."

"But it looks good."

"It's too early to know how it looks."

"That's not encouraging."

"I got the case yesterday. The police don't even have the autopsy report yet, and their investigation is ongoing. For my part, I hired a private investigator this morning and am finding out what I can. Making bail is my immediate concern. It doesn't have to be cash. You can put up securities or real estate, or we can use a bail bondsman."

There was a silence on the line, the clean silence of a perfect connection. It occurred to me that we'd been speaking without noticeable delays—none of the second-long pauses you'd see on TV when the news anchor was asking questions of an overseas correspondent.

"Where are you, Mr. Stevens?" I asked.

"Guangzhou, China. I hope to leave for the States in a few days, but there're some things I have to finish up here first."

"I'm surprised at how instant our communication is. I would have expected delays while the signal traveled."

"We did have delays when I got started in this business. They had to bounce the signal off a satellite. Now it's all fiber optics. Cables link the continents, and the distance is much shorter now that the signal doesn't have to go out into space and come in again."

"Ah." You learn something new every day.

"I understand Chloe's written you a check? You have the resources you need going forward?"

"For my fees and expenses, at least for now. When this case is over, I'll send you a statement, letting you know the total charges and either remitting the difference or billing you for it."

"Fair enough. You work with Chloe until I get back. She's told me good things about you. You've got my complete confidence."

"Will she be able to help with…"

But Mr. Stevens had hung up the phone.

"…bail," I finished lamely. I put the receiver back into its cradle. "Well, that was strange."

"What was strange?" John and Brooke were crowded together in my doorway.

"I guess you heard all that?" I said.

"Just your side of it," Brooke said. "We couldn't help overhearing, what with your door open and my door open."

"And both of us staying very quiet," John said.

"Was that Natalie's father? What did he say?" Brooke said again.

I shrugged. "Not much. 'Carry on. You have my complete confidence. I'll be back in the States someday.'"

"What was strange?" John asked.

"That doesn't sound strange to you? This was Natalie's father. He should have been agitated, worried sick, trying to keep me on the line to milk me for every little bit of information there was to get. Instead it was, 'Hello, this is Mark Stevens. Natalie holding up? I hear great things about you. Keep up the good work.' I couldn't get in a word edgewise about posting bail."

John came back in and sat down.

"Shouldn't you be at work?" I said. "How are you billing anyone for this?"

"I'm on my way to court in Dinwiddie. The traffic is terrible."

"You've got to be kidding me."

"I am, I am. I'll have to work late tonight to make up for it. I wanted to see you in your new digs, though. I've been worried about you."

"I'll get by."

"Babe, there's not a doubt in my mind."

I looked over his head at Brooke, who was still in the doorway. She raised her eyebrows at me, tilting her chin.

"So what were you worried about?" I asked John.

"It's just a manner of speaking. I wanted to see you, okay?" He gave me a little-boy smile that once would have melted me like butter. Even now, I was glad to be sitting down.

Chapter 7

Thirty minutes later, John was on his way to Dinwiddie. Brooke was back in her own office optimizing Salesforce software for the particular needs of a client—unlike me, she had more than one. I was looking at the not quite finished game of spider solitaire. I couldn't see how John had done me any good.

I exited the game and pulled over a yellow pad to jot some notes. I didn't have enough thoughts to fill the page. Pulling over my keyboard, I clicked LinkedIn on my favorites bar, then did a search for Kim Beecher. There weren't as many as you'd think: a few Kimberly Beechers, a K Beecher, one Kim Beecher. I clicked on it and found myself looking at a picture of a long-faced man with a full head of thick, somewhat oily hair, the same man I'd seen the evening before. According to his profile, he lived in Richmond, had a B.B.A. from the University of Richmond, and was a licensed C.P.A. So his story checked out.

Neither Garrett Holloway nor Brett Jennings, the party hosts of Sunday night, was in the phonebook. I could find them neither in the physical director nor online, so I called Rodney Burns.

"This is Rodney Burns," he said as he picked up the phone.

"This is Robin Starling. I'm trying to get a couple of phone numbers—probably mobile numbers."

"What are the names?"

I gave them to him. I waited. In about sixty seconds he read me off a number. In thirty more he had the other one.

"Some time you're going to have to show me how you do that," I said.

"No secret. I subscribe to a database."

Ah. "Well, thanks a lot."

I called Garrett Jennings first. He didn't answer and had a voice mailbox that had not been set up yet. I tried Brett Holloway, who, as luck would have it, also had a voice mailbox that had not been set up. I thought about it a minute, then sent a text to each of them: "This is Robin Starling. I'm an attorney representing Natalie Stevens, who is in trouble and really needs your help. Call me."

My phone rang ten seconds later.

"This is Garrett. You called about Natalie? I'm sorry I didn't pick up a minute ago, but I didn't recognize your number."

"I understand."

"What's going on with Natalie?"

"Right now she's in jail."

"Jail?"

"You didn't know?"

"No, how could I?"

It was in the paper, but I knew not many college students read the paper. "She's accused of running over someone Sunday night and then leaving the scene."

There was a silence. "She hit someone on the way home from our party?"

"I don't know. What time did she leave your party?"

"Shortly after ten? It couldn't have been later than ten-thirty."

It's what Natalie had said.

"Hit and run doesn't sound like Natalie. Even if she'd been..."

"If she'd been drinking?" I prompted.

Another silence.

"Did the beer make her sick?" I asked. "Is that why she left the party early?"

"She did feel sick," Garrett said.

I had the impression that he was leaving something out.

"What time did the accident happen?" he asked me.

"The police say between one and two o'clock."

"Well, that couldn't have been Natalie. She'd have been home by eleven anyway."

"Are you home? Could I stop by and see you some time this afternoon?"

"I guess so. I'll be here studying till six at least. I'm taking an online accounting class over the winter term, and it's a bear."

"I'll be there early rather than late. Not long after lunch."

"Okay. See ya."

Brooke was in my doorway. "Did I hear you say something about lunch?"

"Yeah, but I'm going home for it. Paul gave me a puppy last night."

"A what?"

"I was up at three a.m. to get him out of his crate and take him outside to do his business. You know how long it takes for a puppy to decide to do his business?"

"What kind of gift is a puppy? That's like telling someone, here, I've chosen a whole new life for you. Hope you like it as well as you did your old one."

"Well, he did. I left him in the backyard, but I'm beginning to worry about him."

"You left Paul in the backyard?"

I gave her a look.

"I'm sorry. What's his name?"

"Paul," I said.

She laughed, came in and sat down. "You're kidding, right? You didn't name your puppy after your boyfriend."

"He's not exactly my boyfriend."

"Whatever."

"Paul wants to call him Deacon, but he's such a little guy I'm thinking about calling him Deeks. You want to come meet him?"

She looked wistful. "Better not. I've got a potential client coming by about one-thirty."

I'd been craving meat, so I picked up a burger on my way home. As an afterthought, I got another burger for Deacon—plain, none of the vegetables, just bread and meat. Probably I should just feed him more of the dog food Paul had left with him, but I was willing to bet Mr. Deeks wouldn't turn down a hamburger.

I dropped my keys on the kitchen counter as I came in from the garage and walked through the living room to the French doors. I'd kind of expected Deeks to be there at the door with his nose pressed against the glass—certainly, the smudges all over the bottom panes suggested he'd spent some time doing just that—but he was evidently off in the yard somewhere exploring.

I unlocked the door and pulled it open. Cold air wafted in, and I felt a sudden pang of unease. Maybe it was too cold for a puppy to be outside all day.

"Deacon?" I stepped outside, holding the sack of burgers. "Deeks?"

He didn't come running, and my uneasiness increased. "Deeks?" There were a few pine trees in the back corner, and somewhere in the middle a crab-apple tree and a tree I'd never been able to identify. A few steps into the yard, and I could pretty much see the whole thing. "Deacon!"

A mental image of him lying shivering and cold on the blanket of pine needles in the back corner caused me to run in that direction, but within a few strides I knew he wasn't there. I went through the gate into the alley and called his name in both directions. I went back in the yard and walked along the fence line, looking for where he might have gotten out. There was no break in the chain link, no gaps, no space underneath the fence that even a squirrel could squeeze through.

Somebody stole him, I thought. Somebody saw the cute little guy all by himself in the yard, and they just reached over and got themselves a puppy.

I walked back through the house and out onto the front stoop. "Deacon!" I called, my eyes scanning. There was no movement anywhere.

I sat dispiritedly on the steps, the sack of burgers hanging between my knees, the top step cold even through my wool dress. As a teenager, I'd helped my dad in his veterinary clinic when basketball didn't get in the way, and I'd been crazy about the dogs. Though at this point in my life I didn't have time for a dog, let alone a puppy, I'd already begun to love the little brown mutt.

I sighed, got up and turned toward the door, then spun at the sound of a yap behind me. Deacon had his paws on the stoop, and his tail was a blur. I stepped down toward him and bent to gather him up.

"You rascal," I said.

He yapped again and nosed the sack with the burgers.

"Yes, one of them's for you."

We ate, and Deeks piddled. Actually, I piddled, too, but it wasn't such a milestone. For a while I sat on the couch, and Deeks climbed over me as he went from one end of the couch to the other, snuffling in the cracks between the cushions enough to make me wonder how much food I'd lost down there over the years.

"I hate to leave you, buddy," I said, palming his head and ruffling his fur.

He backed out of my hand and panted up at me.

"You wanna go for a ride?" I said. Why not? I worked for myself; I was going to talk to a college kid. What would he care?

Garrett and Brett lived in a townhouse in Short Pump. There were lots of empty parking spaces in the early afternoon. As I got out of the car, Deeks bounded into the seat I had vacated and made a few tentative motions as if he wanted to jump down, but was a little uncertain about the distance. I had planned to leave him in the car, and probably I ought to. It was safe enough on a cloudy, forty-five degree afternoon.

"Come on," I said. I swept him up and set him on the asphalt. He squatted immediately and pooped. I rolled my eyes, but squatted beside him immediately to rub his ears.

"Bathroom," I said. "Good boy."

The middle of a parking lot wasn't the ideal place for him to do his business—I needed to remember it when I came out so I didn't step in it—but it beat the heck out of the passenger seat of my VW Beetle.

"I need to start carrying plastic bags," I cooed at him as I rubbed his head. "And get you some treats so you'll always want to be a good boy." I stood up. "Come on, then."

He followed along beside me. Puppies were pretty good about staying with you, but I'd have to work to keep him doing it as he got older.

A guy opened the door as I came up the sidewalk. He looked from me to Deacon and back to me. "You wouldn't be Robin Steering, would you?" he said.

"Starling."

"I'm Garrett Jennings. I didn't expect you to bring a dog." He had neatly trimmed brown hair and a downy mustache that made him look like pictures I'd seen of the young Walt Disney.

"It came as a surprise to me, too," I said. "Do you have a dog of your own that he might not get along with?"

Garrett shook his head. "No pets. Come on in."

I followed him and Deacon followed me, the steps shallow enough for him to clamber up on his own.

It was a nice apartment, but typical college guy digs. A pizza box was on the coffee table. A backpack was on the floor directly in front of a 42-inch TV. A half-dozen water bottles lay and stood around in various stages of consumption. Deacon ran to the coffee table, tumbling over himself once in the process, and pointed his nose at the pizza box. When he put his feet on the side of the coffee table in an effort to reach it, I swept him up so his claws wouldn't scratch the wood—which, though it wasn't in great shape, wasn't his to scratch.

I sat on the sofa, avoiding the biggest grease stain, Deacon on my lap. He immediately started trying to escape my clutches as Garrett took a seat in a bean-bag chair at the far end of the coffee table.

"Sorry about the dog," I said. "I just got him yesterday. It's occurs to me that pets probably aren't allowed in these apartments."

"Probably not," he said. "I'm afraid I can't let you move in with me."

I cocked an eyebrow at him.

"A feeble joke. Sorry."

"How late did your party run Sunday night?"

"Right to business. Okay."

I waited.

"One or two o'clock," he said.

"But Natalie was feeling sick and left at ten or ten-thirty."

"Somewhere in there. I wanted to drive her home, but she wouldn't let me. She said she felt like she was going to puke and it was the kind of thing she preferred to do in private. She is going to be all right, isn't she? You can get the charges dropped?"

I moved my shoulders fractionally. "I'm working on it. Tell me about the party."

"What do you want to know?"

"Whatever it is you don't want to tell me. You had a keg, I take it?"

He shifted on his bean-bag chair, looking suddenly uncomfortable. He shrugged, nodded. "Brett, my roommate, is twenty-one."

"But a lot of your guests weren't, including Natalie."

"I don't think she had very much."

"You say that, but I assume people were helping themselves, and you don't really know?"

"I was keeping a pretty close eye on Natalie."

I waited.

He gave me a defensive smile. "I guess I always keep a pretty close eye on Natalie."

I nodded. "So what else don't you want to tell me?"

"What makes you think—" He broke off. "Oh, hell. You get a bunch of college kids together, coming back to town from all over…" He broke off again, took a breath. "Someone brought edibles."

He seemed to feel he had dropped his bombshell.

"Munchies?" I said.

"Space cakes."

A light dawned, though the couple of times they'd shown up at parties I'd been to, they were called cosmic brownies.

"You know, hash brownies. Brownies laced with cannabis," he explained unnecessarily.

"And Natalie had some."

"She didn't know what they were."

"But she ate enough to make her sick. And you let her drive home."

"I didn't want to. And I told her to call me, let me know she made it."

"Did she?"

"No."

"Did you try to call her?"

He hesitated. "I guess I got distracted."

"So we don't know if she got home in twenty minutes, or if she was still driving around at two in the morning trying to find her way."

He looked like he was going to cry. Finding myself not at all sympathetic to him, I waited to see if he would.

He recovered, wiped his hands on his pants legs. "No," he said firmly. "No, I know. She went straight home."

"How do you know?"

He swallowed, cleared his throat. "I followed her."

"You followed her home," I repeated.

"Sure. I'm half in love with her, like I said. When she won't let me be with her, well, I guess I stalk her."

I studied him.

"So Sunday night I followed her home. I must have sat outside her house for fifteen or twenty minutes, even after her car disappeared into the garage."

"So she could have gone out again," I said.

"No. I know she didn't." His eyes shifted, and his tongue appeared briefly between his lips. "Like I said, I stayed outside fifteen or twenty minutes, you know, nervous. Then I thought, what the heck. I went around to the front and rang the doorbell. When she answered, I grabbed her and I kissed her."

"How did she take that?"

"Pretty well. Wonderfully well. She kissed me back. And things developed. You know. We ended up in her bedroom."

"Where things continued to develop?"

His mouth twitched and his shoulder jerked in what was either a muscular spasm or a shrug. "I didn't leave until six or seven the next morning. I woke up, suddenly alarmed about where I was. I mean, what would happen if her father found me there, right there in his own house?"

"He's in China, I understand."

"Sure, I knew that. I didn't know when he was coming back, though. And what about her stepmother? Who knew where she was?"

"You've met Chloe?"

"Oh, yes. And she's a piece of work."

"Meaning what? Scary, quick to anger?"

"Well, no, nothing like that. I won't say she comes on to me, nothing like that either. But her manner always seems, you know, seductive. Not just with me."

Deeks escaped me as I studied Garrett, and he tumbled to the carpet. "Not bad," I said to Garrett.

"What do you mean?"

"I assume you're trying to give Natalie an alibi, and really it's not a bad first effort."

"You're...are you calling me a liar?" His chest swelled as he inhaled.

"Indignation's not your strong point. Better go easy on that."

He deflated. "What gave me away?"

"Nothing in particular. As I say, it's a good first effort. You're talking to a skeptic, though."

"Meaning if I practiced a bit..."

I shook my head, one corner of my mouth rising. "It's not the way to go. Your story breaks down, and you're in trouble, I'm in trouble, and Natalie's in even worse trouble. She really can't afford worse trouble. Deeks!"

He was at the door, squatting and piddling as he looked out through the sidelight at the bright outdoors. He was done by the time I reached him.

"I'm sorry," I said as I picked him up.

"No problem. Mikey Dobbins vomited in almost exactly that spot Sunday night. He was trying to get outside and didn't make it."

"You did a good job cleaning up. I don't smell anything. I mean, I didn't. Now I smell piddle."

Garrett lifted a half-full roll of paper towels from where it had rolled against the front of the couch. "Here's part A of the solution." He dog-legged over to a bookshelf on his way to the door to grab a spray bottle of something called Odoban. "Part B," he said.

Chapter 8

I moved the passenger seat all the way forward so Deeks could stand with his front paws on the dash and see out. We were both keeping an eye on traffic as we headed for home. The difference was that Deeks saw a lot to wag his tail about, and I didn't.

As I drove, I called the office to say I wouldn't be in the rest of the day, but that I'd call before five to get my messages.

Carly said, "You've got one right now. A Mr. Rodney Burns called."

"Okay, thanks." Burns was on my Favorites list, just as my office was, so in moments I had him on the phone.

"This is Rodney Burns."

I knew who he was. "This is Robin Starling. Let me give you my cell, so next time…"

"I've got your cell. I just didn't want to interrupt in case you were in the middle of anything."

"Oh. I had a message you called."

"Yes. I thought you'd want to know that Natalie Stevens rented a motel room in south Richmond Sunday night."

"This past Sunday night? The night..."

"Yes. The night of this alleged hit and run. It was the Best Western at the corner of Chippenham Parkway and the Midlothian Turnpike."

"What would she be doing with a motel room?"

"You might ask her that. Whatever you do, though, you might want to do in a hurry. The Richmond Police have this, too."

"How did they get it?"

"I think someone called them."

"How did you get it? Another subscription service?"

He hesitated. "Sort of," he said.

"That clears that up."

Paul Soldano's cell was on my Favorites list, too. I never called his office number at the Federal Reserve Bank, because bank examiners don't answer the office phone at certain times of day—after four for example or anytime during the hour before they plan to go to lunch. There might not be much chance of getting caught with something that would extend into their personal time, but some chances just aren't worth taking.

When I got off the phone with Rodney, I tapped Paul's name, then dropped the phone when Deeks climbed onto the wheel to help me steer.

"Holy crap, Deeks," I said, pulling back into my own lane and redepositing him on his side of the car. I was going to have to get a doggy seatbelt for my own safety if not for his. Keeping my eyes on the road, I felt around between my feet for the phone and came up with it.

Paul was there, saying, "Robin? Robin?"

"Hi, Paul. Something funny's happening with my new case. When are you coming over?"

"That sounds almost like an invitation."

"Well?"

"Friday."

"Come again?"

"We're at a bank in Hampton Roads. We just got here around lunchtime, so it'll probably be Friday before we can head back."

"Let me get this straight. You drop a puppy on me, and the next day you leave town?"

He sighed. "Does that mean you and Deacon aren't getting along?"

"No. It means he's a very needy puppy. Never mind. I'll deal with it." I hung up and glanced over at Deeks, my cheeks puffing out as I exhaled. He caught the glance, and the cadence of his tail-wagging went up a notch.

"What am I going to do with you, big guy?"

He gave me a yap.

I didn't have time to take him home, which meant he was coming with me. "It's cold enough I can leave you in the car," I said, as if he might be worried about heat exhaustion.

He wagged his tail. It's hard not to like a guy who's happy with everything you say.

The motel was a two-story L-shaped structure of tan brick. The girl at the desk—young woman—was as tall as I was and had long, straight hair with a silky sheen, which is how I like to describe my own hair, though my hair is shoulder length, and hers went halfway down her back.

"How may I help you?" she said with a sunny smile.

I returned the smile. "My name is Robin Starling. I'd…"

"You have a reservation," she said, tapping a couple of buttons on her computer.

"No. I'd like to talk to someone about the room Natalie Stevens rented Sunday night."

Her smile fell, leaving her with a pouty, slightly sour expression that seemed more natural on her long face. "I'll call Michael." She picked up a cell phone, slid her finger across the screen, and touched a button. "Hi," she said, turning away from me and cupping a hand in front of her mouth.

I kept my eyes on her and my own expression sunny. After about a half-minute of murmuring, she punched a button and put the phone down.

"He'll be right here."

"Thank you."

"You police?"

"No. Lawyer."

"District attorney's office?"

I shook my head again. "I'm representing Natalie Stevens."

Her sour expression deepened. When a young man came in—I put him in his mid-twenties—she said, "She's that woman's lawyer."

"Hi," I said, holding out my hand. "Robin Starling."

"Michael Vasquez," he said. He was one of the best-looking guys I'd ever seen, with coal black hair and skin nearly as pale as mine, which was pretty pale.

"I'm told Natalie Stevens rented a room here Sunday night," I said. "Are you the one who checked her in?"

"No, I was," the girl behind the counter said.

"Ah," I said, focusing on her name tag. "Devon. Was she alone?"

"Alone when she came in here."

"But not later."

"Evidently not," she said archly.

"But you never saw her with anyone."

Her lips compressed. "No."

"Would you know her if you saw her again?"

"Of course."

"Something about her caught your attention?"

"Just her manner. You could tell she thought she was something special."

"Would you be willing to look at a picture?"

"Sure."

I pulled out my cell phone and thumbed through my downloaded photographs. I paused on a picture of Natalie Stevens, then on impulse flipped through a couple more. I handed the phone to Devon, and she stared at the screen intently.

"It's a small picture," I said. "There's another one behind it, if that helps."

She slid her thumb across the screen and studied that picture as intently as the first. "This is her," she said. "Natalie Stevens."

I took the phone from her, glancing at the screen to see that it still displayed a picture of Natalie's stepmother Chloe. Whatever else I was accomplishing, I was playing hob with the state's eyewitnesses.

"She's about five years younger than you are?" I said. "Maybe twenty or so?"

Devon snorted. "She wishes."

"You never saw her?" I asked Michael.

He shook his head. "Not that I know of."

I handed him the phone, and he looked at the picture of Chloe a moment before shaking his head. "No. Sorry."

I wanted to show him a picture of Natalie, but then Devon would want to see it, too. "What room was she in? Do you think I could see it?"

He shrugged. "Sure. The police said they were done with it."

Devon said, "Michael. Do you think they would want…" She tilted her head in my direction. "She's representing *her*."

Michael looked at me, and I gave him a half-smile. "We're all representing truth and justice to the best of our ability," I said.

"I understand. Let's go this way."

I followed him out, and we left Devon snarling behind us—not literally, of course, but something about her had put me in a catty mood. When we walked by my car, I could see Deeks in the driver's seat chewing methodically on the rubberized steering wheel.

I stopped. "I'm sorry," I said. "My new puppy seems to be trashing my car."

He moved up beside me. "You brought your dog?" he said.

"I just got him last night. We're still figuring out how things are going to work." I beeped the door unlocked and opened the door. Deeks looked up at me, then, too quick for me to react, darted to the edge of the seat and tumbled out.

"Ouch," I said, bending for him, but he scrambled to his feet and ran a few steps to where a weed was poking through a crack in the asphalt. He squatted and peed on it. He hadn't had any water since we left the house, so I don't know where he got it all.

Beside me, Michael laughed. "That's going to be a great dog," he said.

"I'm sorry."

"No, no. He's probably saved me getting out the Round Up."

Deeks finished and toddled back toward me. I picked him up. "I don't suppose he can come with us," I said.

"Sure, we're pet friendly."

Natalie had been in room 238 at the back of the hotel. Michael slid his keycard into the lock, then replaced the card in his pocket as he pushed open the door, standing to one side to let me enter first.

It was a motel room, completely typical except that it had a king-sized bed instead of two queens or two fulls. There was also a dark stain on the striped carpet a few feet inside the door, a pale spot in the middle of the stain.

"Is that blood?" I asked.

"I think so. The police technicians talked about cutting out a piece of the carpet, but in the end they put something on the stain, to liquefy it, I think, and sucked it up with some kind of handheld vacuum cleaner."

As I stepped over the stain, Deeks began squirming to get down. I held him so we were nose to nose, his rear legs kicking the air, and growled at him. He went still, and I turned him again so I was holding him in the crook of my arm.

"Very impressive," Michael said.

"I'm the alpha dog."

"Isn't that another way of saying you're a bitch?"

We turned to the new voice: Devon, in the doorway. "I don't think the police would like her being here," she said to Michael.

"They said they were done with the room and we could re-rent it," he responded mildly.

"Then you might as well show her the bullet hole, hadn't you?"

Michael continued to look at her a moment before turning to me. "It's in the wall right above Devon's head there. See it? It was just about the diameter of a pencil before the police dug the bullet out."

Now the hole was about the diameter of a ping pong ball. "How did the police come to be digging a hole in your wall? Did you call them?"

"Yeah. Housekeeping called me when the maid found the blood. I could smell it when I walked in."

"What did it smell like?" I asked, suddenly curious.

He shook his head. "Can't describe it, but it was unmistakable."

"Why do you want to know?" Devon asked. "What difference does it make?"

"No difference. In crime novels, the smell is always coppery."

"It was kind of coppery," Michael said.

I was looking past Devon at the hole in the wall. "Take a couple steps forward, will you?" I asked her. "I want to see something."

She glanced at Michael, then complied. Two steps brought her past the bloodstain.

I walked back into the room. When I turned, the hole was above Devon's head, and the bathroom door was directly behind me. I stepped backwards so that I was almost in the doorway. When I bent my knees slightly, the hole disappeared behind her head.

"What?" Devon said.

"If that's a bullet hole…"

"Oh, it's a bullet hole," said Devon. "The police dug a bullet out of it for heaven's sake."

"And the victim was coming into the room when the shot was fired," I continued.

"Then the shooter was coming out of the bathroom," Michael said.

"Oh, please," Devon said. "You can't tell anything about direction from that hole, and anyway, how do you know the victim wasn't leaving, and this woman's client shot him in the back of the head?"

Michael looked at me.

"As for direction, we can draw a line from the hole to the bloodstain to the bathroom door."

Devon said, "He could have been going in or coming out. Or just standing there, for that matter. How do we know it was a he, even?"

"Do you know who the victim is?" Michael asked me.

I shook my head. "No." My fear was that it was Natalie's hit-and-run victim.

I started my car and drove around to the back of the motel to stare up at room 238. The whole case was changing on me. Before, it had looked like Natalie had accidentally run over someone who wasn't carrying ID or any other identifying effects, maybe a street person. If he'd been shot before being run over, though ... Could she have shot him up in that motel room, then dragged his body along the concrete balcony to the steps, bounced him down to the parking lot, hoisted and shoved him into the trunk of her car...If the police found any of the victim's blood or hair or clothing fibers in Natalie's car, it was no longer a case of felony hit-and-run, it was murder. She would be found guilty and sentenced to twenty to life, and there was nothing I or anyone else could do about it.

Already I was assuming the blood in the motel room matched the blood of the supposed hit-and-run victim and that the autopsy report was going to show he had died from a gunshot wound rather than being hit by a car. Maybe not. But if so, Natalie had been in a motel room with him for some reason—a romantic tryst? pickup sex?—had shot him, had emptied his pockets, loaded his body into her car, dumped it out in the street somewhere, and mutilated the face to delay identification and perhaps avoid it completely. If the gun that had fired the bullet turned out to be Natalie's, then she had taken the gun with her to the motel. That looked like premeditation.

Deeks, after discovering that the scene outside the car wasn't changing, climbed over the console into my lap and put his paws on my chest in an effort to reach my face. I pulled my chin back to avoid his tongue, but stroked the top of his head with a couple of fingers.

"It's blowing up on me, bud," I murmured, looking down into his eyes.

He wagged his tail uncertainly. I sighed, put him back in the passenger seat. When I exited the motel parking lot, I circled back into the neighborhood, mixed residential and commercial, and found myself on Everglades Drive two blocks from Kim Beecher's house. I stopped in front of the house and craned my neck to look back down the street. I could see the back of the Best Western; it was the same motel I'd noticed the last time I'd been here.

Someone tapped on the glass on the passenger side of the car. I jumped, and Deeks threw himself at the window, yapping. It was Beecher. I reached across and dragged my dog away, then lowered the window halfway.

"You're back," Beecher said. "And once again you've brought company."

"I can't seem to stay away."

"Did you have more questions?"

"I don't know. Do you have more answers?"

He laughed. "I did the lineup this afternoon. I tried to call you."

"What happened?"

"Nothing. I saw your client, but I couldn't say positively it was her."

"How did you know which one was my client?"

"I guess I don't. I saw the girl the police had shown me a picture of."

"But you didn't identify her?"

"No. It could have been her, but like I told you, my impression was of an older woman. Look, would you like to come inside? I can offer you some sweet tea. It's mango flavored."

I turned him down—I couldn't afford to spend my days letting men pour liquids down me—but I did do my best not to hurt his feelings.

I felt the need of something more substantial than salad, so I put the oven on 400 before going back to change clothes. Deeks trailed me to my bedroom, then back to the kitchen, where I got a chicken pot pie out of the freezer, put it on a cookie sheet, and slid the whole thing into the oven.

"Now, we wait," I said to Deeks. One advantage of having a puppy, I reflected, is that I didn't need to talk to myself anymore. I tore up a couple of slices of deli turkey and put the pieces in the pocket of my warm-ups.

There was an old can of tennis balls on the floor of the foyer closet, which was also where I kept my tennis racquet, a racquetball racquet, a well-worn softball glove, and a couple of basketballs. There were only two tennis balls in the can, but I got out one of them and rolled it across the living room. Deeks scrambled after it.

He was such a little guy that he couldn't quite get his mouth around it, but he did manage to pick it up by the fuzz. I squatted down, my forearms on my thighs, and called to him.

"Deeks," I crooned. "Dee-eeks."

He waddled toward me with the ball, and I continued to say his name. When he reached me, I said, "Good boy," and held out a piece of the turkey as I put the other hand on the ball. He made the exchange willingly.

"Good boy," I said again. "Fetch." I rolled the tennis ball back across the living room, and Deeks went after it. We played fetch until the timer on my oven beeped, then we went into the kitchen where I had chicken pot pie and Deeks had kibble while I thought about my case.

When I was done with dinner, I found the number of Garrett Jennings in my phone and punched it. When he answered, I said, "You aren't really dating Natalie, I take it."

He was silent for several long seconds. Perhaps it would have been quicker to engage in a few preliminaries: How's it going? Have you remembered anything else about Sunday night I might be interested in? Here's a thought...

Finally he said, "No. I'm interested, that much of what I said was true, but we're not."

"Do you know who her boyfriend is?"

"She's got a lot of guy friends, but I don't know that she's going out with any of them."

"Have you seen her with any guys you don't know?"

Another pause. "I don't think so. If this is important..." His tone suggested he didn't see how it could be. "...you might want to talk to her roommate about it. If anyone knows anything about guys she was seeing, it would be her."

"Her roommate at Longwood? What's her name?"

He gave me a name.

"Do you have any contact information for her? A phone number?"

"Sure." After a moment he gave it to me. "I think she lives in Fredericksburg."

"Thanks. One last question. You don't know whether any of Natalie's guy friends have disappeared, do you? Just in the last day or two."

The silence this time really stretched out before he said, "Just what are you getting at?" His voice sounded unnatural.

"Is that a no?"

"I thought you were on her side," he said. "Are you suggesting some kind of sick..."

"I'm not suggesting anything. If there's anything to find out, though, I want to get to it ahead of the police."

Natalie's roommate, one Austin Reed, had a voicemail box that had not been set up. I sent her a text telling her that Natalie was in jail, that I was Natalie's lawyer, and asking her to call me. I waited, but after ten minutes I still hadn't heard from her, so I pulled on a hoodie and hooked Deacon's leash to his collar. "Go for a walk?" I asked. He seemed agreeable, so I led him outside. We walked down the sidewalk to the street. It was already dark enough that the streetlights had come on.

"Ready?" I asked. "Okay." We started running. Almost immediately Deeks fell behind to the length of the leash. I glanced back and saw that he was missing a step every couple of paces, leaving the ground and coming back to earth like a plane cruising the runway at just under take-off speed.

I slowed to a walk, and he tumbled forward into the back of one of my legs. I stopped, and he looked up, panting, his tongue lolling.

"Some running buddy," I said.

He wagged his tail, as content to listen to my even-toned criticism as he had been flying along in my wake.

"On the other hand, you're the most agreeable male I know, of any species." I walked him back to the house, where we rooted around in three different closets until I found a backpack I hadn't carried since law school. I put Deeks in it. Before he could scramble out, I swung the backpack onto my shoulder, hooked my other arm into it, and settled it onto my back. After a bit of scrambling, his head poked out just above the level of my shoulder.

"Okay?" I said.

His expression was still agreeable, so I went out the door again.

I started off slowly, jogging as smoothly as I could, but Deeks's weight shifted on my back as I ran, which threw off my gait. It wasn't awful, but it was fatiguing enough that I cut my usual loop short. I dropped into a walk about a block from my house, breathing hard despite having gone less than a mile. As I approached my house, I met Dr. McDermott coming down his sidewalk with some letters in his hand. He was a family-practice doctor who had retired before I moved into the neighborhood.

"Hello," he said. "I timed it right."

"Hi. I'd like you to meet the new boy in my life. Deacon, meet Dr. McDermott." I twisted to get Deeks out of my shadow, cast by the streetlamp.

Deeks yapped and tried to climb out of the backpack up onto my shoulder, but he didn't make it.

"Hey, little guy," Dr. McDermott said. He reached out his hand, but drew it back when Deeks gagged, then vomited undigested kibble onto my shoulder.

Dr. McDermott looked at me, his lips pursed.

"It's probably not a good idea to jog right after eating," I said, using the edge of my hand to sweep off the kibble that had stuck to my shoulder.

"No, probably not." He took a step back.

"He's harmless. Has little needle-sharp teeth, but he's gentle with them."

"I'm not worried about his teeth. I'm thinking about that vomitus you're slinging everywhere, not to mention the possibility that you might throw up next. I've got to protect my new shoes. Like them?" He turned his ankle out. "I got 'em at Academy."

They looked like black walking shoes.

"Very nice," I said.

"Twenty-five bucks," he said.

"They have some good deals at Academy."

"What do you do with your dog during the day?" he asked.

"We're still figuring that out." I told him about Deeks getting out of the backyard.

"Is he house-trained?"

"We're working on that, too."

"Well, when you get it worked out, let me know. I may be able to help you."

Chapter 9

I didn't know what to do with Deeks when I left for work the next morning. As of right now he was evidently too small for the backyard to hold him. Somewhere there was a gap in the fence undetectable to the human eye, yet large enough for the little guy to wriggle through. Between the time he got too big to push through the gap and the time he got large enough to leap over the fence, there should be a month or two when I could leave him outside, but I hadn't yet hit the magic window.

I moved his crate to where he could see through the French doors, then called Dr. McDermott.

"You still have a key to my house, don't you?" I asked after identifying myself and ascertaining that he had had a good night's sleep.

"Yes, I've still got it. Is this about the dog?"

"Deeks, yes."

"I thought you said his name was Deacon."

"He's such a little guy for a name like Deacon. About half the time I call him Deeks."

"Okay. What can I do for you and the little guy?"

"I'm leaving him in his crate, but I don't think he can last the day. If I don't make it back for lunch, could you let yourself in and let him out in the backyard for a little bit?"

"I guess I can do that."

I stopped by the police station on my way in. McClane was alone in the homicide division, and he didn't look all that pleased to see me.

"Hi," I said brightly.

He didn't answer until I got to his desk. "You've been busy," he said.

"Oh?"

"Talking to witnesses, showing them pictures of some random woman and asking if it wasn't Natalie Stevens."

"I never mentioned Natalie's name. I just asked if it was the woman they saw."

"With no reason to think it might have been."

"I wanted to know what the woman looked like. I had to start somewhere. I asked what about the woman was different from the woman they saw. No one could identify any differences."

"So whose picture was it?"

"Chloe Stevens, Natalie's mother-in-law."

"You think maybe I should put her in a line up?"

"You could."

"Course now they'd just be identifying your picture."

"If they'd picked out Natalie, they might just be identifying the picture you showed them," I said.

He chewed the inside of his cheek as he studied me. "I don't think I like the way you do business," he said.

"Did Beecher pick out Natalie?" I asked.

"No. He couldn't be sure, he said. I've got someone else coming in this morning, but I understand you've been out to the motel now, you and your cell phone."

"It may go better than you think. Devon's seen your suspect's photograph and knows who you wanted her to identify. Most people want to help out the police."

"Not Beecher, evidently. Not enough."

I had to think that was a good thing. "The reason I came by, I wondered if the autopsy report had come in."

"You might have called, saved yourself a trip."

"I like to give my winning personality a chance to do its work."

"Your looks, you mean?"

"I like to think my personality is my real asset."

"Give me a break."

I didn't know whether he was complimenting my looks or dissing my personality. "So the report hasn't come in?"

"I didn't say that."

"What then?"

"As I said, I don't like the way you do business. From now on, I'm gonna let you get your information through the district attorney's office."

He rubbed his forehead, and I noticed that the wedding band was back on his ring finger. It didn't look like we'd be discussing the case over coffee anymore, or discussing his exercise routines, either. As I walked to the door, all but feeling the focus of McClane's eyes, I decided I was okay with that.

My phone rang a little after ten o'clock. "Ms. Starling, there's an Austin Reed here to see you."

It took a second for the penny to drop. "Thanks, Carly. I'll be right out."

The girl who stood when I came out into the lobby was tall, a six-footer maybe, and thin to the point of gauntness.

"I'm Austin Reed," she said, not smiling, keeping both hands thrust into the pockets of her down jacket.

"Robin Starling. Come on back."

She seated herself in one of the client chairs and crossed her legs. Her jeans were in tatters, and I could see most of one thigh. "So what's this about Natalie?" she said.

As I related the story Kim Beecher had told, her almost lipless mouth curled in apparent disbelief.

"Doesn't sound like Natalie?" I asked.

"Not at all."

"Is she dating anyone?"

"How is that relevant?"

"The case may not be a hit-and-run. There was a motel room rented in her name Sunday night. It may be that the victim was killed in the room, then transported to where it was found and dumped."

"That sounds like a hit man, not Natalie. Are you suggesting she was hooking up with someone in the motel room? And something went wrong, and she what—bashed him on the head? Stuck him through the ribs?"

"Shot him. Right now I'm just guessing as to cause of death, though. Pretty much everything else, too, for that matter."

"Well, Natalie isn't seeing anyone. She has friends of both sexes and probably does things one-on-one with any number of them—not sexual things, if that's what you're thinking."

I turned my hands palms-up on my desk. "I'm not thinking anything."

"She was going out with some guy for about three weeks back in the fall."

"Who?"

"Do you really need to know that? It can't be him."

"Why not?"

"He proved to be a very unsatisfactory boyfriend. There's no way she would have gone back to him."

"Why not?" I asked again.

"Well, take their first date, for example. They were going to do dinner and a movie, and he was supposed to pick her up at seven. You know when he showed up? Nine-thirty. She'd already changed out of her date clothes, but she put them back on and went with him."

"Which did she get, dinner or the movie?"

"Popcorn at the movie. He'd fallen asleep on the couch, he said. Woke up, jumped on the phone all in a panic. She was like, okay, anybody can make a mistake. Second date, he picks her up for dinner, and he's got a buddy with him, a guy Natalie doesn't even know. All through the meal, the two guys talk about some dumb-ass video game and pretty much ignore her."

"That doesn't sound very satisfactory," I acknowledged. "You're sure she was over him?"

"As sure as I am of anything."

"How long have you known Natalie?"

"Since the beginning of the year. We're both on the soccer team, and they put us in the same dorm room."

"But you feel like you know her well?"

"Yes."

"Why would Natalie be in a motel room?"

"What's her alternative? Home alone with stepmom while daddy's out of the country?"

I hadn't thought of that. "Did you know she was renting a room?"

"No, actually. I'm surprised to hear it."

"But you think—"

"I can't think of any other reason she'd have done it."

"The boy she was dating," I said. "Is he over her? Is it possible he's continued to pursue her, to show up here and there, maybe at the motel? Maybe he didn't take rejection well, maybe he—"

Austin looked suddenly interested. "Was Natalie marked up pretty bad?"

"Well, no. Not at all that I could tell."

"I don't see it then."

"He's out of it for sure?"

She nodded decisively.

"But you won't give me his name."

She shrugged.

"Why protect him? At worst, I call him or go see him, and he's a little annoyed."

She rolled her eyes. "Have it your way." She gave me a name. "I think he's from Lynchburg."

A two-hour drive. It seemed nobody could just be from Richmond.

"Let me bounce one other idea off you," I said. "I don't know anything about this dead man, his age, his race, his hair color, anything. I had the impression, though, I don't know where it came from, maybe it's just a completely unfounded assumption on my part…"

"Are you gonna say it?"

"Before I knew anything about the motel room, I was thinking this hit-and-run victim was older, not a college kid."

"How old, were you thinking?"

I shook my head. "I don't know."

"You mean like thirty or something?"

"Maybe. Is it possible Natalie was seeing someone in his late twenties, early thirties, maybe someone who had a wife…"

Austin was shaking her head. "No way," she said. "There's no more chance of that than that she was seeing a woman. Or a hermaphrodite."

"And she's not…"

She glared at me, her mouth a straight line. I raised a hand in an effort to placate her. "I won't say anything else," I said. "I'm in a hole, and I'm just going to stop digging."

The phone rang when I was looking through my computer files for an old Request for Production I could use as a model for the discovery document that would get me a copy of the autopsy report. My eyes still on the screen, I picked up my phone.

"Robin Starling."

"Ms. Starling, this is Chloe Stevens. I think you need to get over here right away." Her voice became a loud stage whisper: "The police are here."

"Where is here? Your home?"

"Yes, the house, of course." I let her give me the address, though I had copied it off the ten-thousand-dollar check she had given me and had already gone out there. "How fast can you get here?"

I calculated. "Be close to twenty minutes," I said.

"They'll probably be gone by then, but hurry."

Chapter 10

There were no marked police cars on the street in front of the Stevens' big sprawling house, but there was a Chevy Impala that looked like Tom McClane's: The backseat held a familiar-looking collection of fast-food sacks and protein-bar wrappers. One of the house's twelve-foot-high double doors was standing open, so I poked my head past the edge of it and, seeing no one, went inside.

An octagonal table was in the entrance hall, on it some kind of crystal sculpture that consisted of towering stalagmites going every which way. It almost obscured the larger-than-life oil painting of Chloe Stevens that occupied most of the wall behind it. I could hear voices, but there were openings going in four different directions, so I paused to try to get a sense of where they were coming from. I took my best guess and went right.

They were in a casual living room with four sofas and a couple of easy chairs surrounding a big, square coffee table that looked as if it might weigh as much as my car. There were three of them, Chloe, McClane, and a thin man with wispy blond hair and watery blue eyes. The conversation cut off as I entered the room, and all of them looked at me.

"It's you," McClane said by way of greeting.

"I was going to say the same."

Chloe said, "They found a gun in Natalie's room."

"Did you give them permission to search?"

"We had a warrant," McClane said. "I think you'll find a copy on a counter in the kitchen."

"What's the significance of the gun?" I asked.

"I think you know enough to figure that out."

"What kind of gun?" I asked Chloe, and she looked appealingly at McClane.

"Glock 32," he said. "Found it between her mattress and her box springs."

"Not a very imaginative hiding place, was it?"

"She was arrested no more than twelve hours after she dumped the body. She may not have had time to explore a lot of options."

So it was no longer a hit-and-run. "Easier to dump a gun than a body," I said. "I'm assuming the bullet you took out of the wall at the Best Western could have been fired by a Glock 32?"

He exchanged glances with his partner, who said, "It was a .32 caliber, so from what we know right now, sure."

"Hi. I'm Robin Starling." I extended my hand, and the thin man took it in a hand with fingers so bony there might have been no flesh on them at all.

"Matt Tarrant."

"You work with Tom McClane?"

He nodded. They were roughly the same height, but McClane probably had forty pounds on him.

"Is the pistol—revolver?—registered to Natalie Stevens, or do you know?"

"Compact pistol. We don't know, not yet."

"I assume you're taking it with you. Leaving the house with anything else?" To Chloe I added, "They're supposed to give you a receipt."

Tarrant moved his head in a quick birdlike gesture. "Some shoes, two towels and two wash cloths."

"Where are they?"

McClane said, "Sergeant Burrow took them with him. You should find the receipt in the kitchen with the search warrant."

"So we're all done here," I said.

They looked at each other.

"Unless someone would like a beer?" Chloe interjected.

We all looked at her incredulously.

"I'm afraid all we have is Bud Lime, which sounds awful, but Mark likes it. He says it reminds him of the radlers he has sometimes in Europe."

"No, thank you," McClane said. "Middle of the work day and all that." He jerked his head at his partner. As Chloe and I followed them out of the room, I lifted a framed eight-by-ten photograph of Natalie with a dark-haired man who looked as if he might be in his mid-forties. I raised my eyebrows at Chloe, asking for permission to take it, but she smiled at me uncomprehendingly, so I tucked it into my briefcase. I could deal with uncomprehending.

We stood in the doorway as McClane and Tarrant got into the Impala and pulled away from the curb.

"I guess that's that," Chloe said.

"What did you tell them?"

"Nothing. What could I tell them? It looks just terrible for poor Natalie, doesn't it?"

"Not if it's a hit-and-run. You don't run over someone with a compact pistol."

"But Tom said..."

I eyed her. She was on a first-name basis with McClane.

"I have a nice zinfandel open in the refrigerator," she said. "Why don't we have a glass?"

"No. Thanks."

"Well, I'm having one."

I trailed her back to the kitchen. "I would like to talk about Natalie's bail," I said. "Have you talked to a bail bondsman? Would you like me to?"

"Well, I haven't yet. It's all happening so fast." The wine glass thrummed as she slipped it out of the rack. She worked the cork out of a half-full wine bottle and poured.

"What are you waiting for?"

"I'm trying to get hold of Mark."

"He called me yesterday morning," I said.

"Did he? What did he say?"

"When did you talk to him?"

"Yesterday morning, I think."

"So you knew about bail being set at seventy-five thousand dollars when you talked to him?"

She shook her head, took a sip of her wine. "It was a short phone call. I didn't think about bail until it was over, and then I couldn't get him back. Are you sure you won't have a glass? This is a really good wine."

I was closer to home than to work, so I headed that way for lunch so I could let Deeks out to piddle. At a stop sign, I punched Rodney's number on my speed dial. Though I'd watched her drink half-a-bottle of zinfandel, I still didn't know what Chloe had been talking to McClane and Tarrant about. I thought it couldn't be good.

"This is Rodney Burns."

"Hi. Robin Starling," I said as I started rolling again. "Have you found out anything yet about Chloe Stevens?"

"Well, no. I haven't really been looking at Chloe Stevens."

"Well, look."

"I did run across a wedding announcement in the Times-Dispatch, but that's it. It was a little over a year ago. Her maiden name was Hodson, if that helps."

"Not much, no. Find out what you can about her, will you? I'd like to know where she came from."

"Any particular reason?"

"No, not really."

He waited.

"Something about that woman makes me want to drown her in the toilet bowl."

"Then you'd have two cases to work on," he said.

The door of the dog crate was standing open, and Deeks was nowhere to be found. I went across the street and rang Dr. McDermott's bell. When he opened the door, he had Deeks cradled in one arm, and Deeks had a piece of something that looked like PVC pipe in his mouth. He gave me a yap in greeting, and the PVC pipe bounced on the floor.

"Hello, to you, too," I said, ruffling the fur on this head and getting my wrist licked in the process. "How long after I called you did you go get him?"

Dr. McDermott shrugged. "Might have been thirty minutes."

"You old softie."

One side of his mouth rose in a half-smile. "Come on in."

As I went in, I stooped to pick up the PVC pipe, which was already looking pretty heavily chewed, and I handed it back to Deeks. "Had any accidents?"

"Not so far. We've been going out in the backyard to mark some territory every ninety minutes or so." When we got to the kitchen, he set Deeks down. "I was about to make myself a turkey and swiss. Do you want one? I can put yours on rye bread or double-fiber."

"I'll take rye."

"Once you've developed a little diverticulosis, you'll wish you'd made more high fiber choices when you were younger."

"I've had double-fiber bread. It has the texture of fiberglass."

"Have it your way." He opened the refrigerator and started pulling things off the door and out of the meat drawer.

"What are you doing with rye bread anyway, if double-fiber is a better dietary choice?"

"A man likes a little variety."

"Women aren't much different," I said.

Chapter 11

Stevens Imports was in Mechanicsville, a little town that was now a suburb on the north side of Richmond. It was housed in an old warehouse of dark, crumbling brick with "Pohlig Brothers" just visible in fading paint on one side of the building. The sign in front, though, was a wooden oval that said Stevens Imports, and I guessed the building hadn't housed the Pohlig Brothers in a generation.

The surface of the heavy double doors was lumpy with many, many layers of old paint.
I half-expected them to be locked, but the door swung inward easily on massive, well-oiled hinges, and I found myself in a modern reception area with a drop-ceiling and framed maps on the walls. At the massive, U-shaped secretarial desk sat a diminutive old secretary with not one, but two receding chins, which made her look as if her mouth were set in her throat above a double Adam's apple.

"Hello," I said. "I'm Robin Starling. I understand Mark Stevens is out of the country."

"He's in China," she confirmed in a thin, reedy voice that made me think of doilies, afghans, and china figurines. The name plate on the desk identified her as Clara Partin.

"Who would I talk to in his absence?" I asked.

"You could talk to David Stevens." She sounded doubtful.

"Would that be his father, his brother…"

"Brother, younger by ten years. They're partners in the business."

"Is David in? Could I speak to him?"

"Actually, he's out of the office at the moment, but he should be in tomorrow."

So I should have called. "I don't suppose I could reach him by phone."

"I don't suppose you could." She sounded doubtful, and I gave it up.

"What times does he have available tomorrow? Anything in the morning?"

"Yes, the morning would be a possibility."

"Nine o'clock? Ten?"

"Why don't we say ten-thirty?"

We said ten-thirty.

When I was back in my car, I called the office. Carly answered, "Law offices of Robin Starling," and I told her it was me.

"Just checking in," I said. "Any messages?"

"Just one. A Ralph Waldo called from the district attorney's office."

I put her on speaker and punched in the number as she gave it to me. "Thanks, Carly."

I punched *Call*, got a secretary, and pulled out of Stevens Imports while I waited for her to put me through. Ralph Waldo came on just as I was swinging up onto I-95.

"Waldo."

"Ah. Found you."

He didn't say anything.

"Sorry. It's a reference to…"

"*Where's Waldo?* Yeah, I get it. You won't believe it, but I've heard that one before."

"Sorry."

"I assume you got the amended complaint," he said. "I had it couriered over to your office this morning."

"No, I've been out of the office."

"We need to schedule the arraignment of Natalie Stevens. Judge Cheatham didn't have any time on his docket after three today, and it's probably too late to grab the three-o'clock spot even if you can make it."

My Beetle's digital clock read 2:44. "I can't," I said.

"How about nine o'clock tomorrow?"

I was coming up on my exit. "Tell me about the amended complaint."

"The evidence no longer points to felony hit-and-run. The amended complaint is for murder one."

I almost missed my exit, but I jerked the wheel to swing onto the ramp and slowed sharply. "You gonna try to get bail revoked?"

"I'm gonna try," he said. "So, nine o'clock? The judge has a trial at ten."

"Actually, I'm tied up until after ten. Does he have any time on Friday?"

Waldo sighed. "Fine. Nine o'clock Friday. I'll arrange it."

I could probably have made the arraignment at nine and been on time for my ten-thirty appointment with David Stevens, and for that matter the appointment with Stevens wasn't set in stone. I hated to commit, though, until I had a better idea of what I was facing. When I got back to the office, I read the amended complaint, then looked up first degree murder in the Code of Virginia. The pistol under the mattress, the evidence at the motel…Somebody had murdered somebody, but right now that was about all I knew.

I drummed my fingers on the desk. My case was on its way to being a basket case, and I needed someone to talk to about it. Brooke wasn't in the office, and Paul was out of town. I could call John Parker, and try to work in some case analysis among all the sexual innuendo. I could go out and talk to Carly. Or I could go home and tell it to Deeks.

It was nearly four o'clock. I went home.

At ten-thirty the next morning, Thursday, I was back at Stevens Imports, and Clara Partin was looking vaguely across the reception desk at me.

"Yes, Mr. Stevens got back into town last night."

"I didn't realize he was out of town."

"I'm sorry, what did you say your name was again? Rollins? I can't seem to read my own writing."

"Robin," I said. "Starling."

"And you're with…"

"It's just me," I said. "I'm by myself."

I thought maybe she would ask what I was there for, but she picked up her phone and touched a button. "Your ten-thirty is here to see you, a Ms. Robin Starling." She put down the phone. "He'll be right out."

"Thank you."

"You may have a seat, if you wish."

I glanced around at the matching leather furniture, but before I could make my selection, the door opened and a man came out.

"Hi," he said. "David Stevens." He looked a bit like a young Alec Baldwin, with a full head of dark, neatly trimmed hair, but his eyes were tired.

"Robin Starling," I said. I shifted my briefcase to my left hand so I could shake his.

"You're Natalie's attorney," he said. "Come on back."

When I'd been seated and had refused a soft drink, I said, "I may have seen a picture of you."

"Really?" He looked politely disbelieving.

"I saw it at your brother's house." I still had the framed photograph of Natalie I had taken from the table in the Stevens' den. I reached into my briefcase for it, looked at it, then turned it toward him. "No, I see. Quite a bit different. There is some family resemblance, though. Your brother Mark?"

He looked as if he would reach across his desk for the picture, but he just shifted in his chair. "Yes, that's Mark. He's almost a decade my senior, but I suppose we do look something alike."

"When did you last talk to him?"

"This morning. Just a few minutes ago, in fact."

"Chloe's been trying to reach him to ask what to do about bail. It's been set at seventy-five thousand dollars."

"Wow," he said.

"Did you and Mark talk about Natalie's situation, or was the call strictly business?"

"A bit of both, though it was hard for us to focus much on the business part of it. As much as he wants to get back here, he's likely to be in Asia a couple more weeks. I think he can hardly stand it."

"I can imagine."

"So you're here for seventy-five thousand dollars?"

"It doesn't have to be cash." I gave him the options, including the possibility of going to a bail bondsman. "Of course, the bail bondsman is ultimately more expensive than putting up the money yourselves."

"Do you think there's any point in making bail?" David said.

"For a nineteen-year-old girl in the Richmond City Jail? Sure."

"Chloe called me about the gun."

I grimaced.

"The charges against Natalie seem likely to be amended soon. Will bail remain at seventy-five thousand?"

"Well, no. Not likely. We might give Natalie a night of freedom."

"That's something," he conceded.

"Are you a lawyer?"

"What makes you ask?"

Answering a question with a question was one indication. "You didn't give me the secret handshake," I said, "but you do seem to know some of the passphrases."

He laughed. "University of Richmond. I practiced for a couple of years before Mark invited me to join this venture of his, but I'm inactive now."

"Where did you practice?"

"Norfolk." It was in the southeastern part of the state, about two hours from Richmond. "Dog law," Stevens said. "I'm well shed of it."

"Dog law?"

"Regulatory law. Jeremy Bentham coined the phrase, I think. He was talking about the common law, but the common law in the eighteenth century had nothing on the modern bureaucratic state. There's no way anyone can know what's allowed and what isn't allowed. We're like dogs in the home of a tyrannical master. We know we're going to be beaten for any number of infractions we can't even know we're committing; we just have to hope our bureaucratic masters don't beat us to death."

"That's a cynical view."

"Sure. That doesn't mean it's inaccurate. You run into the regulatory maze in the import-export business, too, of course. That's a big reason Mark needed me here. I kept my license active for maybe five or six years before the fees and the continuing legal education began to outweigh the negligible benefits. If you're not using your license to earn your living, it's hardly worth the trouble and expense of keeping it up."

I could see that. "I'm surprised Mark didn't get you to find Natalie a lawyer," I said. "Rather than relying on Chloe."

"Don't underestimate Chloe." He smiled. "I did play a part in your selection, though. You've made the paper more than once. The last couple of times were pretty high profile murder cases." He nodded at his computer screen.

"They were dramatic, not really high profile."

"Murder cases all the same. And before that you'd begun to make a name for yourself in commercial litigation."

I found myself beginning to like the guy. "So Chloe came to the Executive Suites looking for me specifically?"

"She did."

"Huh. Well, I misread that one. So your brother's going to be out of the country another couple of weeks."

"At best."

"When I talked to him Tuesday morning, he was in Guangzhou," I said.

"This morning he's in Chengdu."

"Is that…"

"Further in the interior."

I exhaled, shook my head. "So for at least two weeks, it's me and Chloe."

"And me. I'm here to help you when I can."

"Thank you. I think I've come to share Natalie's lack of faith in her stepmother."

David put his head back and laughed. "*Lack of faith* is putting it mildly as far as Natalie goes. To be fair, I don't think Chloe has a high opinion of Natalie either."

The character of Natalie seemed to be the great unknown. "Any reason for Chloe's opinion?" I asked.

He shrugged. "Teenaged girls, you know."

"I guess I should know, since I was one myself, but even ten or twelve years ago the category covered a lot of ground." He didn't say anything, so I tried a more direct prompt: "Does your brother put much confidence in his daughter?"

"Oh, sure, probably more than he should. Fathers and their little girls and all that."

"So do you know things he doesn't, or do you just lack a pair of his rose-colored spectacles?"

He laughed again. "Well put. Natalie's mother died eleven years ago, so she's been without that steadying influence."

"How long ago did her father remarry?"

"Little over a year. It came as a surprise to all of us, maybe Natalie especially. Mark seemed to be settling comfortably into bachelorhood, and then he met Chloe at a reception, and everything changed."

"What kind of reception?"

"It was a party thrown by our bank for some of its customers."

"So Chloe is a banker?"

"Chloe? Hell no."

"Did the bank hire her to, ah…"

He was shaking his head. "Nothing like that. She was a professional conference-goer. She had saved up a little money waiting tables or hostessing or something, and she used the proceeds to go to banking receptions, investment conferences, anywhere there was likely to be a gathering of well-off men. She'd strike up conversations where she could, and if a man seemed interested in her, she'd tell them she was a fashion consultant specializing in men's wardrobes and give them her card. Most of them never called, and some of those who did were married, but Mark did and he wasn't, and things developed from there."

"Who told you that story?" I asked. "Mark?"

"Yeah. He knew all about it before they were married."

"Did he get a new wardrobe out of it?"

David nodded, smiling. "And then some. He was proud of her, you know, when he found out how systematically she'd set about improving her situation. And for her part, I think Chloe has played fair. She wanted marriage, financial security, and a certain level of compatibility. What she offered in return, well, you've seen her. She's committed herself to being as graceful and pleasant companion as she knows how to be."

I thought about it. "Do you know where she grew up? Is she from Richmond?"

He shook his head. "I'm sorry, I don't know that."

"Mark and Chloe both still happy with their bargains?"

"Oh, yeah. Natalie never took to Chloe, of course, and that's produced its share of difficulties."

"Is not getting along with Chloe Natalie's only real flaw, as far as you know?"

He shrugged.

"I know, teenaged girls. What do you mean by that? Is Natalie wild, or what?"

He made a face. "She never got any tattoos— that I know of, anyway—never dyed her hair blue, used black make-up, put a stud through her eyebrow. Nothing like that. To look at her, you'd think she was a conventional young woman with her head on straight."

"Yes, you would."

His middle finger tapped the desk. "Let's go for a walk," he said. "Our bank's just a block and a half from here. I'll get you a cashier's check for seventy-five thousand dollars, and you do what you can with it."

"Sounds good." I stood and buttoned a button on my coat as he shrugged into an overcoat, then let him usher me from the office.

"Be back in twenty, thirty minutes," he said to Clara on the way out.

David didn't say anything for the first block. The sky was clear, and the sun felt good on the top of my head. I could already see a branch of Wells Fargo up ahead, when he said, "When Natalie was sixteen she had an affair with one of her high school teachers."

"Uh oh."

"Yes. It changed the whole father-daughter dynamic that had developed since Natalie's mother died."

"This was before Chloe, wasn't it? Does she know about it?"

"I don't know. She wasn't in the picture at the time, and Mark might not have told her more than he had to. He wants so much for Natalie and Chloe to get along."

"I guess this affair would have been at St. Catherine's," I said.

He looked at me sharply.

I said, "Who was the teacher, do you know?"

"No. I don't."

"Did he teach math or history or—"

"I have no idea."

"Don't know whether he lost his job over it?"

"I'd think he would have, but I really don't know the details. I wouldn't know anything about it if Mark and I hadn't been having a few cups of warm saké with dinner on a trip overseas last year. In vino veritas, you know."

We were at the bank. David pulled the door open and held it for me. It's hard to deal with people on an equal footing when they're solicitously holding doors for you, but I don't know what to do about it other than meekly accept the proffered courtesy. It's hard to deal with people at all once you've marked yourself as a feminist bitch.

It took about fifteen minutes to get the check. David signed the necessary paperwork, took it from the teller, and handed it to me. I tucked it into my briefcase.

"I'm going to show you something," David said when we were on the street again. "I've been debating it ever since you showed up this morning, but I've decided the thing to do is to put it all in your hands and let you deal with it as you think best."

Another uh-oh moment. I felt the weight of the pending disclosure. "What?" I said.

"It's in the back of my car."

Already we were almost back at Stevens Imports, and the trunk of a navy-blue BMW popped as we approached it. I held back. Though I had no reason to believe David was a crazy kidnapper, there was something about the opening maw of the car trunk that made my heart rate kick up a notch.

David bent to lift out a plastic grocery sack. He handed it to me.

"What is it?"

"Take a look."

Reluctantly, I held open the sack. Inside were a leather wallet and a key ring with a half-dozen keys on it.

"I found the sack in Natalie's bathroom, tucked behind the rolls of toilet paper in the cabinet. Unfortunately, I missed the gun under the mattress."

My eyes cut toward him. There was no way this was anything but bad.

"You want to look inside the wallet?" he asked.

"You already have, I take it."

"Yeah."

"Wearing gloves?"

He shook his head. "By the time I thought of it, it was too late."

"Whose wallet is it?"

"There's no driver's license, but judging by the credit cards and whatnot, I'd say somebody named Larry Smith."

"You don't know him?"

He shook his head. "There're four in the Richmond phone book, plus an L. Smith and an L.M. Smith. I haven't called any of them."

"There are probably a dozen more in the rest of Virginia."

One corner of his mouth lifted. "At least."

Chapter 12

I didn't go straight to the jail. Once I bailed Natalie out, I was going to have to talk to her, and before I did that I needed time to assimilate the latest bomb blast. Back at my office, I took David Stevens' cashier check from my briefcase and squared it neatly on the desk. It would be good for less than twenty-four hours. Even if Waldo couldn't get bail revoked, I was pretty sure it wouldn't stay at seventy-five thousand.

One handle of the grocery bag with the effects of the late Larry Smith protruded from my briefcase, and I pulled it out, too. Larry Smith wasn't necessarily the late Larry Smith, I told myself. The wallet and keys didn't necessarily have anything to do with the man Natalie was accused of killing.

Who was I kidding? She was going away for life.

Or maybe not. Maybe not. Don't let despair beat you before the facts do, I told myself. I fished my gloves out of the pockets of my coat. They were thin, close-fitting gloves with a special fabric on the index fingers that allowed me to use my smart phone without taking them off. More bulky and awkward than surgical gloves, but they were what I had. I reached into the grocery sack for Larry's keys and set them on the desk. Five keys, none of them a car key, which was consistent with the original homeless-man-hit-and-run theory of the case. And why shouldn't' it be? In her brownie-induced stupor, Natalie could have run over a homeless man. The resulting panic sobered her up enough for her to think about taking his wallet and keys to delay identification. No need for me to envision her bouncing a corpse down the stairs at the Best Western.

On the other hand, two of the keys were marked *Schlage* and had the same distinctive, roughly diamond-shaped bow as my house key, and what did a homeless man need with house keys? Four of the keys could be house keys, in fact: house keys or office keys. The fifth was a smaller key that might have worked with a locked cabinet or a padlock. I pushed the key with my finger to turn it over and saw the word *Master* printed on the bow. I inhaled, exhaled, then bent to take out the leather wallet, which was dark brown, worn lighter in places. A little square in the corner said *Salvatore Ferragamo, Made in Italy*, and it looked expensive, but what did I know? Even if it was expensive, it could have been donated and resold in a Goodwill store for pennies on the dollar.

I flipped the wallet open. There was money in it, but of more interest were the credit cards, one American Express and one Visa, the SunTrust cash flow card, the Starbucks gift card. The name on the bank cards was Larry Smith, just as David had said. The cash came to eighty dollars in four crisp twenties. Digging deeper, I found two business cards, both of them Larry Smith's. There was a phone number on the card, but it looked like a cell number, and the address was a P. O. Box.

Larry Smith wasn't looking like a homeless man. I called the number on the business cards and learned that the wireless customer I had called had a voicemail box that had not been set up yet, which seemed to be what everybody had these days. Having a working voicemail box just showed that, at thirty, I was as behind the times as an old lady wearing a cloche hat.

"No driver's license," I said aloud. "No Sam's Club card." Nothing at all with a picture on it, not even a grainy, indistinct one, nothing to give any clue what this Larry Smith might have looked like. In that, Larry Smith bore an eerie similarity to the man Natalie was accused of hitting with her car and might soon be accused of shooting. His face too had been all but obliterated.

Brooke stuck her head in. "Lunch?"

My eyes went to the cashier's check on my desk. "I shouldn't."

"Oh, come on. Just a quick bite."

I went with her, tucking the check into my briefcase and taking it with me, but I wasn't much company. I wasn't ready to talk about Larry Smith, and I couldn't think about anything else. When we got back to the Ironfronts, I didn't go up with Brooke. "Why don't we meet at Enrique's for dinner?" I said, stopping on the sidewalk.

"Are you going to be as talkative as you were at lunch? It's hard for me to keep up."

"Sorry. I may have a surprise for you. Will you call John, see if he wants to come?"

"Not Paul?"

"Paul is out of town until tomorrow."

It reminded me of the furry little forget-me-not Paul had left me on his way out, and I called Dr. McDermott on my walk to the parking garage. "If I was to be a little late getting home this evening, could you…"

"He's right here. Not a problem."

"Ah. Well, thanks. It may be eight or so before I get there."

"I got Deacon a nice bone with some dried meat on it. He can work on it while I watch TV."

I felt a pang of jealousy at the amount of time he was getting to spend with my dog. "You're the best," I said.

"That's what they say."

I took East Main to North 18th and turned left. The Richmond City Jail was no more than ten minutes from downtown. It looked a bit like the high school I'd gone to, except that my high school wasn't surrounded by a chain-link fence topped with razor wire. The gate was open, though, and unmanned, so I drove into the parking lot and parked.

There was a short queue inside the administration building, and a young woman and a middle-aged couple occupied the two benches. After ten minutes the guy in front of me, who'd been glancing at me off and on, said, "The line may not be long, but at least it doesn't move." I was a little put off by his wild hair and torn shirt and the tattoo of a green monster tearing through his flesh in an apparent effort to get out, so I smiled at him perfunctorily. He didn't follow up.

Fortunately, the line did move, just not very fast. In thirty minutes I had presented my cashier's check and was filling out paperwork. In another ten, I was sitting in a waiting room off the main lobby, waiting for Natalie. That's where time stopped. I sat, I paced, I looked at my watch. Finally, I got my phone out, touched the icon for a game app I had, and ran over zombies. I'd killed hundreds of zombies by the time Natalie came in.

I half-expected her to be in an orange jumpsuit, but when the matron led her into the waiting room, Natalie was wearing the same torn jeans she'd been wearing when I saw her last, and the same flannel shirt. She was carrying a plastic bag with a cell phone, keys, and a wallet in it.

"You made bail for me?" she asked.

"Your Uncle David did."

A smile touched her face. "Uncle David."

"Your father called me Tuesday morning."

"Is he…"

I nodded. "Still in China."

She lost the smile.

"Where are you taking me?" she asked when we were on the road.

"Home?"

"Home to Chloe?"

"Good point. How about the Best Western on Chippenham?"

She looked at me quizzically. "I guess it is Chloe or a hotel."

"The Best Western is actually a motel." The light turned green, and I turned right.

"Why would I go to a motel on Chippenham? That's on the Southside."

"I don't know," I said. "Why would you?"

"You're the one who suggested the Best Western on Chippenham."

"I had a reason for suggesting it." I took the ramp onto the Downtown Expressway, heading out toward the West End.

"What was that?"

"You don't know?"

She made a frustrated sound.

"You checked into it last Sunday."

"I did not."

"Somebody named Natalie Stevens did."

"So? What does that have to do with me?"

"She paid with your credit card."

"Not my credit card." Natalie pulled out her wallet, showed me her MasterCard. "See? It's right here."

"Do you just have the one card?" I asked.

"Just the one."

"And you weren't at the Best Western."

"I wasn't there," she said.

I got off at the exit for Wyndam. When I turned onto Magnolia, the Stevens' street, a white Lexus was coming toward us, and Natalie slid lower in her seat.

"Chloe," she said.

It was indeed. She went past us with her hands on the steering wheel at two and ten and her eyes on the road.

"I don't think she saw us," I said, watching the rearview mirror as Chloe turned the corner.

"You never know what Chloe sees."

"She didn't react anyway. I don't think she's coming back." We drew to a stop in front of the house. "You and Chloe have the same model car, don't you?"

"No. Hers is an IS-250. Mine is a size smaller, the CT-200."

"Catchy names those Japanese come up with."

We got out of the car. Natalie stopped at the end of the sidewalk, her eyes on the house.

I said, "You don't have to stay here, you know. If you want, we can pack up a few changes of clothes, then go to my place."

"You'd be willing to put me up?"

"It's probably just for the one night. Your arraignment's tomorrow at nine."

"I don't understand. I thought I was out on bail until...until whenever."

"Let's go inside."

We went into the foyer, circled the crystal artwork at its center and passed under the painted eyes of a dazzling Chloe.

"That must be hard to live with," I said, nodding at it.

"You have no idea." She led me into the kitchen. "Want a beer?"

"All you have is Bud Lime, I think."

"It's not so bad."

Evidently, at nineteen she was a more experienced drinker than I'd thought. "Okay, I'll take one."

She got them out of a small refrigerator in the bar area that separated the kitchen from yet another living area.

"This house is incredible," I said as I twisted off the cap. "I may have to give up law and get into the import-export business."

"Daddy seems to do all right. So. What do I need to know about the arraignment tomorrow?" She stepped up onto one of the bar stools that stood in front of one long counter and settled her weight on her elbows, the beer bottle held in her right hand between thumb and forefinger.

"They found the gun."

"The gun?"

"The Glock 32 tucked under your mattress."

She straightened on her stool. "What Glock 32 tucked under my mattress?"

I sighed. "There's attorney-client privilege between us," I said. "Nothing you say here goes any further."

"What Glock 32 tucked under my mattress?" she said again.

"The police searched your bedroom."

"And they found a gun under my mattress?"

"Do you own a Glock 32?"

"I'm nineteen. I don't even know if I can own a gun."

I moved my head. "Actually, I don't either."

"Daddy owns a Glock. I don't know what kind."

"Is it a big gun?"

"I don't think so. Kind of smallish I think. He's got a couple of pistols, but it's been a few years since I've seen either of them."

"The police have come up with a new theory of the case against you. It adds up to more than felony hit-and-run."

"Tell me."

I did: One Natalie Stevens had checked into a motel room on the Southside and was joined by a man at some point. That man was shot dead inside the motel room, dragged out to a waiting car, driven a couple of blocks and dumped. "This woman then did what she could to delay identification of the body, removing the wallet and keys and running over the man's head a few times. That was when a man came out of a nearby house and saw her. He gave the license number of her car to the police. The police found the car belonged to a Natalie Stevens who lived right here in this house. They found her car had a broken headlight, blood on the bumper which at this point may or may not match the blood of the victim…"

"This is incredible."

"Isn't it?" I said.

"So why did they charge me with hit-and-run?"

"I'm not sure. The bullet passed through the body, so it wouldn't have shown up when they x-rayed the body bag. What with all the carnage, the M.E. might have missed the bullet track—though as far as I know nobody's seen an autopsy report yet. It may be that the M.E. missed the bullet wound at the scene, but picked up on it as soon as he got the body on the table."

"And they found the gun in my room."

"A gun. They found a gun and dug a bullet out of the wall in the motel room rented in your name. If the two match, we've got trouble."

Natalie stood abruptly, went around the counter into a casual den, then turned onto a staircase that ran along one wall. She took the steps up two at a time.

I followed. At the top of the stairs was a room that overlooked the den. It had a TV and a couple of bean bags eight feet across. On the other side of the room was a short hall with a bathroom on one side and an open door at the end. Natalie was in the doorway, standing with her hands in fists. Her bedclothes were piled in the middle of a bare, queen-sized mattress. Books and clothes were in heaps on the floor.

"Evidently they didn't clean up after they searched it," I said.

She didn't respond.

"I'm sorry."

She jerked her head in acknowledgement.

"I've got something else to show you."

She followed me back to the bathroom, where one of the doors on the cabinet below the sink stood open and the lid on the toilet tank sat crookedly.

"It's like they were trying to be ugly about it," she said.

There was no toilet paper under the sink. I opened the cabinet above the toilet and found the toilet paper neatly arranged. "They were in here, too. I know they took some towels and wash cloths, but at least they didn't find anything incriminating."

Her eyes cut toward me.

"Because the police weren't the first to search," I said.

"I don't understand. Who was?"

"Your Uncle David. He found a man's wallet and a ring of keys."

"What? Whose?"

"The wallet belonged to someone named Larry Smith."

"I don't know a Larry Smith. His wallet and keys?"

I nodded, and she reached up to shift the toilet paper around in the cabinet.

"There's nothing here now," she said.

"No. He took them. Gave them to me actually."

"What are you going to do with them?"

"I don't know. I'm afraid they belong to the man you're accused of running over."

"Who is now the man I shot in a motel room."

"Maybe."

"Well, crap." She went back out into the upstairs TV room and flopped onto one of the enormous beanbag chairs. I hesitated, then dropped into the other one. For a while we just sat and looked at each other. It was Natalie who broke the silence.

"So what now?"

"You still don't have to stay here."

"You really want me staying with you? I'm obviously some kind of monster."

"Austin Reed says you're not a bad roommate. In fact, she was pretty adamant that it would be out of character for you to shoot someone and dump his body on a side street."

"You've talked to Austin?"

"When I've got a case, I run around talking to everybody. It's a character flaw."

"Who else have you talked to?"

"The people at the motel. The man who got your license number as you drove away from the body. Garrett Holloway. He's the one who told me about the space brownies."

"You talk like you think I'm guilty."

"Not really."

"You're still taking the possibility of my innocence under advisement?" One corner of her mouth lifted, but only for a moment. "I'd almost rather you think I'm a cold-blooded killer than to think I'm such a ninny as to keep a murder weapon under my mattress and my victim's personal belongings tucked behind the toilet paper in my bathroom."

"It's possible to be both a killer and a ninny."

"That would be a pretty deadly combination, wouldn't it?"

"It would."

Chapter 13

Natalie changed clothes. She packed a gym bag with underwear, a change of clothes, a hairdryer, assorted toiletries, and a phone charger. We stopped in the kitchen, where she got a handful of protein bars, a couple of Greek yogurts, and a plastic spoon. She threw those in on top of her clothes. "What I really want is a steak," she said. "I'm starved."

"How does Enrique's sound?"

"Like fajitas here we come. I'll save this stuff for late night."

Oh, to be a nineteen-year-old athlete again, I thought.

We beat Brooke and John to the restaurant. The waitress brought us chips and queso and big glasses of ice water with lime wedges on the side of the glass. "Like a margarita," Natalie said, squeezing the lime into her water.

"You've had their margaritas?"

"Well, not theirs. This is the kind of place that checks I.D.'s."

"You've been places that don't?"

"There are some. Usually it depends on who you're with. I'm with college friends, I'm gonna get carded no matter where I am."

I nodded. "Speaking of which, we're likely to be joined by some friends of mine."

She wasn't happy about it, and I didn't really blame her. She especially wasn't happy to hear that they knew her situation. "How many did you say were coming? Two?"

I told her their names again. "John and Brooke and I had dinner right here in this restaurant the day I got him out on bail."

"I thought you said he was a lawyer."

"He is. Surely you've heard of criminal lawyers."

Her eyes relaxed, and I got the hint of a smile.

"And don't even get me started on all the laws written to cover men and their specialized hardware."

"What…"

"You've heard of the Penal Code."

It took her a second. Then she snickered and squirted water out her nose.

"And here's Mister Exhibit A himself," I said as John worked his way across the room.

Natalie was actually smiling as she looked up to greet him.

"Hello. I'm John Parker." He held out a hand. She giggled and took it. He looked at me.

Natalie said, "I'm sorry. I'm Natalie Stevens."

"I'm very pleased to meet you." He winked at her, which sounds smarmy as all get out, but it's the sort of thing that works for John Parker.

He sat, signaled the waiter, ordered a pitcher of margaritas. Brooke showed up before the margaritas came, and I introduced her. "Brooke stayed with me awhile over the summer."

"Was she another client of yours?"

I smiled, shook my head. "I did get her arrested once, if that counts."

The waiter brought the pitcher with three mugs, saw Brooke and went back unasked to get a fourth. By the time he got back, John had already poured and presented a mug each to Natalie, Brooke, and me. When he had his, he held up his glass and said, "To crime."

I looked at him.

"I'm sorry. That was in bad taste."

But Natalie was holding up her mug. "The Penal Code," she said. She giggled, this time without her nose making like a garden hose. John and Brooke looked at me quizzically, but I just smiled and we all drank to the Penal Code.

We went through that first round surprisingly fast. I told John and Brooke about Natalie being a freshman at Longwood College and about her playing soccer. John said, "I could tell you were an athlete," and Natalie blushed faintly and poured herself another margarita.

"He's thirty years old," I told her. "A few more years, and that will come across as kind of creepy."

"How do you know?" John asked. "I'll have you know I expect to retain my charm well into middle-age."

"And I expect to carry college-girl boobs well into my forties," I said. "That doesn't mean it's going to happen."

In vino veritas. In margaritas, merriment. We laughed and talked, occasionally veering into the inappropriate; we drank margaritas and ate our food. I found out Brooke had a tattoo of a humming bird on her hip, something I had somehow never seen in three months of living with her.

"Is this recent?" I said.

"Not too."

"I find that hard to believe. I mean, I've seen you in your underwear."

She tilted her head and raised her eyebrows in a what-can-I-tell-you sort of look.

"I've got a soccer ball tattooed on my butt," Natalie said, and we looked at her.

"It's real small," she said in a more subdued voice. "All the girls on the team got one."

"Has it got your number on it?" John asked.

"How did you know? My cleats, too."

"I was just picturing it. Sounds like it can't be that small a tattoo."

"I know what you're thinking," Brooke told John, "and you can forget about it. You're not going to be looking at tattoos this evening."

He looked at her, then at me, in wide-eyed innocence.

"That's one of the things your uncle told me about you," I told Natalie.

"That I had a tattoo?"

"No. Specifically, that you were a straight-laced girl who didn't have any tattoos."

"It's been awhile since Uncle David's seen my butt."

John stopped drinking his margarita in mid-sip, his eyes on Natalie. What Uncle David had actually told me, I reflected, was that Natalie *seemed* like a straight-laced girl, in part because of the absence of tattoos.

"Wasn't there some kind of hullabaloo about you and one of your teachers back at St. Catherine's?" I asked.

"How do you know about that?" After a moment she said, "How did Uncle David know about that?"

I shrugged. "Was there anything to it?"

"No. Or not very much. Mr. Blonk had a great relationship with a lot of his students."

That was a phrase that could have more than one meaning. "Mr. Blonk taught…"

"Theatre. He had us over to his apartment sometimes to listen to music or watch a movie or something. Sometimes some of the guys would sleep over at his house."

"But never you," I said.

"No. Not any girls that I know of, but it was the father of one of the girls that thought the whole thing was weird and tried to stir things up with administration."

"How old was Mr. Blonk?" I said.

"Twenty-eight or so. I don't know."

"And he never hugged you, or…"

"Of course he hugged me! This was theatre. Everybody hugged everybody."

"But he never kissed you."

She shook her head in evident exasperation, took another swig from her mug. "He may have. I don't know."

"On the mouth?" John said. We looked at him, and he shrugged defensively. "Hey, I'm just trying to get a picture."

"You're thinking maybe you went into the wrong profession," Brooke said.

He shook his head emphatically. "I know better. If all the girls at St. Catherine's look like Natalie, and they were all on hugging and kissing terms with me…"

"You'd be in big trouble before you turned around," I said.

"You're telling me."

"That's one thing about John," Brooke said to Natalie. "At least he knows his weaknesses."

When we had left the restaurant and were on the way to my house, Natalie said, "I like your friends."

"Thanks. Me, too."

"I had a good time, and I wouldn't have expected to."

I grinned across the console at her. "It was the margaritas. We shouldn't have had them, what with you being under age."

"But then you might not have been able to get me talking about my tattoos and Mr. Blonk."

"I wasn't after anything in particular. I just wanted to get a better feel for you as a person."

"Because you think I might be guilty?"

"Because I think you might be innocent, yet the circumstantial evidence keeps piling up on us, making things look blacker and blacker."

"It matters to you, doesn't it? Whether I'm innocent."

"It shouldn't. If I'm going to represent you effectively, what I need are the facts—good or bad."

"It shouldn't matter to you, but it does?"

I moved my head, reluctant to be pinned down. "I'd rather you be innocent than some kind of monster. It makes the world a better place."

"One less monster at a time," she said.

Deeks's crate was standing open.

"You have a dog," Natalie said on seeing the cage. She sounded delighted rather than dismayed, which I took as a good sign. She went to the French doors and flipped on the light for the back patio.

"My neighbor keeps him during the day," I said. "Old retired guy. Let me change out of my work duds, and we'll go get him."

I changed into sweats and sneakers, and we walked across the street to Dr. McDermott's.

"This is a nice neighborhood," Natalie said.

It was nothing like hers, but I thanked her. At Dr. McDermott's we mounted the steps and rang the doorbell. When the door opened, Deeks ran past me and squatted to wee on the lawn. Then he came back to greet the new person, his tail wagging. Natalie squatted to pet him.

"Seems like he always needs to go," I said to Dr. McDermott.

"This afternoon, he lifted his leg on a flowerpot out back. He didn't squat."

I felt a pang at having missed another big moment in Deacon's life. "They grow up so fast."

"They do. The average lifespan of a lab is twelve-and-a-half years. I found it on the internet. As old as I am, I've got a decent chance of outliving the little guy."

"Now you're just trying to make me cry."

His chuckle sounded old, which really did make me sad. Over the past couple of years, Dr. McDermott had become a fixture in my life.

Natalie stood up to shake his hand and introduce herself. Deeks came over to stand on my foot.

"So you're having a sleepover," Dr. McDermott said.

"Sort of," I said, bending to pick up Deeks. "Natalie's dad is out of town, and her stepmother…" I paused in search of the right word, tilting my head back to keep the dog from licking my mouth.

"Say no more."

To Natalie I said, "I shock Dr. McDermott sometimes with what he calls my free way of talking. I try to watch it around him."

"Have to be careful of my heart," Dr. McDermott said.

We crossed the street back to my house. Natalie played fetch with Deeks. The two of them wrestled. Deeks came and looked at me from time to time, and I tossed him a piece of deli meat. "Good boy," I said. My goal was to get Deeks to form pleasant associations with my "good boy." I wouldn't always have treats in hand, but, once there was a phrase he loved, I could always reward him verbally.

When he had calmed down a bit, and we had settled on the couch and recliner, Natalie said, "Do you have them here? The things Uncle David found in my bathroom?"

"Yeah." I pulled over my briefcase and got out the grocery sack. "Until I decide what to do with them, we probably ought to handle them with gloves. Just a minute." I went to my coat, hanging over a hook by the door going out into the garage, and got my gloves.

Natalie pulled them on, looking solemn. She got out the wallet first. One at a time she took out the cards and looked at each.

"Ring any bells?"

She shook her head. "It doesn't seem like a real wallet to me. No driver's license, nothing personal like a receipt or a Costco card."

"There's the Starbucks gift card."

"Okay, he drinks coffee." She put her index finger through the key ring and spun the keys about her finger. She shook her head again.

"What?" I said.

"I can't believe this was behind the toilet paper in my bathroom."

"Kind of points the finger at you or Chloe, doesn't it?"

Chapter 14

The arraignment the next morning was at the John Marshall Courthouse. Natalie was pretty silent on the way in. I knew how she felt, because the same sense of dread was weighing on my own spirits. I, of course, was likely to leave the courtroom on my own recognizance.

At the courthouse we waited in line for the metal detector and took the elevator to the second floor. We reached the courtroom at a quarter till, but Ralph Waldo from the D.A.'s office was there ahead of us, seated at one of the tables with a red folder in front of him.

"Hey, Ralph," I said as we pushed through the bar, and he gave me a nod.

"Starling."

The court reporter got up from his desk beside the judge's bench and disappeared through a doorway.

"What you got for me?"

Ralph opened the folder and took out a document stapled at the corner. It was a grand jury indictment, charging that Natalie Stevens did feloniously kill and murder one John Doe against the peace and dignity of the Commonwealth. They still hadn't been able to identify the body.

"Murder one?" I said.

He nodded soberly. "In light of the developing evidence, we've dismissed the charge of manslaughter."

"It has been developing," I said. "Did you get copies of my discovery motions?"

He got another document out of his folder and handed it to me. "This is what I've got so far."

It was the autopsy report. On the front page I saw that John Doe was a white male between the ages of 35 and 50, which really didn't do much to narrow it down. Several pages further in, the cause of death was listed as a gunshot wound to the head. The time of death was between eleven p.m. Sunday night and two a.m. Monday morning. It left Natalie without an alibi, but it answered all the questions I had at the moment. Monday's felony hit-and-run had evaporated completely, leaving a much more sinister pattern in its place.

The court reporter came back in, and a sheriff's deputy took up his position beside the bench. The judge entered, and the deputy sheriff announced, "Oyez, oyez, the 151st District Court is now in session, the Honorable Eric Cheatham presiding." *Oyez* has been announced in English courtrooms since the Norman invasion and means something like "Hear ye."

It had been four or five years since I had appeared before Judge Cheatham, which was back when I'd been doing collection work for Northcutt,

Hambrick and Larsen. The judge had a name made for lawyer jokes, like the one about the law firm of Dewey, Cheatham & Howe. He also had a full head of silvered hair and was a lot better looking than the average judge, though I realize that's pretty faint praise. The judge sat. Waldo, Natalie, and I remained standing.

"We're here for the arraignment of Natalie Elizabeth Stevens on the charge of murder in the first degree, is that right?" Judge Cheatham asked.

Waldo said, "Yes, your honor."

"Ms. Stevens is present in the courtroom?" He looked at Natalie, and she nodded. I nudged her.

"Yes, your honor," she said.

"You are represented by counsel, Robin Starling of the firm of…" He looked down at the paper in front of him. It was just Robin Starling, no firm. "By Robin Starling?"

"Yes, your honor."

"You have been charged with murder in the first degree which is punishable by imprisonment for life or for any term not less than twenty years." To me he said, "Do you waive the reading of the indictment?"

"No, your honor."

He stopped with his mouth open. He blinked. "You don't waive the reading of the indictment?"

"No, your honor. We'd like to hear it read."

"Very well." He put on his glasses and began, "Commonwealth of Virginia, City of Richmond, to-wit…" I watched Natalie's face tighten as he read, not sure why I was putting her through this. The indictment wasn't long, but by the time the judge was done, she was noticeably paler.

The judge asked Natalie, "Do you understand the charge against you?"

She swallowed and nodded. After a short pause she said, "Yes, your honor."

"You understand that you have the right to remain silent and that anything you say can be used against you in a court of law?"

She nodded. "Yes."

"Understanding that right, is there anything you would like to say at this time?"

Natalie looked at me, and I shook my head.

"No, your honor."

"Very well. How do you plead?"

"Not guilty."

"So recorded. Now, I understand you have been released on bail in the amount of seventy-five thousand dollars."

Waldo said, "Your honor, that bail has been discharged. It was based on a manslaughter charge."

The judge looked for a moment as if he might react to the interruption, but he only said, "You wish to have bail set on the new charge?"

"Yes, your honor. It is the commonwealth's position that seventy-five thousand dollars is inadequate for a murder charge. Moreover, the defendant has a passport and has at least some fluency in French, German, and Chinese. Her father, a principal in the import-export firm of Stevens Imports, is currently out of the country on business. She is clearly a flight risk, and bail should be set at one million dollars."

French, German, and Chinese. I didn't know. The judge looked at me, and I said, "As counsel has pointed out, Natalie's father is a successful local businessman with a significant stake in the community. Natalie is a student at Longwood College, where she is on the soccer team. She is not just a good student, but an exceptional one, as her proficiency in three foreign languages would suggest. Bail should be set in an amount sufficient to insure her appearance, but no higher. One million dollars has nothing to recommend it other than being a big round number. One-quarter that would represent a significant financial commitment on the part of the defendant and her family, one that will be more than sufficient to assure her appearance."

The judge tapped his teeth with his pen. "Counselor?"

Waldo said, "Two hundred fifty thousand dollars is clearly inadequate given the financial resources of the defendant's family."

"You have evidence as to the financial resources of the defendant's family?"

"Uh, no, your honor. The case has really been developing too fast, and as I said, the defendant's father is out of the country and unavailable."

"I see." The judge looked at me a moment, then looked at Natalie. "Bail is set at five hundred thousand dollars. The defendant is remanded into the custody of the sheriff."

As the judge left the courtroom, I blew out my pent up breath and smiled bleakly at Natalie. "I'm sorry."

"Five hundred thousand's just another big round number. He pulled it out of his butt, didn't he?"

"I think that's where a lot of judicial decisions come from," I said.

At my request the deputy sheriff gave us fifteen minutes to confer. He put us in a conference room the size of a broom closet with two plastic chairs and a table the size of a TV tray. Neither Natalie nor I sat down.

"So I'm back in jail," she said.

"The man you're accused of killing was shot, not just run over."

"In a way it makes me feel better. I've been torturing myself with the thought that I'd been driving all around Richmond running over people, but I was so out of my head I just couldn't remember. But I know I didn't shoot somebody and load his body into my car and dump it."

"The autopsy report says the man was between thirty-five and fifty."

"And that's just offensive. What do they think I was doing in a motel room with a middle-aged man? That's disgusting."

I liked Natalie, and it depressed me to see the deputy sheriff handcuff her and lead her off down the hall on her way back to jail. I called David Stevens on my way back to the office, but had to leave a message with his dried-up secretary. He would be getting his 75,000 dollars back. What I hoped was that he'd be willing to walk down to his bank again to get a cashier's check for half-a-million, but I wasn't counting on it.

Once I got back to the office, I found myself adrift, with nothing to do on Natalie's case and nothing else to work on either. I really needed more business to walk through the door, but, if more business was ambulatory, it sure wasn't strolling in my direction.

"Lunch?" Brooke asked me from my doorway, and I looked at my watch. Eleven-thirty.

"Where have you been?" I asked.

"Servicing clients."

"You might want to work on how you phrase that." I stood up and grabbed my coat and my purse.

"You've just got a dirty mind."

"I won't argue with you."

We had lunch at a Thai place that recently opened up in Shockoe Slip, then walked back to the office in sunshine that made for a pleasant contrast with the crisp winter air. Brooke went into her office to work. I sat behind my desk and thought. I liked to develop a case by going places and talking to people, but it seemed to me that I had run out of people to talk to.

I played a couple of games of spider solitaire while I ruminated. Though I didn't come up with any ideas pertaining to Natalie's case, I did win two games out of three before the phone rang. Paul Soldano.

"Back in town?" I asked.

"I told you I would be. How's the little guy?"

"Deeks? He's fine. A bit too creative to stay in the backyard, but he's been hanging out with Dr. McDermott during the day."

"Hey, that's a solution. I bet the old guy enjoys the companionship."

"I hope he does. It's a big imposition if he's just doing me a favor."

"I thought I'd drop by tonight. See how he's settling in."

"But you changed your mind?"

"Uh, no."

"You used the past tense: You thought you'd drop by."

"Okay. I'm thinking I'll drop by. What's gotten into you?"

"I'm just depressed."

"Tell me about it over dinner?"

"I could, but it seems all I do is eat."

"We could go bowling, skating, walk around the lake at the U of R…"

"You'd go skating?"

"Well, with you. I can't say it'd be my top choice."

"Why don't you pick up a pizza on your way over, and we can watch a movie."

My plan was to stop by Rodney's office on the way home to give him the wallet and the keys David Stevens had given me. He might not be able to find out anything about this Larry Smith—talk about your needle in a haystack—but he could look.

A flat tire derailed my plan. It was my left back tire, and it was so flat the rim was resting on the ground. I walked around the car to make sure it was the only tire that was flat, then I debated: Call a tow-truck or change the tire. I looked at my watch and sighed.

I put my briefcase in the car and popped the trunk. When I had rolled back the trunk liner, I found myself looking at a compact spare. I got out the owner's manual, which had instructions for changing a tire. It also had a number for Volkswagen Roadside Assistance: Evidently, I had free towing for as long as my car was under warranty. I called the number.

By the time my tire was fixed, it was six-thirty. I'd lost two hours.

"What was wrong with it?" I asked the service person.

"It was flat."

Duh. "Did you fix it?"

"We aired it up. Thirty-two pounds all around."

"What cause it to go flat?"

"Can't tell. Valve stem was fine, couldn't find a leak. It looks like someone just let the air out."

Chapter 15

Deeks's crate was standing open as per usual. I changed into sweats and sneakers, then headed over to Dr. McDermott's to pick him up. Deeks was excited to see me, to judge by all the jumping and twisting. I picked him up, turning my head so he could reach my neck and chin but not the rest of my face.

"Sorry I'm late again," I said.

"You had a flat. Not much you could do about that."

"You don't have to bring him over here every day, you know."

"Do you mind? There's no point in us both being alone right across the street from each other."

"I guess not."

"What do you feed him?" Dr. McDermott asked. "The two of us just split a ham-and-cheese omelet."

"Good grief." I held up Deeks so I could look him in the face. "Did you just have an omelet?" To Dr. McDermott, I said, "You're going to spoil him."

"Well, I could tell he was hungry, and I didn't want to go prowling through your cupboards in search of dog food."

"I'm not sure you'd have found any. I need to go shopping."

"Maybe I can pick something up, too. What kind shall we get? Do you know anything about Evo? From what I've read, it may be the best kibble on the market."

"It's one of the more expensive kibbles on the market, from what I remember."

"Well, sure it may cost a little more. But we want widdle Deacon to have the best." He reached out to turn Deeks' head toward him. "Don't we, widdle guy?"

I made a mental note not to talk baby-talk to my dog.

"Is that your boyfriend pulling up?" He nodded. Paul Soldano was across the street getting out of his Camry.

"He's just a friend," I said automatically, raising a hand to wave to Paul.

"And he's a boy," Dr. McDermott said, "or at least he looks like one."

"Have it your way."

Paul was crossing the street to join us. Deacon noticed him and started wriggling. I put him down, and he ran down the sidewalk to greet him. Paul squatted to pat him. "Hey dare my widda buddy," he said, pushing him from side to side, not letting him get his mouth on his hand. "Hey my widda widda buddy-boy."

No baby-talk to dogs, I told myself again. "Pick him up, and let's go eat," I said. I looked back at Dr.

McDermott, raising my eyebrows, but he held up a hand.

"Like I said, I've eaten."

"I brought pizza like you said," Paul said.

"You've got to love a guy who follows instructions," Dr. McDermott told me.

We ate at the coffee table tossing bits of crust to Deeks, who gobbled them voraciously.

"Refined flour's probably not the best for him," I said as Paul surfed the TV channels.

"Probably not the best for us, either," Paul said. "How about this one. It looks like it's just starting."

"What is it?"

"Hitchcock, 'Shadow of a Doubt.' Look, 'Psycho's' going to be on right behind it. Do you like Hitchcock?"

"I think I saw 'To Catch a Thief' once."

"You're a real aficionado. This one's actually my favorite, and Turner Classic Movies doesn't have commercials."

"You've sold me."

The pizza box was on the coffee table. Deeks, who had been trying to get up there with it, gave up and tried to get onto the couch. But when Paul lifted him onto the couch, he immediately tried to cross the chasm between the couch and coffee table. He tumbled to the carpet instead.

"You know he just wants to get into the pizza," I said.

"Who wouldn't?"

"I'm not saying I blame him, just that I'd like to keep him from doing it."

"Okay, we'll leave him on the floor."

Deeks had a paw on Paul's leg and was looking up at him soulfully.

"Don't gimme dose puppy-doggy eyes," Paul crooned at him.

"I thought we were going to watch the movie," I said.

"Are you all right?"

"It's just been a long day. Let's watch."

"Sounds good."

So I nestled in beside him with my paper plate and my pizza. I set my empty plate aside at some point and was vaguely aware of Deeks licking avidly at the grease-spot. Somewhere about the time young Charlie went walking with the detective, I fell asleep.

The next day was Saturday, a day off I badly needed. I woke in my own bed with no real memory of how I got there. I was alone, though, and still wearing my sweats, so I'd evidently avoided any new complications in my personal life. Deeks yapped at me through the bars of his crate.

"Good morning to you," I said.

He yapped again, which I took to mean, "Let me out, I need to go pee-pee."

I got up and let him out.

After breakfast, I went running with him, alternating him between the backpack and the leash. Neither was entirely satisfactory, but he didn't barf on me again, which was progress. He went grocery shopping with me and stayed in the car, safe from heat exhaustion on a December morning. We played fetch, I did a little house-cleaning, then we went for a walk along several of the neighborhood alleys. After lunch we took a nap on the sofa, Deeks snuggled in beside me. All the time, the phone didn't ring, I stayed off my laptop, and I tried not to think about Natalie and her case.

The doorbell rang at about five-thirty. Deeks, who seemed a lot more excited to see who it was that I was, beat me to the door by a wide margin. It was Paul Soldano. He was carrying a sack of food that even I could smell.

"I brought Chinese." Deeks was bouncing onto his hind legs in an effort to touch his nose to the sack.

"Good boy," I said.

"Are you talking to me or him?" Paul bent to pat Deeks, holding the sack out of reach. "Is she talking to me or you?"

"Oh, I think it hardly matters," I said. I took the bag from him and began putting the boxes on the coffee table. "There's an awful lot of food here, isn't there?"

"Not for three people."

"I don't think Deeks should eat Chinese food."

The doorbell rang. Deeks barked and ran for the door.

"Why don't you get the paper plates from the kitchen?" I said to Paul. "I'll get the door."

Deeks stood with his head extended, his eyes fixed on the edge of the door and his tail a blur. I opened the door. Brooke was on the doorstep.

"Paul and I were thinking the case was getting you down," she said. "We decided to come cheer you up."

"Come in, then. Fortunately, I don't have a life."

We ate around the coffee table, largely in silence but for the audible breathing of Deeks, who moved from one to another of us with his hopes for a handout writ plain on his furry face. When we had slowed down a little, Paul said, "So tell us about the case."

Brooke said, "She's not supposed to think about the case tonight. Wasn't that the point?"

"Look at her. She's hardly said a word. She can't help thinking about the case, so we might as well think about it with her."

"Maybe you're right."

"Don't I get any say in this?" I said.

Brooke said, "Sure. After all, you're attorney-of-record."

Paul said, "I understand the case changed on you this week."

I exhaled. "Yes, it did that."

"And it wasn't even your fault," Paul said.

"What do you mean by that?"

"Well, to be fair, all your cases tend to thunder along like a pack of greyhounds."

I rolled my eyes.

"Just tell us the story," Paul said. "Start from the beginning, right where this exquisitely beautiful woman walks into your office."

My eyes slid to Brooke.

"Describe her body in as much detail as you'd like," Paul said. "I don't mind. Start with her slim, silky legs, and work your way up."

"This doesn't seem likely to be very productive."

"No, no, it's good. I'm enjoying myself already."

"As long as you're enjoying yourself."

"Oh, just tell us," Brooke said. "I like a good story. You can leave out the descriptions of Chloe." To Paul she said, "She has a picture of her wearing leather on her phone."

"No way."

"Oh, good grief." I snatched my phone off the end table and tucked it under my leg. Then I told the story, starting with Chloe coming into my office but touching only lightly on her physical attributes, being careful not to reveal anything Natalie had said to me that I wouldn't want repeated on the witness stand, since neither Brooke nor Paul was covered by attorney-client privilege. When I was done, Larry Smith's wallet and keys were on the coffee table.

Looking at them, Paul said, "So when you got the case a week ago, it was felony hit-and-run. Now it's first-degree murder."

"But it's not her fault," Brooke said.

"Is it?" Paul asked me.

"Of course not. Why would it be my fault?"

"Just making sure I understand your bad mood."

"I'm not—"

"It's her first case since going solo," Brooke said. "She has to win it."

"Well, I'll tell you who I don't like in all this," Paul said. "It's David Stevens. There's something wrong there."

"What do you mean?" Brooke said. "He's under forty, handsome, rich…"

"You don't know he's rich."

"He walked down the street and got a cashier's check for seventy-five thousand dollars."

"Of his company's money."

"A company he part owns."

"Well, here's what's wrong. He's got this incredibly incriminating evidence, and what does he do with it?"

"He turns it over to his niece's attorney."

"Yes, and leaves Robin holding the bag or...or grocery sack or whatever."

"What would you want him to do, give it to the police?"

"He could deep-six it. I was trying to save my niece, it's what I'd do. And he didn't have to search for it in the first place. What made him do that?"

"You're just jealous," Brooke said.

"Me? Why would I be jealous?"

"You heard how Robin described him. He sounds wonderful."

"I think he had doubts about Natalie from the beginning," I said. "He seems to think she's more of a wild thing than you'd think by looking at her."

Paul said, "I'm really sorry I missed her the other night. You say you were talking about tattoos in places nobody sees?"

"You see what he focuses on," I said to Brooke.

"I don't get it," Paul said. "What's the point of a tattoo if nobody sees it?"

"He wants to see your tattoo."

"Brooke has one too? You're kidding."

I raised my eyebrows at Brooke.

"Well, I'm not going to show him. I didn't even show you."

"You don't have a tattoo, too, do you?" Paul asked me. "A butterfly or a squirrel or a spider or something?"

"A spider!"

"A cute spider, maybe right next to your—"

"I think we've talked enough about tattoos," I said. "Back to the case."

Paul took a breath, evidently pulling himself together. "Okay, so what you're telling me is that you trust this David Stevens," he said.

I considered. "No, I wouldn't say that. I don't like to make snap judgments."

Brooke snorted.

"And I know you don't like Chloe Stevens," Paul said.

"She doesn't like her because of her smoking hot body and her smoldering looks," Brooke said.

"Man. I picked a bad week to be out of town."

I was done talking about tattoos and silky legs and smoking hot bodies. "Let's just say I don't trust her to have Natalie's best interests at heart. I think she's helping because her husband's going to be back some day, but wouldn't stop at undermining her stepdaughter if she could get away with it."

"That's a lot of distrust."

"As strange as it seems, the person I feel most inclined to trust is my client, except that Natalie…"

"…shot a man, dumped his body in the road, and ran over him a few times," Brooke said. "At least, if the charges are true."

"And had the murder weapon and the dead man's wallet hidden in her room," Paul added.

"If it was the dead man's wallet," I said. "And, remember, the one eyewitness to the hit-and-run part didn't actually see her run over him."

"There are some indications she likes to walk on the wild side," Paul said. "But try this. Assume everything she's told you is true. Where does that get you?"

"Somebody planted incriminating evidence in her room."

"And—"

"If Natalie's telling the truth, Chloe must be in it up to her eyeballs."

"The woman with the silky legs."

"I didn't say she had silky legs. You're the one…"

Brooke said, "Don't forget that two witnesses identified her."

We both looked at her.

"Not really," I said after a few moments. "Kim Beecher couldn't rule her out—couldn't rule Natalie out either, for that matter, or you. The girl at the motel was so anxious to implicate my client she would have identified a female gorilla."

Paul said, "That motel room is where it all went down. That's where the crisis occurred, whatever it was."

"I think we ought to go there," Brooke said. "Right now."

"To the motel? All of us?" I asked.

"I'm game," Paul said.

I rolled my eyes, but really couldn't see the harm. It's not like I'd done so great out there on my own.

Chapter 16

It would have been nice if Michael Vasquez had been at the desk, or at least a stranger, but of course it was Devon. Her face lit up as we entered, and we were almost at the desk before she recognized me and her expression curdled.

"It's you," she said.

"And my little dog, too." Though it was Brooke who held up Deeks for inspection.

"Michael's not here."

"Maybe you could help us."

"What do you want?"

"Could you tell us exactly what time Sunday Natalie Stevens checked in?" Natalie had been at a party for several hours that evening. If Natalie Stevens had checked into the motel during that time, then it wasn't my Natalie. My Natalie would have an alibi.

"Maybe," Devon said.

I waited. Her eyes went from me to Brooke to Paul.

"Who are these people?"

"My investigative team. And my dog."

"What kind of lawyer are you anyway?"

"The kind who has friends and a dog who loves her. We're a rare breed."

Devon rolled her eyes toward the ceiling.

"So you'll help us?"

"I guess."

"Thank you."

She punched buttons on her computer, sighed deeply. "Stevens," she said. She clicked her mouse as she said, "Natalie…"

"Is there another one?"

She blinked at me. "What?"

"Did another Stevens check in that night?"

"Do you think that's any of your business?"

"Was it Chloe Stevens?"

"No, it wasn't, for your information. It was a man."

"David Stevens?"

"No."

"Mark?"

Her eyes cut back to her computer screen. She didn't answer.

"Mark Stevens checked into this motel Sunday night?" I said. "What room was he in?"

"Look, you can't just come in here and…"

"What room?" I said, stepping toward her.

She stepped back from the desk, putting distance between us. "240."

"Natalie was in 238, wasn't she?"

"Let me check." She extended her arm to lay a hand on her mouse, keeping her distance as if I might come over the counter at her. "Yes," she said. "238."

"Where is 240 in relation to 238?"

She gestured at the pad of maps of the hotel that was on the counter. "Right next to it. See?" She tapped on the map and stepped back.

Paul said, "Is there a connecting door?"

"I wouldn't know," Devon said.

"Can we go see? Is anyone in there?"

"I can't leave the desk. And I don't know if room 240 is rented or not."

"We'll do better if we come back when Michael's here," I said.

"Oh, let me check." Devon typed something, waited. "It's empty. Would you like to rent it?"

"We can't just have a key? Five minutes."

A man and a boy came through the door and stood waiting behind us. "Look, Daddy, a doggy," the boy said in a loud whisper.

"It sure is a doggie. He's a pretty dog, isn't he?"

Deeks was straining his neck to sniff at them. Devon poked a cardkey into the gadget next to her computer and slapped it on the counter. She raised her eyebrows at me and gave me a nasty smile. "Five minutes."

"Thank you," I said. Brooke let the boy pat the dog, and then we got out of there.

There was a connecting door between room 240 and room 238. We could open it on our side, but all that revealed was another door, this one blank and knobless. We couldn't get into 238 unless someone opened the door on their side.

"What does this tell us?" Brooke asked.

"We never did find out what time Natalie checked in," Paul said.

"I don't know what it tells us. It seems like too much of a coincidence that someone with the name of Natalie's father happened to be in the room next to hers that night."

"So you think it was her father?"

"Her father, coincidence, or someone using her father's name."

"Let's say it was Natalie's father," Paul said. "Why would he be spying on her?"

"Suppose it wasn't Natalie?" I countered.

"Who would it be?"

"Devon identified Chloe. Suppose he was spying on his wife?"

Brooke slapped my shoulder. "Because Chloe was having an affair!" I noticed she wasn't holding Deeks and looked around just as he went out the door.

"Deeks!" I ran after him.

The man and boy we had seen in the lobby were just coming up the stairs, the man lugging a suitcase. He put it down as he reached the top of the steps and snagged Deeks.

"Almost got away," he said as he handed Deeks to me.

The boy reached up a shy hand to pat the dog and seemed delighted when Deeks licked it.

The man pulled up the handle of the suitcase and started to roll it. "Come on, Martin."

The boy gave me a quick smile and hurried after him, but they didn't have far to go. They were in room 238. Devon was playing with us. As Martin's dad pushed open the door, I put Deeks down and then grabbed at him so that he scrambled away. Both hands reaching, I started after him.

He ran, delighted at the offer of a game of chase, and darted through the open door of room 238. "Sorry," I said, following Deeks. "Sorry." I managed to get past the man and his son without throwing elbows, but let Deeks get deep into the room before I caught him. "He's a squirmy little thing," I said. "Slipped right out of my arms."

Not even his tail was squirming at that particular moment, but he was panting a little.

"There's a connecting door to our room," I said. "I can just go right through here." I pulled it open, expecting to see Paul and Brooke on the other side, but the connecting door into 240 was closed.

"Maybe not," the man said.

"Robin?" It was Brooke. She and Paul were on the walkway at the door of room 238.

"I'm sorry," I said again to the man whose room I had invaded. This time I think I managed a bit more sincerity. "Hey, look. There's a hole in your wall." I reached up and poked my finger through it as I went past. It was on the same wall as the connecting door, which didn't quite fit my theory of Mark Stevens coming through it with his gun blazing, but unless the connecting door had been open in room 238, it was hard to see how he'd have managed it anyway.

Both Paul and Brooke glanced at the hole, then backed out of the doorway.

I turned. "I really am sorry about busting in on you and your boy."

"It's quite all right," the man said.

The boy said, "Do you like my daddy?"

"What? Yes, your father seems like a very nice man."

The man put a restraining hand on his son's shoulder.

"Do you want to marry him?" Martin asked me. "He's thirty-four."

I shot the man a glance. "I don't know your father well enough to marry him."

"You could get to know him." Kids had an answer for everything.

"I'm sorry," the man said. "He lost his mother a year ago."

"Oh." I felt a stab of sadness and tried to rally. "Well, you've got quite an agent working for you there."

"Yes, he's all of that." The man patted the boy's head.

"Bye bye now." I pulled the door shut behind me. Took a deep breath. Jerked my head at Paul and Brooke and got out of there.

We went by my car on the way back to the motel office. Everything having to do with the case, I kept in my briefcase, which at the moment was in the car.

Devon wasn't at the counter, but when we got closer we could see her in an office behind the counter and to one side.

"We're returning the key," I called, putting it on the counter.

She nodded, but didn't come out.

"I had another question."

Her eye-roll encompassed her whole head, but she did come out to the counter.

"We got sidetracked," I said. "The whole reason I came tonight was to find out what time Natalie checked in."

"Why do you need to know that?"

I shrugged and gave her what I hoped was a disarming smile. "I need to know everything."

"Of course you do."

She tapped at the computer. "Six-thirty-six," she said.

"Six-thirty-six Sunday evening?"

She smiled, but didn't answer.

"One last thing." I set a framed photograph face-up on the counter. It was the one of Natalie and her father I had taken from the Stevens home. Devon glanced at it, then up at me.

"Recognize either of them?" I asked.

"Not the girl. I've seen the man before."

"Is it Mark Stevens?"

"Mm, who knows, you know? I check in a lot of people in a week."

"But this man has been a guest at this motel," I said. "You think."

She nodded. "I'm pretty sure."

"How did Mark Stevens pay for his room Sunday night? Credit card?"

"I can't give you his financial information. That would be a breach of motel ethics."

"I wouldn't want you to breach motel ethics." I tried hard not to sound sarcastic. "All I really need to know is cash or credit card."

She looked. "Cash," she said.

"Cash." I was disappointed. "Would he have had to put down a deposit, present some sort of ID? You wouldn't have made a copy of his driver's license, would you?"

"No, we don't do that."

"What if they trash the room, run off with the bedding, something like that?"

She shrugged. "It's a risk, I guess. As far as I know, we don't get stung very often."

"How did Mark Stevens come to have the room next to Natalie Stevens? Did they check in together?"

"No, I'm pretty sure they didn't. They paid separately anyway."

"Who checked in first?"

She referred to her computer. "Mark checked in at nine-twenty-one."

"Did he ask about Natalie, request the room next to hers? Ask for Room 240 specifically?"

She made a face, tilting her head. "I can't remember."

"Would you remember a man asking for a specific room?"

She shrugged. "Maybe? It might depend on how he broached the subject."

"Uh huh," I said.

Chapter 17

We went back to the car. Paul once again offered to take the back seat, Brooke once again demurred. "You're taller than I am," she said.

"Yes, you said that before. It's not really true, you know. What I am is fatter than you. It does make me less agile when it comes to scrambling into the back of this Beetle, but I can do it."

"I didn't want to say you were fat," Brooke said.

"Ouch."

When we were underway, Brooke in the back seat holding Deeks, she observed, "That girl doesn't like you."

"I thought she was beginning to warm to me a little."

Paul said, "There're a lot of people who don't like Robin. She has a knack for irritating the crap out of them somehow."

"Thank you, Mr. Soldano. She may just be jealous, though," I said. "She's very possessive of the owner's son, who's a really good-looking guy. Nice, too."

"Maybe I should be jealous," Paul said.

"There's nothing for her to be jealous about," Brooke said. "She's a really pretty girl—or she is when she smiles."

"You have to look quick to catch her doing that," I said.

Before I left for work on Monday, I walked Deeks over to Dr. McDermott's house to save Dr. McDermott the trouble of walking over to get him.

"Come here, I've got something to show you." The something was a forty-pound bag of chicken-flavored Evo. "I can't wait for him to try it. Have you fed him breakfast?"

I nodded. "Some. I'm sure he'd be happy to eat a little more."

"I got another bag for you. Deacon and I will walk it over in the wheelbarrow later on this morning." To Deeks, he added, "Won't we Deegy-weegy?"

Deegy-weegy wagged his tail. I tried not to wince. "How much do I owe you?"

"These first ones are on me. A thank-you for letting me choose the brand for your dog to eat."

"I'm beginning to think he's our dog."

"All the more reason for me to chip in."

I went into town on West Broad Street so I could make the stop I'd meant to make on Friday before the flat tire intervened. For once Rodney Burns wasn't in his outer office, but the coffee pot was, and it was half full.

"That you, Starling? Grab you a cuppa and come on back."

I went to the door of his office without detouring by the coffee pot. Rodney was kicked back in his chair, his Edgar Allan Poe mug in one hand, the fingers of the other tucked into the waistband of his trousers. One foot was propped on the edge of an open drawer.

"Take a load off," he told me. "Tell me what's up."

"Maybe I should ask you that."

"Maybe you should," he said, ogling me with owlish solemnity.

"What do you have in that mug?" I asked.

"Good question." He took a slurp. "What I have in this mug is some of the best damn coffee you'd ever want to drink."

"Krispy Kreme?"

"Not just any Krispy Kreme. It's their signature dark roast, a rich Arabica blend of African, Indonesian, and Central American coffees."

"And what do you have in it? Shot of Jack Daniels?"

"Huh. I wouldn't put anything in this coffee to adulterate it. It's a rocking hearty roast for the sophisticated sipper."

I moved a stack of papers out of one of his client chairs and sat down. "They ought to put you on the payroll."

"So," he said. "You tell me what you've got for me, then I'll tell you what I've got for you."

"My big news is that Mark Stevens occupied the room next to Natalie's Sunday night. Mark Stevens is the name of her father."

"Okay."

"Someone who gave the name of Mark Stevens, anyway," I continued. "He paid cash, so I have my doubts. Not only does Mark Stevens seem like the sort of man who'd use a credit card, but he's out of the country."

"So you said. In China, heading deeper into the interior. I'll try to track him for you. In the meantime, I found out something about Stevens Imports." He reached for a folder and a legal pad. "I can email you a written report, but here's the short version. Mark Stevens didn't start out importing from China. He got his start importing windows from Austria. It was a style of window that opened like a door if you turned the handle one way and tilted inward if you turned it the other way. He evidently noticed them when he was on a celebratory trip abroad after finishing his MBA—which he got at UVA by the way, but he was there a number of years before you were."

"How in the world do you know what he noticed during a celebratory trip abroad?"

Rodney hesitated. "I hate to reveal trade secrets, but that tidbit's actually on the company website. After several years of importing windows from Austria, Mark Stevens decided to make his own windows, and he contracted with a factory in China because he didn't want to have to deal with European labor laws. His brother David joined him about six years into it, and about that time they started importing other things, not just their own windows."

"What kind of things?"

"They started with beer."

"Tsingtao?" Even I had heard of Tsingtao.

"No, evidently somebody already had that. They started with Sinkiang Black Beer. Mark drank some in a Xinjiang restaurant—I don't know if I'm pronouncing that right—fell in love with it, decided there had to be a market for it in the States."

"Can't have done too well with it. I never heard of it," I said.

He looked surprised. "I didn't realize you drank beer."

"Well, I don't. Not really. I had a bottle of Bud Lime the other day."

"Ah, well. I'll defer to your expertise."

It was the first time he'd ever been at all snide with me, and I liked him rather better for it. "Touché," I said.

"Sorry."

"No, no. Don't apologize. I had it coming."

He grinned. "Anyway, they've continued to branch out. They import several brands of beer, wine, and teas now. A few children's toys. Ever heard of Baby Bibi, the doll with the demonic face?"

"I can't say I have. As you may be about to point out, though, I haven't played with many dolls over the last twenty years."

"It's a closely held company, so financials aren't readily available, but it's possible their revenues are in the neighborhood of eight or nine million dollars a year. Maybe even twice that."

I stared at the ceiling as I considered whether this kind of background was useful to me. At the moment I couldn't see how, so I got the grocery sack out of my briefcase and handed it to Rodney. He dumped out the wallet and keys on the secretarial desk that held the coffee pot.

"What am I looking at?" he asked.

"A wallet and keys. That's all I can tell you, except maybe you ought to handle them with gloves. Actually, you can dust them for prints, can't you?"

"I can try."

"Then I want to know everything there is to know about Larry Smith."

"Who is…?"

"Larry Smith is the owner of the wallet, or at least of the cards that are in the wallet."

"What else do you know about him?"

"Not a thing."

"A name like Smith, you're not giving me a lot to work with."

"Hey, if it was easy, I'd do it myself."

Later that morning I was in my office making sure I had filed all the paperwork I needed to in the Natalie Stevens case. Carly buzzed me and told me there was a woman waiting to see me. In a low voice—it sounded like she was cupping the phone with her hand—she added, "She wouldn't tell me her name."

"Would she tell you what she wanted?"

"Unh unh. Not that either."

"I'll be right out."

The woman was about five years older than I was with a slightly angular face and hair of an almost neutral color that she probably thought of as light brown.

"Are you Ms. Starling?"

"I am. What can I do for you?"

She pulled her chin in.

"Or come on back and tell me about it," I said.

When she was seated, she said, "You're not what I expected. I expected some kind of petite little thing."

"Well, I don't often get called petite."

"No. I imagine you get called a lot of things, but not that."

"What can I do for you, Ms...."

"Mrs."

"Mrs...."

"Mrs. McClane. Does that name mean anything to you?"

I had a sinking feeling. It was beginning to.

"I came to ask you about your intentions concerning my husband."

"Tom McClane?"

Her eyes narrowed. "Oh, don't play dumb with me."

"When I saw him last week, I was hoping he'd show me a case file."

"I'll show you mine, if you'll show me yours. Is that it?"

"Uh, no. Look, we stopped for a cup of coffee on the way back from the impound lot one morning last week."

"Is that what you call it these days? Stopping for a cup of coffee?"

"Starbucks has that room in the back with all the mattresses, but I try not to go in there." Her face tightened. "I'm sorry," I said. "You're in pain. I didn't mean to make light."

"Tom and I have had our problems, but we're working through them. It doesn't help when some long-legged..." Her mouth worked before she could spit out the next word. "...vixen comes along swinging her hips—"

I held up a hand, hoping to cut her off before she really hit her stride. "I won't have coffee with your husband ever again," I said. "And when I see him in the course of doing my job, I'll do my best to keep my hips under control."

She breathed in and out through flared nostrils. "Okay," she said finally. "Okay." She gathered her coat and her purse against her chest and stood up. "Good bye." She staggered on her heels just a bit as she went through the doorway. Her hips didn't swing when she walked, I noticed. She was a thin woman, and it was actually hard to tell whether she had any hips to swing.

When she was gone, Brooke came in and sat down.

I exhaled through puffed cheeks. "Do you hear everything that goes on in this office?"

"You really need to close the door."

"It's a small office. With two people in here, I feel like we'd suffocate."

"Did you really have coffee with her husband?"

I shook my head. "Yeah," I said. "He took me to see Natalie's car at the impound lot, and at his suggestion we stopped for coffee. I saw the indentation in his ring finger. I should have known better."

"How do you think his wife found out about it?"

"I don't know. I guess he told her."

"Why would he do that?"

"Because men are stupid? How would I know?"

Brooke smiled and stood up. "Life would be simpler if we were lesbians," she said from the doorway, and I raised my eyebrows.

"Except for the sex thing," she said. "That would be gross."

That afternoon when I pushed through the door of Rodney Burns, Private Investigations, Rodney was sitting in his outer office with a cup of coffee.

"You look like Yurtle the Turtle," I said. "King of all you can see."

"I feel like Yurtle."

"Aren't you going overboard with this new coffee pot? How do you manage to sit still? You should be jitterbugging all over your front office."

"I only drink half-caf after lunch. I get regular and decaf, and I mix them together."

"Shrewd," I said.

"You don't know the half of it."

I sat. "Tell me."

"You never mentioned just when Mark Stevens is supposed to have left for China."

"I never knew."

"Monday," Rodney said.

"Pardon?"

"Mark Stevens left Richmond for China on Monday."

"This past Monday? A week ago today?"

Rodney nodded. "Probably about the same time Mrs. Stevens was in your office hiring you to represent her stepdaughter. At 9:20 a.m. Mark Stevens was on a plane taking off from Richmond International Airport. He flew to Dallas, changed planes, flew to LAX, changed planes, flew to Hong

Kong. If he went into mainland China from there, he didn't fly. I'm assuming he took a train in, but I can't verify it and may not ever be able to."

"You're sure about this?"

"He used his frequent flier numbers."

"When did he purchase his tickets?"

"Roughly a month ago."

"I'd have liked it better if it were three a.m. that morning."

"He does the deed, then gets out of town?"

"And leaves his daughter twisting in the wind. Yes."

"Well, he'd planned the trip at least a month in advance. But you never know: Maybe he also planned what happened in that motel room."

Chapter 18

I didn't know if Mark Stevens had committed murder or not, but everybody I had talked to had given the impression he had been out of the country for some time. Natalie, Chloe, Mark's brother David...I was ready to confront someone and unload. I couldn't sleep for being ready to confront someone.

The next morning on my way into work, I drove through downtown and took I-95 ten minutes north to Mechanicsville. The septuagenarian secretary looked up as I came in.

"David Stevens?" I said.

"I'm afraid he isn't..."

I spun as the door opened behind me, and David Stevens came in.

"Ms. Starling!" he said.

"We need to talk."

"Okay. Come on back."

We went through the door into his office. Now the polished mahogany and clean desktop had a more sinister feel to me, speaking of pretentiousness and having something to hide.

"How's the case going?" he asked as he settled back into his chair.

I wasn't sure I wanted to sit. "As I said on your voicemail, the charges have been changed from manslaughter to murder. Other than that, it's going swell."

"You don't sound like you're making progress."

"I'm not. I have to spend my time uncovering information that should have been given me right off. You're real helpful when it comes to handing me a grocery sack full of things that supposedly came from Natalie's room. Not so helpful about letting me know your brother was in Richmond last Sunday night. I don't know if you explicitly told me he wasn't, but you sure led me to believe it."

"And now you don't?"

"Now I don't. Mark Stevens was in Richmond that night. Moreover, he was in the Best Western on Chippenham Parkway. Did you know that, too? Did you also know that, coincidentally or otherwise, he was in the room next to Natalie's?"

David had a hand out. "Calm down. No need to get angry."

"I'm not angry." I dropped into a client chair. "What I am is pissed off royally."

He started to speak, then hesitated. "What's the difference?"

"Beside the point. Did you know Mark was at that motel, or didn't you?"

"I didn't know it. Of course I didn't know it."

"But you did know he was in town."

He sighed. "Yes, I did know that."

"Did Natalie? Chloe?"

"Maybe not. It's possible they thought he left the previous week. He did, actually, but it was to talk to a distributor in Philadelphia. He came back the Friday before all this unpleasantness, but…" He shrugged. "He may not have gone home."

I waited.

"Look, I've told you about Natalie, what a worry she was to her father."

"You've told me."

"If she thought he was out of town, she'd be more likely to be herself, and Mark would have a better chance of finding out what was going on with her."

"What did he think was going on?"

David moved his head in apparent discomfort. "He thought she was having an affair with a married man."

"He thought Natalie was having an affair? Are you sure he wasn't suspicious of Chloe?"

He looked shocked. "I don't know why he'd be suspicious of Chloe. She hunted down her sugar daddy and married him. She wasn't going to jeopardize that."

"So you think Natalie was having an affair with this Larry Smith. What's your theory of the case? Natalie was meeting married Larry. Her father got wind of it and booked the room next to hers in order to confirm his worst suspicions. Then what? He burst into their room and confronted them? A shot was fired, and Larry was killed. Who fired the shot in your view? Natalie or her father?"

"Does it matter?"

"What do you mean, does it matter? It's pretty much the only thing that matters."

"Either way, the two of them had to work together to dispose of the body."

I thought it through. Pictured Natalie and her father in a panic, stripping the body of anything that might identify it. They drag him out to the parking lot, run over his head a few times, spin the tires against his face, do whatever it takes to delay identification as long as possible and forever if they're lucky. They drive the body a couple of blocks into a residential neighborhood and dump it—or maybe Natalie does that part alone. The only person Beecher saw was a woman…

"It won't work," I said.

"What won't?"

"Your theory of the case. As far as I know, it's possible that Natalie checked into that motel at six-thirty. It's possible that she was out disposing of a body sometime after midnight. In between those times, though, she was at a party. She wasn't shooting someone and mutilating his corpse."

"You sure about that?"

I wasn't sure. If she'd gone straight from the party to the motel, if her father had burst in on them at eleven o'clock or so…Maybe there was time. It might seem improbable merely because I didn't have all the facts.

"Let me give you a theory," I said.

He shrugged.

"Mark was suspicious of his wife."

"I told you. That doesn't seem at all likely to me."

"It's all too likely. A professional man-chaser, everybody's idea of a sex kitten. Why not Chloe? Something arouses Mark's suspicions—callers that hang up, Chloe disappearing from time to time, a letter, a memento, it could be anything. So he leaves town on an extended trip, takes care of some business in Philadelphia, but comes back before he has to leave for China. Doesn't tell his wife. The cat's away, the mouse may play, he thinks. He breaks in on Chloe and this Larry Smith, is outraged, takes his revenge. Maybe lover boy even attacked him, and it was self-defense."

"Who mutilated the body and then dumped it?"

"Chloe, Mark, the two of them together? What do I care? Either way, it exonerates my client."

"If you can prove it. Don't forget this took place in Natalie's motel room."

"A room that was registered in Natalie's name. How difficult would it be for Chloe to have a credit card with Natalie's name on it? She applies for a card, it comes in, she signs the back of it and puts it in her purse."

"How does she get a driver's license? Suppose the motel asked for identification to go along with the card?"

"She leaves that motel and tries another one? I'm not saying I have this all worked out. At this point, I'm just speculating, but I don't know that my theory is any more farfetched than yours. I've met Natalie and Chloe, and based on my impressions of both women I like my theory better."

David drummed his fingers on the desk. I'd never noticed before, but it looked to me as if he'd had a manicure.

"Natalie's not going to thank you for trying to smear her father with this," he said finally.

"I'm not after her thanks. My job is to get her acquitted."

That evening, when I went to get into my car at the parking garage, I had another flat tire. I made the call, waited for the tow truck, rode in the cab to Discount Tire. "Something's wrong with my tire," I told the guy. "I was in here last week. Clearly, I've got a leak."

"We'll check it out." When he called me back up to the desk, he said, "You're right. It's a leak. Want to come look?"

I followed him out into the service bay. The back of my car was in the air, my tire off and lying horizontally on a spindle tool..

"Here it is." He took a pencil out of his shirt pocket and poked it through the hole in the side of my tire. "It's through the sidewall. We can't fix it."

"What did it?"

"Off-hand, I'd say a big nail, or maybe a screw."

"Can I see it?"

He shook his head.

"Wasn't it inside the tire?"

He kept shaking his head. "If I had to guess, I'd say somebody drove a nail into your tire, pulled it out, and took it with them."

"Why would anybody do that?"

"Could be that they don't like you very much."

I was silent.

"Shall we go look at tires?"

"Driving a nail into the tire wouldn't make it explode or something?" I asked.

"People drive over nails all the time. Their tires don't explode. You can get some blowback, I understand. Depending on the tire pressure and the cross-section of the nail or screw or whatever, it could shoot the nail back out at you."

"You mean there could be someone walking around Richmond with a nail sticking out of his forehead?"

"Well…"

"At least I can hope."

The next morning, I looked around the parking garage for surveillance cameras, thinking maybe I could get the recording and see who was sabotaging my car, but there were no surveillance cameras. Though I hadn't thought about it, a parking garage with no cameras didn't seem very safe. Suppose I was attacked?

When I came back to the garage that evening, my windshield was an opaque sheet with a web of cracks running all the way across it. I called roadside assistance again, waited.

"Discount Tire doesn't do windshields," I said when the tow truck got there. "Can you recommend a body shop?"

Fortunately, the body shop didn't close until six, but I had to leave my car.

"We can have it for you by tomorrow at this time," said the man across the desk. "Can we drive you somewhere?"

"You don't rent cars, do you?"

"No, but there's an Enterprise about a mile that way." He pointed. "Want me to call them for you, set something up?"

"Please."

I didn't get home until after seven, and when I did I was driving a Ford Focus. Deeks had already been fed, but he was delighted at the prospect of going for a ride. I set him in the passenger seat, and we went to Best Buy.

Nobody messed with the Ford Focus on Thursday. I didn't have an assigned space, so probably no one knew it was mine. On Friday I had my Beetle back, but nobody messed with it, which was actually a disappointment since I had two security cameras set up inside, one on the front dash and one in the rear. On Monday, I had four flat tires. I felt anger mixed with a savage triumph as I waited for the tow truck. I had the bastard.

When I got home, I plugged my camera into my laptop and sat with Deeks in my lap as I watched the shadowy image of a man walk into the frame, grow larger, then bend and drop out of the frame. It looked like he had something over his head or his face, but the image was too dim for me to tell what. "It's too dark," I told Deeks. Too dark to shoot video through my tinted windows. It had been a mistake to let an amateur like me set up the security cameras, I told myself. Pennywise and pound foolish. I watched the video again and again, but I couldn't make out anything that would help me identify the vandal.

The next day, I took a drill, some screws, and some concrete anchors to work with me, and I mounted one of my cameras high on the wall in front of my car. When I came back to my car at the end of the day, I had one flat tire—a hole through the sidewall again—and a missing video camera.

"This is taking a toll," I told Brooke that evening over wine and salad. "I'm going to have to give up and park somewhere else."

"If this vandal is following you, it won't work."

"At least it might slow him down. This is costing me a fortune, and I can hardly think about my work."

"Maybe that's the point. Maybe you're getting somewhere on the Natalie Stevens case, and somebody doesn't like it."

"Why the Natalie Stevens case?"

"Isn't that the only one you have?"

Unfortunately, it was. "I may be at the point when I can cast suspicion on Natalie's missing father, but I really have no idea what happened that night."

"Have you talked to her about implicating her father?"

"Not yet."

"Not looking forward to it?"

"Not really, no."

I moved my car to the parking lot outside the mall in Shockoe Bottom that had once been the old train station. It gave me a half-mile walk uphill to get to my office, but the vandalism stopped. I drafted more discovery motions and hand-delivered copies to the clerk's office and the D.A.'s office. I got a copy of the D.A.'s witness list—most of their witnesses seemed to work for the police or the medical examiner's office—and I sent them my witness list. I called around and traveled around to talk to all the potential witnesses, but I didn't learn anything that seemed particularly helpful.

Deeks and I spent Christmas in Charlottesville with my mother and my brother and his family. My father, long estranged from the family after leaving my mother for his veterinary assistant, showed up for lunch, bringing presents. Nobody told me he was coming, and his expression was cautious when he spoke to me—or even looked at me.

"Look," I said finally. "I'm not the scary bitch you seem to think I am."

"Said the scary bitch in her most belligerent voice," my brother said.

"You're not helping," I said.

"Sorry." Though he didn't look it.

Daddy had gotten me a dog training collar with a remote, so somebody had told him about Deeks. I hadn't gotten him anything.

"I would have," I said. "I didn't know you were coming."

"I think everybody was afraid you wouldn't come if they told you."

"This is my family. Even you."

He held out his arms, looking tentative. When I stepped into them, he hugged me hard enough squeeze the breath out of me.

Natalie spent Christmas in jail. When I saw her the day before, I gave her a George R.R. Martin paperback, since during one of our conversations she'd said she liked fantasy. When I saw her the day after Christmas, she said she'd finished it.

"Isn't about 600 pages?"

"More like 800, but it's not like I have a lot else to do. Are there five books in the series? Can you get me the next one?"

I nodded. "Sure. Has Chloe been to see you?"

"No. She's not even pretending anymore."

"Your uncle?"

"Twice."

"What do you hear from your father?"

She pursed her lips and exhaled through puffed cheeks. "Nothing," she said. "Nothing since all this started. Uncle David says it's been more than a week since he's been able to get hold of him."

"Your father's disappeared?"

She shrugged. "Daddy loves me and can't bear what's happening to me, and he'll get back just as soon as he possibly can."

"That's what your uncle tells you?"

"Yes."

"Except that now he's dropped out of touch with everyone."

Tears welled in her eyes and spilled over. "I need him."

It didn't make what I had to say next any easier. "The night someone rented a room at the Best Western in your name, someone else rented a room in your father's."

"What?"

"Your father, or someone using his name, rented the room right next to the room rented in your name."

She shook her head, clearly bewildered.

"Airline records show your father didn't leave for Hong Kong until the next morning." I told her everything I knew.

"You're wrong. Daddy wouldn't have killed someone and then left me to go to prison for it."

"I'm not saying he did."

"What are you saying, then?"

"Maybe he's staying away to provide us a red herring."

"What do you mean?"

I said, "Your father rents a room. A man next door is shot. Your father leaves the country. He may be staying away to give us the chance to save you by throwing suspicion on him."

"I wouldn't want to do that. If it worked, he could never come home."

"He can't be convicted in a trial against you. We just use him to raise reasonable doubt. It may be that he's got an alibi or something he can use to clear himself when he needs it. If he used it now, though, we couldn't implicate him in order to save you."

"You don't know he has an alibi."

"I can't know that. I can't get hold of him."

Chapter 19

The trial started on a Tuesday morning in the second week of January. The front rows of the courtroom's gallery were filled with prospective jurors. Ralph Waldo was at the prosecutor's table, but he was not alone. Aubrey Biggs, the curly headed district attorney himself, sat beside him, which meant that Waldo was second chair.

The bailiff called the court into session with an "Oyez, oyez." Everyone stood up, and the judge came in and sat down. He waited until the jury pool was seated and the rustling and foot-shuffling had abated.

"Greetings," he said in his resonant voice. "I am Circuit Judge Eric Cheatham. At the table to your right is Commonwealth's Attorney Aubrey Biggs, who will be representing the government in this case, and beside him is his associate Ralph Waldo." Aubrey stood, and then Ralph stood beside him, at six-foot-one or two, a head taller than Aubrey. When the judge introduced me and then my client, we each stood to smile and nod at the potential jurors. At such times I try to negotiate the line between looking genial and likeable and looking simple-minded, but it's a fine line.

"The charge in this case is one of murder in the first degree," the judge said. "Twelve of your number will sit in judgment. In choosing those twelve, we will be asking you a number of questions…"

The potential jurors had filled out questionnaires the day before, and I had been up late entering the information into a database. As the judge called each juror's name, I tapped the name on my iPad, and a juror summary sheet popped up with basic information like name, address, age, marital status, and occupation. I could get more information by scrolling down: organizational memberships, religious affiliation, whether they had ever been in court or ever been a victim of a crime. The questionnaire itself went on for fifteen pages, though my summary was considerably condensed. Color-coding helped. Mildred Lees, for example, was a member of Mothers Against Drunk Driving, and her summary was outlined in red. Natalie had been driving the streets of Richmond in an impaired state the fateful Sunday night. Though I would do my best to keep that out of evidence, I was also going to do my best to keep Mildred Lees off the jury, just in case.

The judge was saying, "Kyla Sander, I see that you are a student at J. Sargeant Reynolds. Is that correct?" J. Sargeant Reynolds was the community college.

"Yes, your honor." According to my summary sheet, Kyla was twenty-three and unmarried.

"Do classes start this week or next? You know that jury service is not mandatory for you."

"This semester my classes are all online and at night. I can do this."

"I see. You don't list any occupation other than student."

"No, ma'am. I mean, no sir. No, your honor." There was a titter, and Kyla's face turned red. "I live with my parents."

The judge moved on to another potential juror. He spent just over two hours questioning them. One prospect had spent six months working as a secretary for a lawyer that did criminal defense work. I rather expected the judge to excuse her for cause on his own initiative, but he did not. She was likely to have formed strong opinions about criminal defendants, either idealistic—the defendant is innocent until proven guilty—or cynical, as in "all defendants are guilty scuz-buckets." She might be a good juror from the defense perspective, or she might be a very bad one.

Another prospective juror had once witnessed the police put a man on the ground outside a bar and cuff him. Another had had his house burglarized. One woman had once been held up at knife-point. One had a bachelor's degree in criminal justice. One, when asked if she had ever been arrested for a crime whether or not that arrest had resulted in a conviction, asked the judge if the arrest counted if her record had been expunged. The judge didn't excuse any of them for an inability to decide the case impartially. I was beginning to think that this judge wasn't going to excuse any prospective juror for cause, at least not unless one of the attorneys asked for it in a sidebar conference, when he hit on a juror whose brother-in-law worked as a patrolman for the police department in Norfolk, Virginia.

"Is it your opinion, Mr. Bridges, that police can generally be relied upon to tell the truth?"

"When testifying under oath? Sure."

"If a defendant in a criminal case were to take the witness stand, would you generally expect that defendant to be truthful?"

"If it helped her case."

"But not otherwise?"

"You can't expect her to say something that's going to put her in jail. She's not like a police officer who has no stake in the outcome."

Judge Cheatham's gaze flicked to me. "Thank you, Mr. Bridges. You're excused from further service in this case."

Jonathan Bridges looked surprised, then angry, but he got up and left the courtroom. Not long after that the judge asked Aubrey Biggs if he had any questions for these fine people.

"Thank you, your honor." Biggs got up and took a breath as he smoothed the jacket of his suit against his sides, a habit of his I'd seen before. "Mr. Hill. You were the one who saw the police handcuffing someone outside a barroom. Is that right?"

"Yes, your honor."

Biggs smiled. "You don't have to call me your honor. I'm Mr. Biggs." I wondered how a man who was five-four could say that with a straight face, but I guessed he'd had long practice.

"Mr. Biggs," the man said.

"What was your reaction to what you saw? Did the police act appropriately, do you think?"

Charles Hill jerked his head. "It was something. They put that man right down on the ground."

"Did it seem to you to be an unnecessary use of force?"

"Well, the man was talking loud and moving around some. I guess so."

"You guess it was necessary or unnecessary?"

"Necessary, I guess."

"Did the incident affect your attitude toward the police?"

"It sure makes me careful. I don't want them to grab me and put me down like that."

Biggs went on to another prospect. I was studying the jurors. Michael Burling, age 26, was wearing a pinstripe suit, which made him stand out, though not as much as the copy of the *Wall Street Journal* he had folded on his knee. It made me think he didn't want to sit on the jury—he worked in the loan department of Wells Fargo and doubtless had better things to do—and was giving me a reason to bump him with one of my peremptory challenges. He was young, though, and kept studying Natalie Stevens and me with apparent interest. Natalie, for her part, looked young and fresh-faced in her dark slacks and her white shirt with its open collar. She'd be able to hold his interest, I thought, and despite his age he had the possibility of exercising a leadership role in the jury room.

By the time it was my turn to ask questions, I already had a good idea about who I wanted on the jury and who I didn't. I asked a few questions to clarify a point or two, asked a few questions along the lines of "You're aware that the defendant doesn't have to prove anything in this trial, aren't you?" I asked the MADD Ms. Lees if she would hold it against Natalie if she didn't testify, and she said she wouldn't, which meant I couldn't get her struck from the panel for cause.

When I had asked all the questions that I thought would do me any good, the judge called us up to the bench. "Counselors," he said. "Are you satisfied with this panel?"

Biggs said, "I would like to excuse Mr. Hill for cause. He's admitted to a changed attitude toward police."

"He did agree the use of force was proper," I said. "I'm careful around police myself."

"Yes," Judge Cheatham said. "If he believed the police had behaved wrongly, I think I'd be more skeptical about his ability to hear the case with an open mind. I'm going to make you use one of your peremptory challenges, Mr. Biggs. Any other challenges for cause?"

I shook my head. "No, your honor."

"Mr. Biggs?"

"No, your honor."

"Very well. We've got a panel of twenty-five, more than we usually have, which means you each have a good number of strikes. Mr. Biggs?"

"Charles Hill." Charles Hill was gone.

"Mildred Lees," I said.

"Kyla Sander." It was my college student, the closest I had to one of Natalie's peers.

"Why Kyla Sander?" I said.

"I'm exercising a peremptory challenge," Biggs said. "I don't have to give a reason."

"The defendant in this case is a young woman, and so is Kyla Sanders," I said. "That's why Mr. Biggs wants her off the jury. J.E.B. v. Alabama."

"Mr. Biggs."

Mr. Biggs' shoulders had come forward, and he'd gotten a bit red in the face. "I can't strike her for her sex, but I can strike her for her age. She's a young college student, and she's likely to identify too closely with the defendant to be objective."

"I'll allow it. Ms. Starling?"

I said another name, and Judge Cheatham marked it on his list. Mr. Biggs said, "Ashley Nichols."

"Another woman, your honor," I said.

Biggs rolled his eyes in my direction. "Your honor, are we going to have to go through this every time? Ms. Starling herself exercised her first strike on a woman."

"If you think that's why I struck her, you should have challenged it."

"Confine your remarks to the court, Ms. Starling. Mr. Biggs?"

Biggs's lips were pressed together and his nostrils were flaring. He looked to me like he was hyperventilating. "She has tattoos on both forearms," he said. "It may be a prejudice on my part, but I just don't see her as a law-and-order type."

The judge nodded.

"John Shields," I said, giving up on Ashley Nichols.

When we had twelve jurors left, the judge sent us back to our tables. He thanked the thirteen panelists Aubrey Biggs and I had challenged, and he sent them back to the jury pool.

The trial proper began right after lunch with opening statements. Paul Soldano, who was in town this week, was sitting with Brooke Marshall on the back row.

To give him his due, Aubrey Biggs was good. He told the story beginning at 6:36 p.m. on Sunday, December 6, with Natalie checking into the Best Western motel. "The defendant has a home here in Richmond, but she lives there with her father and stepmother. That Sunday she did not go home. Early in the evening, she checked into a motel on the south side of town. At some point between eleven p.m. and two a.m., a man was shot to death in that motel room. He fell and bled extensively into the carpet, but his body didn't stay there. By two a.m. he was lying on a street several blocks away in an area zoned residential and commercial. His head had been crushed and most of his face peeled off by a spinning car tire." A woman in the jury flinched—Melanie Scarborough, age thirty-four. Biggs followed up on it. "You don't want to see those pictures—I didn't want to see them myself—but it is our duty to look at them, to see exactly what was done in an effort to block identification of the body. So far those efforts have been successful. We still don't know who the murder victim is…"

I was waiting for him to start arguing his case, talking about what evidence should weigh heavily in the jurors' minds and what should not, but, as required in an opening statement, he stuck pretty well to the facts he expected to prove. What I wanted was an opportunity to object, to break the flow of his story, but he didn't give me the opportunity.

"A man living in the neighborhood saw a young woman matching the defendant's description bending over the body on the street outside his home. He saw her drive away, and he got the license number. The car was registered in the name of Mark Edward Stevens, Natalie's father. The next morning police went to the residence of Mark Edward Stevens. They saw the car, which had a broken headlight and blood on its bumper. DNA testing tells us it was the blood of the man that Natalie Stevens had left lying in the road."

Some of the jurors were eyeing Natalie, who was sitting with her hands in her lap and her eyes on the table in front of her, with mingled disbelief and horror. I didn't have to be a mind-reader to know what they were thinking: *She looks so young and innocent. You can never tell, can you?*

"This was about one p.m. December seventh, the day after Natalie checked into that motel room. The police rang the bell at the Stevens' residence and pounded on the door until the defendant opened it. She admitted that the car in question, the car with the broken headlight and the telltale smear of blood, was hers."

Biggs sat down after speaking just forty-five minutes, his opening statement more effective for its brevity, a concept most lawyers can't seem to get their heads around. It was my turn.

I stood and moved toward the lectern, but turned in front of it and stood between it and the jury. Rule number one, a speech professor had told me once: Show your body. "Hello, I'm Robin Starling," I began conversationally. "In case you've forgotten. I'm representing Natalie Stevens, the accused in this case." My mouth twitched, but I got no return smiles. "She shares something in common with you. Do you know what it is? The law presumes her innocent of the crime of murder. It presumes her innocent of any crime. The law does not require her to testify; it does not require her to put on any evidence whatsoever. The entire burden is on the prosecution to peel away, strand by strand, the cocoon of presumed innocence with which the Constitution of the United States surrounds her. If the prosecution fails to remove a single strand, any reasonable doubt, then it is your duty to acquit. You may not find her guilty because you think she probably is. You may not find her guilty because you think it is important to get whoever might have committed such a monstrous crime off the streets. You may only find her guilty if the facts are such that no reasonable person could doubt her guilt.

"What we have in this case is a great deal of circumstantial evidence. There is no direct evidence. A woman checked into the Best Western using Natalie Stevens' credit card. A man saw a woman who could have been Natalie Stevens standing over a body outside his home, but nobody has positively identified Natalie Stevens as either of these women. The prosecution is able to prove a number of facts about this crime, and from those facts it wants you to infer Natalie's guilt. You may do this only if there is no other reasonable interpretation of those facts. If there is another interpretation, then there is reasonable doubt as to Natalie's guilt. Then you are duty-bound to acquit her of this horrible crime of which she stands accused.

"This probably seems to you like a good time for me to give you an alternate interpretation of the prosecution's facts. I wish that I could." One member of the jury sat up a little straighter, impressed, I hoped, by my unexpected candor. "I will be listening to the testimony of the witnesses with as much attention as you will, because there are certain facts that just don't add up. They don't add up to Natalie's guilt. At the moment, they don't seem to add up to any kind of coherent story."

Standing, Biggs said, "Objection, your honor. She's arguing her case."

"Sustained."

I nodded my acquiescence. "The prosecution will offer evidence that a woman calling herself Natalie Stevens—in fact, a woman using Natalie Stevens' credit card—checked into Room 238. Mr. Biggs has already told you that a woman driving a car registered to Mark Edward Stevens was seen driving away from the body of the deceased. What he has not told you is that on that same Sunday night Mark Edward Stevens was checked into Room 240, the room immediately next door to the room registered to Natalie Stevens."

Aubrey Biggs was on his feet again, his face already turning red. A paper disturbed by his braced hands floated from the table to the carpet between our two tables. "Your honor, I…" He stopped, evidently already doubting the wisdom of such a strong reaction. I bent to pick up the paper and, walking to the table, held it out to him.

"You didn't know?" I said.

"Your honor, I'd like a sidebar."

Judge Cheatham motioned us forward, pushing a button that turned up the level of white noise in the courtroom.

"Your honor," Biggs said. "The opening statement is no place for the defense to be springing surprises on the prosecution. Assuming the facts bear out Ms. Starling's statement and she's not making it up out of whole cloth. My understanding is that Mark Stevens is in China."

"He may be," I said. "But someone giving his name rented a room at the Best Western that Sunday night."

"Then that fact should have been in the discovery materials turned over to us."

I said, "What should have been turned over? I think the witnesses on the prosecution's list will be sufficient to prove the point, and if it doesn't come out in the prosecution's case, those same names are on the defense's witness list. I am frankly amazed that Mr. Biggs didn't know who was in the room right next door to where this murder was committed. He's talked to the same people I have. I assumed he was up to his usual game of hide-the-ball."

"That's enough, Ms. Starling. You will refrain from personal attacks in this courtroom."

"Yes, your honor." Though Biggs had accused me of making up facts out of whole cloth, such an accusation evidently was fair play.

"If facts don't bear out your assertions, Ms. Starling, you are going to be in a world of trouble," the judge said.

"I would expect the jury to hold it against me, your honor."

"You may proceed with your opening statement."

I went back to my position midway between the lectern and the jury box. I smiled at the jury. "You no doubt wonder what that was all about. I'm afraid it's unlikely to be the last sidebar you experience. As I was saying, rooms right next to each other were registered to a Natalie Stevens and a Mark Stevens that Sunday night. No doubt there is some narrative that explains that. At this point, I don't know what it is. I do know that the facts don't seem to fit the prosecution's narrative. During the trial, I will be doing my best to uncover enough facts so that a sensible narrative emerges. I believe that narrative will exonerate Natalie Stevens and make it clear that she had nothing to do with the events of that night. It may not. We may be left with a collection of facts that could fit any number of narratives. If in one of those narratives, Natalie is innocent, then there is a reasonable doubt of her guilt and you must find her not guilty. Listen closely to the witnesses. Keep an open mind. Make the prosecution prove its case."

Chapter 20

"I wanted to stand up and applaud," Brooke said afterward.

"I'm glad you didn't." She, Paul, and I were standing in the parking lot outside the courthouse, stepping from foot to foot as our breath condensed in front of our faces.

"When did you decide to drag Natalie's father into the picture?" Paul asked.

"When Aubrey Biggs stood up and objected to my arguing the case."

"You hadn't planned it in advance?"

"I'd like to say yes, but something about that little twerp makes me want to smack him in the face with a large, wet tuna. The main thing I wanted to accomplish was to keep the jury from buying his narrative of what happened so completely that they couldn't keep open minds. You notice I didn't say anything about Chloe. I didn't want to telegraph my next surprise."

"I think you achieved your purpose. Where shall we have dinner to celebrate?" Paul asked.

"Can't. I'm a family woman now, remember? There's a little guy at home depending on me."

"So we eat at your place. I'll pick up Italian nachos on the way. You have wine, don't you?"

"Does a fish have gills?" Brooke said.

I got home just after five and retrieved my pup from Dr. McDermott. I changed clothes, opened a bottle of cabernet, then, with Deeks trailing after me, headed back to my bedroom to change clothes.

It took Paul and Brooke longer to get to my place than I expected. I found myself drowsing in the big, stuffed chair in my living room, Deeks lying across one foot and gnawing on a flip-flop he had found in my closet. I found myself too lethargic to take it away from him. It was an old flip-flop, I told myself, probably not worth more than a buck or two at a garage sale.

I must have fallen asleep, because when the doorbell rang, Deeks was in my lap, and his claws racked my thigh through my sweats as he launched himself to the floor. His toenails clicked on the wood floor as he left the area rug, and he yapped when he reached the door and couldn't get to whoever was on the other side of it. I took a deep breath and exhaled it. The doorbell rang again, and I pulled myself to my feet.

When I opened the door, Deeks ran out past Paul Soldano, who was on the porch with a big sack that said *Carino's*.

"Whoa," Paul said. "Hey, buddy." Brooke Marshall was coming up the sidewalk carrying a gym bag, but Deeks wasn't interested in her either. He cut onto the grass and began to pee.

"Does he always do that?" Paul asked. "Do his business outside I mean. Has he had an accident since that first day?"

"Not that I know of. He's spending the days with Dr. McDermott, though, and I haven't asked him."

"Hi, Robin," Brooke said. "Have you done P90X?"

"The workout video?"

"I brought it in case you want to try it. I just got it in the mail."

"Sorry we're late," Paul said. "Have you gone running yet?"

"No, I've got a dog now, and I'm waiting for him to get big enough to keep up. Why? Did you come to work out, too?"

"You could carry him in a backpack or something," Brooke said.

"I've done that, but all the bouncing upsets his little tum-tum. He threw up on me."

"Oh." Her face brightened. "This is perfect then. We get our workout, and we don't have to leave your dog alone or anything."

"What about him?" I said, jerking my head at Paul. "He gonna work out with us?"

"Can we eat first?" Paul asked.

"So you are going to work out with us?"

"No, no. Don't worry about me, though. Deacon and I are content to watch." He put the Italian nachos on the coffee table. I got the wine and three mugs—wasn't going to risk stemmed glassware with Deeks around. Paul nested his smartphone in my Rocketfish speakers, and we listed to the eclectic work of Artic Monkeys while we ate.

"This would be good music to work out to," Paul said.

"You thinking about it?"

"I guess what I meant is that it's good music to watch you work out to. Good music, a canine companion, sipping wine from a square, white mug— where did you get this anyway?"

I rolled my eyes and didn't answer.

After dinner we watched an episode of Grimm on Netflix while we gave our food time to digest. Then Brooke went to the guest bedroom to change. I already had gym shorts and an exercise bra on underneath my sweats, so I just stripped out of them there in the living room. I should have been able to ignore Paul watching me out of the corner of his eye.

"Okay, I'm done," I said. "Striptease is over."

"Sorry." He gave me a smile, but I thought he wasn't really.

About thirty minutes later, Brooke and I were in the middle of the plyometrics workout (jump training), slick with sweat, blowing like horses, and bouncing up and down. Paul told Deeks, "This is better than a floor-show in Vegas."

I didn't have the breath to react. Tony Horton was moving us to the next exercise, demonstrating a variation for lower intensity, and I was thinking maybe lower intensity was called for.

By the time we were done, my clothes were wet enough to wring sweat out of. "Time to hit the showers," I said to Brooke as I rolled our dumbbells under the coffee table. "You take the guest bath."

Paul stood up.

"Where do you think you're going?"

"I was going to take Deacon outside," he said with some dignity. "He might need to piddle." He looked from me to Brooke. "If, however, either of you needs someone to wash her back, I will do my best to expedite his toilet."

Brooke gave him a raspberry, which, I thought, was all the reply he was entitled to. We showered and put on fresh clothes, and Brooke and I talked about how sore we were going to be the next day. Brooke suggested ice cream.

"Doesn't that defeat the purpose of the workout?" Paul asked. "Not that I'm objecting. I like ice cream."

Brooke said, "We need to replenish our glycogen stores."

"Burn the fat, feed the muscle," I said.

"Hey, whatever. It works for me." To Deeks he said, "It sounds like gobbledygook, but if it's a reason to eat ice cream, I'm for it."

"You skipped the burn-the-fat part and are skipping straight to the feeding," Brooke objected.

"We do what we can."

Soon we were sitting around the living room with our ice cream. Actually, as Paul pointed out, it wasn't ice cream, but a coconut-milk, nondairy frozen dessert. "Which really doesn't taste too bad," he said, licking his spoon. "I just don't see the point of it. If you're going to eat ice cream, why not eat ice cream?"

"She's doing what she can to indulge herself and still eat clean," Brooke said.

"Everybody talks about that, but I don't get it. Eat clean."

Brooke started explaining the concept to him. My bowl was empty, so I got up and took Paul's and

Brooke's, which were also empty. Deeks, who hadn't gotten any coconut-milk, nondairy frozen dessert, looked up at them longingly, and gave a little whine.

"Sorry, buddy. I don't know if coconut milk is good for doggies. I need to look it up."

The front window cracked. I felt a tug at my hair, my legs went limp on me, and I fell. I found myself on my side, staring wide-eyed at the front window, wondering how it could still be intact and not shattered after getting smacked so hard with what sounded like a baseball bat.

"There's a hole right at the edge," Brooke said in a voice that sounded unnaturally calm. "See it?"

The hole in the glass swam into focus just before Paul reached up and turned out the floor lamp. "Get the light in the kitchen," Paul said. Brooke headed that way in a crouch while he hit a wall switch to kill the light in the hallway. Deeks started barking.

"Robin? Are you hurt?" He started toward me, but the kitchen light went out just as a pane of glass in the French doors broke inward with another crack, this one with the echo of a gunshot behind it, and Paul fell forward across the sofa. We were fish in a barrel.

I tried to shout. My mouth was moving, but I wasn't sure I was actually saying anything.

Deeks ran at the French doors, driving his head into a pane of glass and falling back. There was a third shot as Paul rose up between me and the sofa and swung his arm in a throwing motion that was followed by the crash of shattering glass and a cry of surprise or pain.

"Deeks," I said, or tried to. He was beside me, licking my ear. I reached for him, but missed. I felt my legs move as I tried to get up, but there was no strength in them.

"Robin." It was Paul, kneeling over me, his face in shadow. "Oh, God." His hand felt wet against my face.

Brooke's voice in another part of the room: "There's been a shooting. We need an ambulance." She recited my address. "I don't know. Yes. Yes. Please hurry…Is she—"

Paul: "She's breathing. Robin?"

I felt my lips move.

"Robin?" The front doorknob rattled, and Brooke yelped. Someone pounded on the door.

"Is everyone all right in there?" Dr. McDermott's voice. "Is everyone all right?"

I couldn't answer. I heard the door open. Dr. McDermott said, "I heard gunshots." He was gasping.

"Robin's hurt."

"Turn on the lights."

Paul was gone, and Dr. McDermott was in his place. His face was a web of fine lines, and wisps of hair stood out from his nearly bald head in high definition clarity. I felt pressure on the side of my head, increasing to the point that it was almost unbearable.

"Can you get me a washcloth? A clean one. Someone get this dog out of the way."

The room began to darken at the edges.

"Stay with us, Robin. You stay with us."

Everything was fading to black. I heard Dr. McDermott say, "I don't know. It may not have breached the cranium," then darkness and silence crowded in on me, blocking out everything.

Chapter 21

"Help me." I was trying to raise a hand to my face, but my hand wasn't moving. I tried to shift my position, to kick my feet, but nothing worked. "Help me." A drop-tile ceiling was above me. No light shone from the fluorescent panel. My eyelids had moved, I realized. I blinked, and darkness alternated with dim ceiling tiles. I made a heroic effort to sit up, to tug my arms free of the bonds that held them, but gave up, gasping. I could turn my head. A window was on one side of me, a brightly lit hallway on the other. There was a sink on the wall at the foot of my bed. I dropped my head back onto a pillow.

I could see people in the hallway, a little distance from my bed. One was a middle-aged woman in scrubs. The other looked like… "Dr. McDermott?"

The two of them were talking, and if they heard me, they gave no sign.

"Dr. McDermott!"

There was no reaction, and I didn't try again. Dr. McDermott said something else, and the nurse nodded, then he turned toward me and opened a door in the glass wall that separated us. He stopped, looking at me.

"Deacon," I said.

He stepped forward and reached for my hand. "Brooke's got him; he's all right. How do you feel?"

"Thirsty."

He nodded, stepped back into the hall. When he came back, I said, "Am I tied down?"

"You've been agitated. It was the only way they could keep the IVs in you."

The woman in scrubs came in carrying a cup with a flexible straw. With a whir, the head of my bed rose. I sipped some water.

The clock above the sink said one-thirty-five. It didn't say a.m. or p.m., but there was no light coming through the window. "Is that right?" I asked, meaning the clock.

"Is what right, sweetie?" Dr. McDermott said. He laid a hand against my face, and I closed my eyes.

When I came to again, I was alone, or I thought I was. I tried to lift my hand to my nose, which itched, but a bracelet of white cloth still held my wrist against the frame of the bed. "Well, crap," I muttered. Dr. McDermott's head rose into my field of vision. A sadness came over me at how old he looked. He wouldn't be around forever.

"You're back with us," he said.

"I'm back. Can you untie my wrists?"

He glanced at the door. "Sure."

The clock above the sink showed that it was five minutes to seven. Dr. McDermott untied one wrist and moved around to the other side of the bed. I said, "I'm starving. Do you think there's breakfast?"

He smiled. "We'll have to talk to the doctor, but I think we can manage it."

"Where are we?"

"ICU. You were shot in the head, but fortunately it wasn't a penetrating wound. You do have a concussion, and you lost a lot of blood, not quite enough that they've given you a transfusion."

I lifted my head enough to see the chair he'd been sitting in, which was half-reclined. "Have you been here all night? Do they allow that in ICU?"

He held the cup with its flexible straw to my lips, and I sucked greedily. "I used to have hospital privileges here. Not everyone I know is retired or dead."

A few people in street clothes walked past in the hall. Paul and Brooke appeared at the door. I raised a hand, feeling almost exultant at the freedom of movement. They came in. There were tears on Brooke's face, and Paul's eyes were bloodshot.

"Are you all right?" I asked them.

"Are you?" Paul said.

"I feel pretty good, actually. Hungry as all get out, but nothing hurts."

Paul looked at Dr. McDermott. "Can she eat?"

"We'll have to clear it with the doctor, but she should be able to."

Paul said, "You're a doctor. Would a protein bar hurt her any?"

"That's not the kind of food…"

I interrupted. "You've got a protein bar?"

He moved his head. "Two of them, actually."

"Gimme."

He glanced at Dr. McDermott as he fished one out of his pocket. Dr. McDermott moved between us and the door, looking out.

"Incorrigible kids," he muttered.

I tore open the protein bar. It was a bit melted from Paul's body heat, but I took a bite and chewed. "Messy, but delicious," I said with my mouth full.

"Do you always carry protein bars?" Brooke asked Paul.

"One of the benefits of having a fat boyfriend," I said, chewing.

"Ouch," Brooke said. "She called you fat."

"She called me her boyfriend."

"So she did." They both looked at me.

"He's a boy, and he's my friend," I said defensively.

"He may have saved your life," Brooke said. "Though there's not much glass left in your French doors, what with the gunfire and the brass bookend Paul threw at the shooter."

"Hit him, too…I think I did," Paul said.

Dr. McDermott was suddenly beside me, one hand closing over the inside-out wrapper in my hands, the other lifting the remaining protein bar from my sheets.

"I don't guess we can do anything about the chocolate on your face," he said.

The door behind him opened, and the woman in scrubs came in. When she saw I was awake and coherent, she told me I'd had a Class II or Class III hemorrhage secondary to ballistic trauma and had required volume resuscitation—lots of saline or something like it—but not a blood transfusion. My heart rate had been in the nineties when they brought me in, but was almost back to normal. My oxygen saturation was fine, but my blood pressure was still just ninety over fifty-five. She pointed to each of the displays in turn.

"That's pretty much my normal blood pressure," I said.

"You can talk to the doctor about it when he comes around this morning."

"When will that be? I've got to be in court at nine-thirty."

She gave me a pitying smile.

"I'm not kidding. I'm in the middle of a murder trial."

"Who's the judge?" Dr. McDermott asked. "I'll call him and explain what's going on."

"The jury was just empanelled yesterday." I looked around at them. "It was yesterday, wasn't it? This is Wednesday?"

Paul was nodding. "This is Wednesday."

I felt a wash of relief that left me feeling suddenly very tired. "The judge is Eric Cheatham," I said. "Maybe I'll close my eyes for just a bit."

Chapter 22

The case of the Commonwealth versus Natalie Stevens was postponed until the following Monday. I was discharged from the hospital late Thursday morning, the day after I'd woken up in ICU, and, though my mind was a little fuzzy, I really didn't feel that bad. Still, I was glad for the long weekend, because I looked like crap. The hair clipped from the side of my head had been cut with no regard for cosmetic considerations. The scalp wound had been closed with Dermabond, which wasn't supposed to get wet for five days, which meant that my oily hair would remain that way until Sunday. On top of that, there was a deep bruise on my temple and some discoloration of the skin around my eyes. Paul tried out "Raccoon-face" as a possible term of endearment, but I glared at him, and he didn't try it again.

When court reconvened on Monday morning, I still had the bruise and possibly the worst bad-hair day I'd ever had. Though I had a persistent low-grade mental lethargy, I thought I was sharp enough and that anyway mental acuity was overrated. If we can rely on Woody Allen for tactical advice, eighty percent of the battle is just showing up.

Judge Cheatham, bless him, referred neither to my appearance, nor to my having been shot, but the incident had made the papers, and some of the jurors were staring at me openly.

"Mr. Biggs," the judge said after the bailiff had called court back into session. "You may call your first witness."

Kim Beecher, the accountant who lived in the cracker-box house on the Southside, took the stand. As he told about standing at his picture window having milk and cookies when he couldn't sleep, a couple of men in the jury exchanged glances.

"This car you saw, can you describe it?" Biggs asked him.

"It was white or at least pale. Smallish. And it was an actual car, not an SUV or anything."

"Two-door or four-door?"

He shook his head. "I don't know. I got the license number."

"But you can't say whether it was a two-door or a four-door."

"I can't. Can't tell you the model either, or even the manufacturer. I don't know cars."

"But you did get the license number. What was it?"

"I don't know."

A ripple of involuntary laughter swept the courtroom, and the judge eyed Beecher disapprovingly.

"I told it to the dispatcher. I have the transcript here." He pulled a folded paper from the inner pocket of his suit coat. "Here it is. 'GBX 1-1-6, could be 1-1-8. GBX 1-1-something.'" He looked up.

"When you first saw the car, the driver's door was standing open?"

"I think so."

Biggs head slumped forward, then he brought it up again. "You don't know? Did you used to know?"

There was more muted laughter. I stood. "Your honor…"

Cheatham held up a hand. "Sustained. Try to refrain from making fun of your own witness, Mr. Biggs."

More laughter, less muted.

"Yes, your honor." Biggs smoothed his jacket against his sides. "Mr. Beecher. You saw a woman standing behind the car, did you not?"

"I did."

Biggs looked relieved at the affirmation. "What was she doing?"

"She took a couple of steps and squatted down next to what I thought at the time was a bundle of clothes lying in the road. I glanced at the trunk, thinking maybe the lid had come open or something and stuff had fallen out, but it looked to be shut tight. I remember now about the car door. She left it standing open."

"Did you get a good look at this woman? Is she here in this courtroom?"

"Pretty good. She was wearing slacks and a short fur, and she moved like she was wearing heels, though I didn't notice her feet particularly."

"Do you see her here in this courtroom?"

"I don't know. This woman was medium height, medium build, dark hair, somewhere between twenty and forty. Actually, of all the people I've seen since, she looks the most like Ms. Starling's girlfriend who came by to talk to me. Except that she has red hair."

"Ms. Starling's girlfriend came by to talk to you? Ms. Starling, the attorney for the defense?" All heads turned toward me. I held up a hand and flashed a smile.

"I don't see her friend in the courtroom today though," Beecher said.

"Her girlfriend," Biggs said.

I stood. "For the record," I said, "I like men."

There was laughter in the jury box and here and there among the spectators. The judge smacked his gavel on the bench.

Kim Beecher said, "I didn't mean to imply...It was just a manner of speaking. This person was a young woman, and she seemed to be Ms. Starling's—"

"Friend," Biggs finished for him. "Yes, we got that. Why was she coming by to see you?"

Judge Cheatham said, "Since this young friend of Ms. Starling's has not been charged and is not in the courtroom, this seems like a pointless line of inquiry."

"I agree, your honor," Biggs said.

Cheatham held out his hands. "Can we move on then?"

Biggs started turning red, but he took a breath and went on, going over the woman's bending over the body, Beecher's movement out onto the porch, the woman returning to her car and driving off as Beecher moved out into the street and called 9-1-1. When it was my turn, I went to the podium.

"You don't know that you've ever seen this woman again," I said.

"No, I don't."

"You said this woman was between twenty and forty. If Natalie Stevens is nineteen—" She was nineteen, but that fact was not yet in evidence.

"That puts her outside the range," Beecher said. "I know. This woman could have been nineteen, but she seemed older."

"How old would you say?"

"I would have said about thirty. It was after midnight, though, and there was just the one streetlight. A lot of what I saw were shadows."

"But for your identification of the license number, all except the last digit, you wouldn't know the car if you ever saw it again."

"That's right."

"When you first saw this car and this woman, the car was stopped, the door was open, and the woman was on the street. You didn't see the car hit this man or run over him."

"No. Once I realized the bundle of rags was a human being, I just assumed—"

I had my hand up, and he trailed off. "I appreciate your efforts to be open and honest about what you saw and what you remember," I said. "But what you assumed isn't evidence."

He nodded. "I'm sorry."

"When the car pulled away, it went forward, away from the body."

"Yes. I went out into the street. The car took a left turn toward Midlothian Turnpike and was gone."

"Did the woman see you?"

"Not that I could tell."

"And she was alone in the car."

"No one else got out. I'll put it that way."

"Your witness," I said to Biggs.

Biggs, officious little toad that he was, got up with his usual amount of extraneous movement. "Mr. Beecher," he said when he got to the podium. "Do you think you might have assumed this woman you saw was older than nineteen because of the way she was dressed, the heels and the fur and whatnot?"

"Possibly."

"Was there anything about her appearance, anything at all, that would rule out the possibility of it having been the defendant in this case?"

"No."

To the judge: "That's all I have."

I half-stood at my table. "No further questions."

Next up was one of the officers who had responded to the 911 call. He and his partner had arrived at the scene at 1:50, just ahead of the fire truck. An ambulance had followed, then the crime techs, then the M.E. He described the scene, indicated they had talked to Beecher.

A police photographer followed to introduce a half-dozen gory photographs. Technically, the pictures were to show that the unknown decedent was dead and the nature of the injuries that had killed him. There were other ways to present that information, of course, but the prosecution valued the photographs for their inflammatory nature, a little something to get the jury in a hanging frame of mind. I'd objected to such photographs before, but never with any success. This time I sat next to my client and tried to ignore the looks of horror that several of the jurors shot at Natalie as they viewed each of the photographs.

Chapter 23

Neither Paul nor Brooke had been in court that morning, but we met for lunch at a little hole-in-the-wall a block off Shockoe Slip. I called Rodney Burns while we were waiting on our food. He was on my witness list and so couldn't be in the courtroom with me. I had not yet subpoenaed him, though, because he had a living to make, and I couldn't afford to pay him to sit in the witness room.

"This is Rodney Burns," he said.

"Hi, Rodney. Robin. Listen, I had a thought."

"Of course you do." I wondered how many cups of coffee he had had. "It's why you always call me."

"You said you checked airlines and trains and whatnot for evidence that Mark Stevens had left Hong Kong for mainland China."

"Yes, and couldn't find anything. He didn't take a flight back to the U.S. either."

"Did you check for other flights out of Hong Kong? To Singapore, maybe, or Bangkok, or Kuala Lumpur?"

He didn't answer immediately. "Perhaps not as thoroughly as I should have," he said.

"I'm thinking he's back in the United States, that maybe he circled back somehow. When I suggested in opening statements I was going to implicate him in this murder, he shot me in the head."

"Well, he hasn't flown back out of Hong Kong, at least not as of a week ago."

"Check to see if he might have flown back via Singapore or some place, will you?"

"I certainly will. How are you holding up?"

"Other than a headache and a little dizziness, not too bad."

I punched off and looked across the table at Brooke.

"You've got a headache?" she said.

Paul said, "You didn't tell us that." He sounded accusing.

"You didn't ask. I'm surprised Rodney did. He's not usually one to get personal on you."

After lunch a pathologist from the medical examiner's office came to the stand. Aubrey Biggs ran him through a moderately impressive list of credentials that included medical school at St. George's University in Grenada. Though I assumed Reginald Birdsong went to a med school in the Caribbean because he couldn't get into one in the U.S., I really didn't know how or whether to exploit that assumption in the courtroom. He had done his residency at the Orlando Regional Medical Center in Florida, which might well cancel out any shortcomings implied by his medical school.

"Dr. Birdsong, could you tell us how the decedent in this case met his death?" Biggs asked him.

Birdsong cleared his throat. "He had a gunshot wound to the head. The bullet entered beneath the chin and exited just beneath the occipital protuberance."

"The occipital…"

"The bony bump on the back of the head."

"Ah." Biggs was feeling of the back of his own head. "It was just the one gunshot? How long after the shooting did death occur?"

"In my opinion, death would have occurred in less than a minute." That was the point of going through all his credentials as a pathologist: Qualifying him as an expert made his opinions within his area of expertise admissible into evidence.

"When you say the bullet entered beneath the chin…" Biggs used his index finger to push up his own chin. "Are you suggesting that the wound may have been self-inflicted?"

"It could not have been self-inflicted. There was no bruising beneath the skin, no tattooing from gun powder on the skin, and the entrance wound wasn't split. The origin of the shot had to be at least three feet from the entrance wound, further away than the length of a man's arm."

"Thank you, doctor." Biggs handed him an envelope. "Is that your signature on this envelope?"

"Yes. My signature and that of Officer Thomas McClane."

"Is the envelope sealed?"

"Yes, it is."

"Could you open the envelope, doctor?"

Dr. Birdsong tore off the end of the envelope and dumped a small metal object into the palm of his hand.

"What are we looking at?" Biggs asked.

"This is the bullet that was delivered to me by Officer McClane. I examined it in his presence, then we sealed it in this envelope and signed our names across the flap."

"What did you find when you examined the bullet?"

Dr. Birdsong was turning it over in his hands. He looked up, appearing almost startled. "I found traces of blood on it."

"Did that blood match the blood of the decedent?"

"Yes, it did."

"When you say it matched, are you referring to blood type or…"

"Well, the blood types matched. We also did a DNA comparison, but I wasn't the one who did it."

"We'll get someone else to tell us about the DNA match, but just for some background, how accurate is DNA analysis?"

"Every person's DNA is unique. It's the best form of identification we have."

"Your honor, I request that this bullet be marked and received into evidence as People's Exhibit 7." The first six exhibits had been photographs of the victim.

There was a pause while that was taken care of, then Biggs returned to the podium. "Dr. Birdsong, can you tell us at what time the decedent met his death?"

"Not with pinpoint accuracy, but I can give you a window."

"Give us a window, please."

"Sometime between eleven p.m. the night of December 6 and the time I examined him, which was 2:18 a.m. the morning of the seventh."

"How did you establish this window?"

"The absence of post mortem lividity, the absence of rigor mortis, and the temperature of the body."

Biggs grimaced in my direction, perhaps intending it as a smile. "Your witness."

I stood. "You say that every person's DNA is unique. Has that enabled you to identify the decedent?"

"No. You have to have something to compare your sample to."

"In this case, you had the body of the decedent, and you had the traces of blood scraped from the bullet."

Dr. Birdsong glanced in Biggs' direction. "Yes. Well, DNA testing can allow us to identify the bullet as the fatal bullet, but that's all."

"It's believed that every person's fingerprints are unique, isn't it?"

"Yes, it is."

"Are you familiar with the work of Simon Cole, the criminologist at UC Irvine?"

"I've heard of him."

"Have you read his 2005 article from the *Journal of Criminal Law and Criminology*?"

There was the briefest of hesitations. "I've heard of it."

"It's a study of courtroom errors in fingerprint identification, isn't it?" During my days of enforced idleness, I'd had little to do besides walk Deeks and surf the internet; hence my sudden courtroom display of erudition.

"I believe it is," Dr. Birdsong said.

Biggs stood. "Objection. Your honor, no fingerprint evidence has been presented in this case. This testimony is irrelevant."

I said, "A great deal of testimony was elicited concerning Dr. Birdsong's qualifications as an expert in forensic pathology. I'm entitled to cross-examine him as to his expertise in the field."

"Are we going to devote very much time to this, Ms. Starling?" Judge Cheatham asked.

I gave him a broad smile. "No more than necessary, your honor."

He didn't quite roll his eyes as he raised a hand in acquiescence. "Objection overruled."

"Thank you. Dr. Birdsong, Professor Cole's article finds that since 1983, the aggregate error in fingerprint identifications has been eight-tenths of one percent. Correct?"

He shook his head slightly. "I'm not familiar with the specifics, but I will point out that those figures suggest that fingerprint identification is 99.2 percent accurate."

"Given the thousands of criminal cases processed by crime laboratories each year, that impressive success rate would still mean that there are hundreds of cases of mistaken identifications."

"I wouldn't say hundreds."

"The article estimated nineteen hundred in 2002 alone."

The doctor opened his hands in capitulation. "DNA comparison is considerably more accurate than that. The chance of an error has been estimated to be in the neighborhood of one in 350 million, which puts the accuracy of the test in excess of 99.999 percent. If you'll let me get out my phone, I can tell you just how many nines."

"You'd be using the calculator function to divide one by 350 million?"

"And then subtracting from one."

"The point of the DNA evidence in this case isn't to identify the victim though, is it? It's to identify the fatal bullet."

"That's right."

"Your testimony links the bullet to the unidentified decedent, but does nothing to link it to Natalie Stevens, the defendant in this case."

"By itself, no. It may be one of the links in a chain."

"And maybe there are weaker links than yours. You may be right."

Biggs said, "Your honor," and the judge said, "Ms. Starling, confine your cross-examination to asking questions."

I gave him a nod. "Of course, your honor. Dr. Birdsong, what I'm really interested in exploring with you is your testimony about time of death." The point of the questions about fingerprints had been to establish some credibility with the jury before I started. "You said that death occurred after eleven p.m. and before 2:18. The end of that window was when you arrived on the scene and examined the decedent, is that right? He had no pulse, he had no heartbeat. He was clearly dead."

"That's right."

"Could he have been killed there at the scene, right on the street where you first examined him?"

"No. There was insufficient blood at the scene. The body had lost between one and two pints, and it simply wasn't there."

"Just one or two pints? Wasn't the exit wound rather large?"

"When death is instantaneous, what blood the body loses simply drains out under the force of gravity. The heart isn't beating to force blood out through the wound."

"So the decedent didn't expire moments before you arrived on the scene. The body was moved post-mortem."

"Clearly death had occurred some minutes before. How long it takes to move a body is outside my expertise, so I made no attempt to calibrate the time of death based on that."

"So the three factors you mentioned—rigor mortis, postmortem lividity, and temperature of the body—they all went to establish the earliest time death could have occurred."

"That's right."

"Let's take them one at a time. Rigor mortis is the stiffening of the muscles after death—correct? It typically begins in the small muscles of the eyelids, lower jaw, and neck, then moves to the joints of the hands and feet, and finally to the elbows, knees, shoulders, and hips. Is that right?"

"It is. Though rigor mortis probably develops simultaneously in all muscles, it becomes apparent in the small masses of muscle much earlier than the larger ones."

"And in this case, when you first examined the body at 2:18, rigor mortis was not yet apparent anywhere. Is that right?"

"That's right."

I flourished the autopsy report. "When you began your autopsy at 4:14, had rigor begun to develop in the small muscles of the eyelids, jaw, and neck?"

"Yes. In fact, by that time rigor mortis was noticeable in the elbows and knees as well."

"Indicating it was already fairly advanced?"

"That's right. By 5:30 it was all but complete."

"Indicating that death would have occurred when?"

"Probably three to six hours previously."

"So, sometime after 11:30."

"Yes."

"When did rigor start to disappear?"

Dr. Birdsong shook his head. "I don't know."

"Are you familiar with Bernard Knight's *Legal Aspects of Medical Practice*?"

"Yes. I believe it's been long out of print. Knight's *Forensic Medicine* is still available in reprint editions."

"Yes. Knight's *Forensic Medicine* was for a long time the standard textbook in the field, wasn't it? In fact, when other people took over the editing job for later editions, it was still called *Knight's Forensic Medicine*. Wasn't it?"

"I believe so. Yes."

"Isn't it Knight's opinion that 'it is extremely unsafe to use rigor at all in the estimation of time since death'?"

Dr. Birdsong shifted in his seat. "I don't believe so."

"I believe that's an exact quote." I went to my table and bent to lift a textbook from the briefcase beside it. I'd ordered the book online on Friday, and Amazon had gotten it to me the next day. "It's on page 123. 'It is extremely unsafe to use rigor at all in the estimation of time since death.' Would you like to see it?"

At a nod from the judge, I took the book to the witness. While Birdsong flipped to page 123, studied it, and flipped back to the beginning of the book, I was giving photocopies to the judge and the district attorney. "This is a twenty-year-old textbook," he said, his finger on what must have been the copyright page.

It was a weakness in my choice of authority, but I hadn't been able to find what I wanted in anything more recent. "So later science has contradicted Mr. Knight?" I said.

"I didn't say that. But this opinion of his is outside the mainstream."

"Can you quote an authority for that?"

I waited.

"P.F. Niderkorn. Francis E. Camps. Those are two."

I felt a surge of elation. Dr. Birdsong had just handed me an unbelievable gift. "Really, doctor?" I said. "Niderkorn and Camps?"

His eyes moved as if he had realized his mistake. "Well, there are others."

I went back to the table for one of my legal pads and flipped through it. "Didn't Niderkorn's primary work on rigor mortis come out in seventy-two?"

Birdsong didn't say anything.

"*Eighteen* seventy-two?" I said. "Wasn't Knight's book published more than one hundred years later? Just who disproved whom?"

There was murmuring in the gallery, some shifting of position in the jury box. When the courtroom quieted, Dr. Birdsong said, "Niderkorn did some of the pioneering work in the field. He's been tremendously influential. And there's been more recent work. I've read dozens of articles on the subject."

"But you can't give us any names."

"Not off the top of my head."

"When you first saw the body, what was the environmental temperature?" I asked, changing tack.

He glanced at his notes. "Thirty-nine degrees Fahrenheit."

"Isn't it true that when the environmental temperature is below 50 degrees, it is unusual for rigor mortis to develop at all? That it is only when the environmental temperature is raised above 50 degrees that rigor mortis begins to develop in the normal manner?"

There was a long pause. "I really didn't put much weight in rigor mortis in determining the time of death," Dr. Birdsong said.

"You relied on postmortem lividity and body temperature." The blood in a corpse remains liquid and never coagulates, so over time gravity settles it in the tissues of the body closest to the ground. Postmortem lividity refers to the darkening of those tissues.

"Primarily body temperature."

"That's because the development of lividity is too variable to serve as a useful indicator of time of death?"

"Well, lividity usually becomes apparent within two hours and is well developed within four."

"But it is highly variable," I said.

"It is highly variable."

He'd given up the point more easily than I'd expected, which was fortunate. I had lucked onto a really good article on rigor mortis that had led me to Knight and other sources, but I didn't have nearly as much on postmortem lividity. I said, "So when you give your opinion that the decedent met his death after eleven o'clock, you were relying on body temperature."

"Primarily."

I took a breath. Natalie had an alibi before ten or ten-thirty, so I needed to move the time of death back as much as possible. I was two down with one to go.

"When did you first take the temperature of the body?"

"At the scene, shortly after I arrived." He consulted his notes. "2:25."

"And the temperature at that time was what?"

"Thirty-two point four degrees Centigrade."

"Which is what in Fahrenheit?"

"Ninety degrees, maybe a few tenths over."

"You assume that the normal temperature of this particular individual was 98.6?"

"Thirty-seven point two Centigrade. I think that's about 99 degrees Fahrenheit."

"Isn't normal temperature 98.6?"

"Well, that's oral temperature. Rectal temperature is about a half-degree higher, maybe three-quarters of a degree."

"You took the temperature rectally?" I had a visual image of the doctor rolling the body over and pulling down its pants, but he'd probably cut a slit in the clothing. My gaze flicked toward the jury.

"In this case, I made an abdominal stab over the lower ribs and inserted a chemical thermometer into the substance of the liver. The temperature readings would be comparable."

I thought I detected a slight exhaling of breath from the jury box.

"So you assume the temperature of the body was 99 degrees at death. At the scene you recorded a temperature of 90 degrees, so you based your conclusions on a temperature drop of nine degrees."

"That's right."

"Though the temperature at death could have been as low as 97 degrees, which would mean it only dropped seven degrees by the time you made your observations. Could the temperature at death have been as low as 97 degrees?"

"It could have been."

"Or it could have been significantly higher. Temperature at death has been recorded as high as a hundred and nine, hasn't it?"

"I'm not familiar with that case. That would be rare."

"But it is possible."

"Highly unlikely."

"But possible. Which would mean the temperature had dropped not seven degrees, not nine degrees, but nineteen degrees."

"If the baseline temperature was one-oh-nine."

"Which is possible?"

He turned over his hands so that the palms were facing up. "This is your fairy tale."

"I don't believe fairies are recorded in the scientific literature, doctor."

The gavel cracked. Judge Cheatham looked annoyed. "Let's refrain from personalities, shall we?"

I nodded. "Body temperatures are usually higher in the evening aren't they?"

"I believe so."

"And after exercise."

"Yes."

"And as the result of infection."

"Yes."

"And due to individual variations in baseline temperatures."

"Yes."

"The decedent in this case might have had a temperature at death of more than one hundred degrees, which by itself would throw off your calculation of time of death by at least an hour. The time of death could have been as early as ten o'clock."

"Combined with the absence of rigor mortis and postmortem lividity..."

"Which we've just thrown out as unreliable," I said.

"They're an indication."

"With too much variability to be reliable."

"Taken individually."

I rolled my eyes. "Let's stick with body temperature then. Tell us about the postmortem plateau."

Dr. Birdsong's tongue appeared briefly between his lips. He took a breath and let it out. "There is an initial maintenance of body temperature. The human body is a large mass, irregular in shape, that is composed of tissues with different physical properties. Observations have shown that there is often an initial maintenance of body temperature, which is followed by a fairly linear rate of cooling."

"This initial maintenance of body temperature may last for some hours, might it not?"

"Generally one-half hour to one hour."

"But may last for as long as three hours. Isn't that right?"

"I don't believe so."

"Please turn to page 118 of that textbook you're holding: Knight's *Legal Aspects of Medical Practice*. Do you see it? I've highlighted it for you."

Dr. Birdsong flipped pages. When he looked up, I said, "Evidently some authorities claim the postmortem plateau lasts as long as five hours."

He cleared his throat. "As I've said..."

"You disagree with another opinion in this otherwise mainstream textbook?"

"Yes."

I waited about ten seconds to let the jury pounder that. I said, "There seem to be two big unknowns in assessing the time of death: the initial body temperature, and the length of the postmortem temperature plateau. Aren't there some authorities who hold that assessment of time of death from body temperature can't be accurate in the first four to five hours after death, because early on those two factors have such dominant influence?"

He held up the textbook. "Am I holding one of them?"

I said, "But we have a third problem in this case, and that's the environmental factor. According to Newton's law of cooling, the rate of cooling of a body is determined by the difference between the temperature of the body and the temperature of the environment. And we don't know the temperature of the environment, do we?"

He hesitated. "It was thirty-nine degrees, as I've said." His voice sounded weak, though, as if he knew what was coming.

"Thirty-nine degrees where the body was found. But you've testified that the body was moved. Suppose the death occurred inside a much warmer motel room, and suppose the body lay there for several hours. Suppose it had only been on the street for a few minutes, which seems likely if the body was dumped by the young woman Kim Beecher saw outside his home. It would have cooled much more slowly, wouldn't it? The time of death would have been significantly earlier than the eleven o'clock you've testified to."

"Not in my opinion."

I gave him skeptical look, held it for a couple of beats. "Thank you for your opinion," I said, and I went and sat down.

Chapter 24

Court recessed for the day. The judge left the bench, the jury filed out, a sheriff's deputy led Natalie away. I sat at the defense table, my papers and pens and legal pads still spread out in front of me, as the gallery behind me emptied of spectators. I found I was suddenly too tired to move. Though I felt like I had done a good job with the medical examiner, the details of the cross-examination were slipping away from me, and I wasn't sure.

"Are you all right?" a voice said from somewhere behind me.

I nodded, kept nodding. I heard footsteps, the squeak of a hinge as someone pushed through the bar.

"I just ask because you're sitting there with your head down and your mouth open."

I knew that voice. I looked up. "Hi, Dad," I whispered.

"What is it?"

I took a breath, sighed it out. I shook my head.

"You should still be in the hospital."

I hadn't seen him since Christmas. Mom must have told him what had happened to me.

He gathered my stuff together and put it in my briefcase. I felt his arm around me and his breath on my cheek.

"Come on," he said. "Let's get you up."

"I'm fine," I said, leaning hard on the table.

"Yes, you look fine."

He carried my briefcase and supported me with his other arm as we pushed back through the bar and made our way to the elevators. Outside the courthouse, he left me sitting on a low brick wall while he went to get his car, a ten-year-old Audi with faded paint. He got out, came around the car, helped me get in.

He drove around the courthouse to the parking lot, which was now mostly empty. "Is that your Beetle? I think it will be all right there, don't you?" He sounded doubtful. I was, too, but I didn't know what we could do about it.

"I guess it will have to be," I said.

"You need to get the trial delayed until you've got your strength back. Can you?"

"I'll be okay in the morning. I just need to rest."

He looked at me a long moment. "You do need that." He put the car into gear and pulled out of the parking lot. As he drove, I relapsed into the stupor that had come over me in the courtroom once the pressure was off.

When we got to my house, there was a Camry parked against the curb in front of it. My father pulled his car to the curb behind it.

"It's your friend Paul," Dad said as Paul got out. I'd forgotten they'd met.

Dad opened his car door.

Paul asked, "What happened?"

"She's tired. She finished a long cross-examination, and when court recessed all the energy went out of her."

"How'd she do?" My door was open, and Paul's hands were on my legs, turning me in my seat and getting my feet out the door. He pulled me toward him, then he was on one side of me, and Dad was on the other.

"Not good?" Paul said.

"She was very good. Don't know what she has left for tomorrow, but today she was brilliant."

"She's always brilliant." Paul got my door open while Dad supported me. When they got me into the bedroom and I'd sunk down on the bed, I said, "I'm going to have to do this part myself."

"This is no time for modesty," Dad said.

"This is the precise time for modesty."

Dad and Paul exchanged glances. "Now that sounded like Robin," Paul said.

They left me. I got into some gym shorts and a T-shirt, but didn't bother with hanging up my clothes. I opened the door, held onto the knob for a moment, then steadied. I walked carefully out into the living room, and both men got to their feet looking ready to spring toward me should my knees buckle.

"It's okay," I said. "You can relax."

They did, but only fractionally. Both sets of eyes remained on me.

"You look as good in gym clothes as most girls look in a teddy," Paul said. He glanced at my father. "Not that I'm familiar with how a lot of girls look in teddies. At least not flesh-and-blood girls. Just photographs, really."

I sank into the recliner. "Let it go. You're not helping yourself."

Paul and Dad sat, one on the sofa, one on the other chair, but both sat forward on the edges of their seats.

"I'm tired," I said. "That doesn't mean I'm about to fall out on the floor."

They sat back, but didn't relax. I closed my eyes.

"She was almost normal at lunch," Paul said. "But this afternoon I had to work. Is she winning?"

Dad recounted the trial from the perspective of a man who had been watching his daughter rather than paying attention to the over-all course of the trial. When he got to my cross-examination of Dr. Birdsong, his account became almost excruciatingly detailed. I wasn't ready to relive it.

"Do you think I did a good enough job with Dr. Birdsong that I don't need to bring in an expert of my own?" I said, interrupting.

"What would your expert say?"

"That death could have occurred before eleven o'clock."

"Do you have an expert who would say that?"

"For twenty-five hundred dollars plus expenses. I've talked to him on the phone, but he's in Texas. I'm not sure how good a witness he would make."

Paul said, "Will he testify the death couldn't have occurred after eleven?"

"No. The best we've got is that death could have occurred anytime that evening."

"Then I don't see the point. If he can testify that it couldn't have happened after eleven, then Natalie has an alibi. If he can't, you right where you are now. The murder could have occurred when Natalie was at the party, but it could also have occurred after. If the rest of the evidence points to Natalie, then the jury's going to conclude it occurred after."

I felt myself drifting off. "Good to know I've been wasting my time," I said.

"I don't think you've been wasting your time," Dad said. "You've widened the time window, partially discredited a witness, strengthened your own credibility with the jury…"

He may have said more about the wonders of me, but I went to sleep in the middle of it. When I woke up some time in the night, the room was dark, and one or the other of them was lying on the sofa.

I got up quietly without sitting the recliner up, went into the kitchen, and got myself a drink of water. I was drinking it when something pressed against my leg, and I spilled most of the water I hadn't drunk. It was my dog. I bent over him and rubbed his back.

"Hey, there, Deeks," I whispered. "When did you get here?"

He licked my hand and wagged his tail, which, while not especially informative, was all the answer I needed. He trailed me back through the living room, where I paused to lean over the figure on the couch. It was Paul.

I went to the front window and looked out through the sidelight. My father's car was gone, which meant he had left a man alone in the house with his unconscious daughter. Paul must have impressed him strongly as either fairly virtuous or completely harmless.

"Maybe both," I said.

Deeks and I went back to the bedroom. I picked him up to put him in his crate, then set him on my bed instead. I crawled in, and he snuggled next to me. I slept.

Chapter 25

Paul drove me to the courthouse the next morning. We drove by the parking lot where my car was—windows all intact, no slashed tires—then Paul swung around and dropped me in front of the courthouse.

I expected Aubrey Biggs to recall Dr. Birdsong to the stand to try to rehabilitate his testimony on redirect. He didn't. Maybe I had damaged his testimony beyond rehabilitation. I feared, though, that he had reached the same conclusion Paul had, that it didn't really matter.

Tom McClane came to the stand to tell about arriving on the scene in front of Kim Beecher's house and about how his attempts to identify the body had been thwarted by the absence of any form of identification on the body and by mutilation of the face.

"How was that done, in your opinion?"

"Well, the skull was cracked in multiple places—that's in the autopsy report—and you can see from the pictures that the shape of the head is distorted. I'd say somebody ran over it with a car a few times, maybe spun the tires against the face."

Out of the corner of my eyes I could see some of the jurors wincing and glancing in Natalie's direction.

"The fingerprints didn't tell you anything?"

"They're not on file anywhere. The murder victim is not in the national database, and he's never held a job that required him to be fingerprinted. He's not a securities dealer or a lawyer for instance."

"He wouldn't have been fingerprinted when he applied for a driver's license?"

"Not in Virginia."

"Concealed-carry gun permit?"

"Again, not in Virginia."

"Could he have a passport?"

"Yes. You don't get fingerprinted when you get a passport."

"So this isn't necessarily a homeless person, despite the lack of identification."

"Not at all. This could be anybody."

"You haven't been able to connect him with any place other than the piece of pavement on Everglades Drive where the body was found?"

"We were able to connect him to a motel room."

I did a mental eye-roll.

"Ah, tell us about the motel room."

So McClane told us about going to the Best Western, making inquiries at the desk, going up to room 238.

"Was there anything unusual about that motel room?" Biggs asked him.

"There was a hole in the wall and a stain on the carpet about a foot across."

Biggs handed him the small manila envelope with the bullet that had been admitted into evidence as Exhibit Number 7. "Do you recognize this envelope?"

"Yes. I've written my initials over the seal along with those of Dr. Reginald Birdsong."

"What's inside the envelope?"

McClane dumped the bullet into his palm. "The bullet the crime technicians removed from the motel-room wall in my presence and under my direction."

"Thank you, detective." Biggs retrieved the bullet and envelope and returned it to the court clerk. When he returned to the lectern, he asked McClane, "Did you ever have occasion to search the residence in Wyndam, where the defendant Natalie Stevens lives with her father and stepmother?"

"Yes, on December ninth. I entered the house pursuant to a warrant and searched the house."

"What did you find?"

"I found a compact pistol underneath the mattress of the bed in the bedroom belonging to the defendant. A Glock 32."

"Is this the pistol?"

McClane took it from Biggs and peered closely at the barrel and the tag hanging from the trigger guard. "Yes, it is."

"How can you tell?"

"This tag on the trigger guard has the serial number recorded in my handwriting and initialed by me, and the serial number I wrote down matches the serial number stamped on the barrel of the gun."

"What did you do with this gun?"

"I took it back to police headquarters and turned it over to Danny Golden, one of our lab techs."

Biggs looked at the judge. "Your honor, I'm not through with this witness, but I'd like to dismiss him from the stand to take Mr. Golden's testimony at this time.

The judge looked at me. "Any objections?"

"I'd like to cross-examine this witness on his testimony so far."

"Your honor, we're not concluded with this witness," Biggs repeated.

"You've concluded with this phase of his testimony," I said.

"The defense may cross-examine," the judge said.

At the lectern Biggs, clearly peeved, shuffled his papers together with rough, jerky movements.

"I really only have one question at this time," I said when I had replaced him at the lectern. "How did you come to go the Best Western on Chippenham Parkway in the first place?"

"We had a tip."

I waited, but he didn't elaborate. "From whom?"

"Anonymous phone call."

"Did you make an effort to trace it?"

"Couldn't. It was a burner phone."

"Would that be a cell phone purchased for cash with minutes already on it?"

"Yes. That would be a burner phone."

"Was the caller male or female?"

"Male. I think. Let me check my notes." He opened the binder he had taken with him to the witness stand and started flapping pages. "Here it is. Male."

"Thank you, Detective McClane."

I sat down, and Biggs called Danny Golden, a big, square-headed man in his late twenties who had the thick neck and massive shoulders of a linebacker. In my previous encounter with him, he'd struck me as competent and too unimaginative to be misleading or deceitful. Biggs ran him through his credentials to qualify him as an expert, then led him through a brief tutorial in ballistics for the benefit of us nonexperts. In manufacturing a rifle or a handgun, a spiral is cut out of the barrel to spin any bullet fired through it, the spin being necessary to give the bullet stability in flight and accuracy beyond a few feet. The spiral, the lands and grooves, left striations on a fired bullet that were distinctive to the model of the gun. In addition, the barrel of a gun became marked from repeated firings. These imperfections left their own striations on the bullet that allowed an expert to tell whether two bullets had been fired from the same gun.

"Did you examine the class characteristics of the bullet that Detective McClane gave you?"

"I did. It was a .32 caliber bullet fired by a Glock 32."

Biggs introduced an enlarged photograph of the bullet and had him point out the striations left by the lands and grooves of the gun.

"There are certain distinctive elements of these striations that can tell you which Glock 32, out of all the Glock 32s that have been manufactured, fired this particular bullet?"

"Yes, there are. For those purposes, you need the gun. You fire a test bullet into a slab of ballistics gel, and then you compare that bullet with your original using a comparison microscope." A comparison microscope is actually two microscopes connected by an optical bridge that brings the two images together

Biggs introduced more photographs.

"We're looking at the sides of both bullets in this one," Golden testified. "You can see how the striations in the one bullet continue unbroken into the striations of the other one. In this next picture, the bullets are turned about ninety degrees. You can see the striations still line up."

When he was done, everyone in the courtroom felt like a ballistics expert. Everyone was also convinced that the bullet first introduced by Dr. Birdsong, the bullet recovered from the wall of the motel room, had been fired by the Glock found under the mattress of Natalie Stevens.

Chapter 26

After lunch a gun dealer was called to the stand to authenticate Form 4473, a firearms transaction record that showed Mark Edward Stevens had purchased a Glock 32 about five years previously. The form was admitted into evidence. Then McClane came back to the stand.

"Have you compared the serial number on the Glock 32 found under the defendant's mattress with the serial number listed on the firearms transaction record admitted into evidence as People's Exhibit 12?" Biggs asked him.

"I have. It's the same."

Biggs asked him, "Mark Edward Stevens purchased this handgun. Who is this Mark Stevens in relation to the defendant? Do you know?"

"He is her father."

"Have you made any attempts to contact him?"

"Yes, but I haven't been able to speak with him. He's in China."

"And you haven't been able to reach him by phone?"

"I haven't."

"Let's go back to the night of the murder. Kim Beecher testified to seeing a young woman with the body of the decedent on the street in front of his house on Everglades. Did you go to that location?"

"Yes, I did."

"And what did you do about locating the young woman he had seen?"

"He had a license plate number. I checked it with the Department of Motor Vehicles, found it was registered to one Mark Stevens, and went to that address early the next afternoon. My partner Matt Tarrant and I did."

Biggs went through the rigamarole of introducing the car registration document into evidence. It was not as big a rigamarole as it could be, since certified copies of public documents are self-authenticating: there was no need to dismiss McClane and call a clerk from the DMV to the stand. He presented me with a copy and I left in on the table between Natalie and me.

"What happened at that address?" Biggs asked.

"In an open garage we found the white Lexus Mr. Beecher had described. We saw that it had a broken headlight and something that looked like blood on the bumper."

"Did you subsequently test that substance to see what it was?"

"I turned it over to the state medical examiner's office."

I had a copy of the report. The substance was blood, and DNA testing showed that it had come from the decedent. To introduce that into evidence, they would have to recall Dr. Birdsong or, possibly put on the lab tech who had assisted with the test. From McClane's mouth it would be hearsay, inadmissible in court.

"What did you do next on the morning after the murder?"

"We rang the doorbell at the Stevens residence and knocked on the door. Eventually, the door was answered by the defendant Natalie Stevens."

"Did you ask her any questions?"

"I asked if that was her Lexus in the garage."

"And what did she say?"

"She said it was."

"Then what did you do?"

"My partner read her her rights, and we arrested her."

"Thank you, Detective. That will be all."

I went to the lectern. Aubrey Biggs hadn't asked about subsequent questions McClane had asked that had not been answered, nor about Natalie invoking her right to remain silent. That would have been to invite the jury to speculate that her silence was evidence of guilt, an inference that was impermissible under the Constitution.

"What's your theory of the case, Detective? That Natalie Stevens rented a motel room, that sometime that evening she shot a man in her motel room, that she carried the body of the man she had shot out to her car, evidently wearing a short fur and heels, that she loaded him into the trunk, drove him a few blocks to the street in front of Kim Beecher's picture window, dumped the body, and then drove home?"

"Something like that."

"Why didn't you introduce her blood-spotted clothing into evidence?" I asked.

"We couldn't find it."

"The fur?"

"We couldn't find that either."

"Surely you found some shoes with heels in her closet."

"We found a good number of those."

"Any of them have traces of blood on them?"

"Not that we could find."

"You have some fairly advanced techniques for detecting blood, don't you? Even if the shoes have been wiped clean?"

"There are some chemicals that can bring out latent blood spatters, yes."

"And were you able to bring out any latent blood spatters?"

"No."

"How about the rags that might have been used to wipe the shoes clean? Or wash cloths? Find anything like that?"

"We found wash cloths and some towels in her bathroom, but there wasn't any blood on any of them."

"Did you check the trash bin outside the house? The washing machine and dryer?"

"Of course."

"So, if this unidentified woman that Mr. Beecher saw was Natalie Stevens, she did a very thorough job of getting rid of the clothes she'd been wearing."

"I would say so."

"But not a thorough job at all of getting rid of the murder weapon. If you hadn't found that gun in her room, Danny Golden wouldn't have had a test bullet to compare in his comparison microscope."

"I guess not."

"You wouldn't have been able to connect the murder weapon to Natalie Stevens."

"We would have known that the bullet was fired by a Glock 32, and that a Glock 32 was registered to her father, Mark Stevens."

"Which would have connected the crime to Mark Stevens, not Natalie."

"Clearly she had access."

"So did her stepmother, Chloe Stevens. Did you show a photograph of Chloe Stevens to Mr. Beecher to see if he could identify her as the woman he had seen?"

"We didn't."

"Did you see if he could pick Chloe Stevens out of a line up?"

"No. You had already tainted that identification."

"I had? How did I do that?"

"You showed him a picture of Chloe Stevens and suggested to him that she could be the woman he saw."

"And that tainted the identification?"

"In my opinion."

"Hadn't you already shown him a picture of Natalie Stevens and asked him if she might not be the woman he saw?"

"It was part of my investigation."

"And didn't you subsequently ask him to pick Natalie Stevens out of a lineup, after you had already tainted the identification?"

"I didn't taint the identification."

"No? Let's go back to your theory that the defendant transported this body in her car. How do you know it was her car, by the way?"

"She admitted that it was hers."

"It was registered to her father, wasn't it? Wasn't it his name on the title documents?"

"Well, sure."

"How many sets of keys were in the house? Do you know?"

He hesitated. "I don't know."

"You found evidence of the decedent's blood in this car registered to Mark Stevens? Fibers from his clothing?" There'd been no report to that effect among the papers the prosecution had turned over to me in response to my discovery motions.

"We found that blood on the bumper." He didn't know of his own knowledge that the substance was blood, but I let it go.

"This was blood on the back bumper that dripped or rubbed off as the body was being hoisted into the trunk of the car?" I asked.

"No. It was on the front bumper."

"Is it your theory that the body was transported in the engine compartment?"

There was little ripple of nervous laughter somewhere back in the gallery.

"Or possibly tied to the front of the car like a deer carcass?"

An outright guffaw prompted the judge to bang his gavel, and the burst of laughter cut off abruptly.

"We assume that the body was transported in the trunk or passenger compartment, but that it had been wrapped in a sheet or something. The blood on the front bumper would have been from when she ran over him."

"Was there a sheet missing from the motel room?"

"No."

"You found the sheet, though, and there were matching fibers in the trunk of the car."

"It didn't have to be a sheet. It could have been a tarp or anything else of that nature."

"So there were no sheet fibers in the trunk of the car. You mentioned a tarp. Does that mean you found one, maybe in a dumpster near where you found the body, maybe in the trash bin behind the Stevens house?"

"No."

"Did you find fibers on the balcony walkway of the motel? Of a sheet, a tarp, or the defendant's clothing?"

"No."

"Did you find blood?"

"No."

"So your theory is that the defendant carried the body in her arms from the room to the staircase, down the stairs, and to her car, possibly wrapped in a sheet or tarp? According to the autopsy report, this body weighed 182 pounds."

"She could have dumped the body over the rail. That wouldn't have required such great strength."

"Did you find crushed shrubbery beneath the walkway, an imprint in the dirt, some blood spatters—anything?"

His eyes moved, then returned to me. "No."

"So your theory is that the defendant, possibly wearing heels, muscled this body down the stairs or over the rail, then up into her car, that after dumping the body she disposed of a tarp or sheet, her shoes, and possibly all of her clothing, somewhere far from the place where she dumped the body and far from her own house, somewhere it would never be found, but that she found nothing better to do with the murder weapon than tuck it under her mattress. That's it, isn't it?"

"It seems to be."

I glanced at Natalie, and she jerked her head at me. I held up a finger. "If I could have just a moment, your honor." I went to the table and put my head next to Natalie's.

"This isn't my car," she whispered, all but inaudibly. She put a hand on the registration paper. "This is Chloe's IS 250. My car is a CT 200."

"You're kidding."

She widened her eyes at me, and I nodded. "Okay," I said, and I went back to the lectern with my copy of the registration paper.

"Could you tell us a little more about this car of Natalie's that you impounded?" I asked McClane. "It was a small Lexus of some sort?"

He checked his notebook. "Yes. License plate GBX 118."

"What was the model?"

"I don't have that here."

"You identified it by the license plate."

"Yes."

"Perhaps you could take another look at Exhibit 12, refresh your memory." The court reporter took it to him.

"Lexus IS 250."

"You still have the car you impounded in the police lot, don't you?"

"I believe we do. I don't think anyone ever picked it up."

"That car is a Lexus CT 200," I said. "You showed it to me."

"No, it's not."

"Both are registered to Mark Stevens. Both are white. Actually, I think the IS 250 is off-white. Your honor, we need a recess to allow this witness to examine that vehicle. I'd like to accompany him."

"No need," McClane said. "I've got the vehicle identification number here in my notes." He ran a stubby index finger along the line of type, eyes flicking back and forth between it and the registration. "Well I'm damned."

"The plates were changed," I said. "Do you think it was before the crime or after?"

He was still comparing his notes and the registration paper.

"If the defendant is guilty of this crime, then it was premeditated. She changed plates with her stepmother's car before going out to commit the crime, though it would have been smarter to change plates with a stranger in a parking garage somewhere. Do you think she was trying to implicate her stepmother? If so, why wouldn't she have changed the plates back and wiped the blood from the bumper?"

McClane looked up and met my eyes with a look of defiance. "People don't think of everything, do they?"

"Let's suppose for a moment that Chloe Stevens, Natalie's stepmother, committed the crime. Let's suppose she was in her own car when she dumped the body, then, after she was seen, she realized she needed to get rid of the plates. She changed plates with her stepdaughter, broke her headlight, and smeared blood on the bumper. Did you check the stepmother's car for blood or fibers?"

"No."

"Because you had a theory of the case, and when you didn't find evidence to support it, you stopped looking. Isn't that right?"

"It's not right. We did a thorough, competent job."

"You got the wrong car!"

"We didn't get the wrong car, we just got the wrong plates."

"The eyewitness didn't identify the car. He identified the plates."

Biggs objected. "Not a question, your honor."

"Your whole case against Natalie Stevens just fell in the toilet, didn't it, detective?"

"Objection," Biggs said, more loudly. "Not proper cross-examination."

"It didn't fall in the toilet," McClane said. "We've got the motel registration, the car, the murder weapon…"

"Your honor," Biggs shouted. "They're arguing the case."

"Yes, they are," Judge Cheatham said. He looked at me. "Are you done questioning this witness?"

I smiled. "I am, your honor. Thank you."

The judge said, "Mr. Biggs, do you have further questions for this witness?"

Aubrey Biggs, on his feet behind his table, was smoothing his jacket with his hands. "Your honor, it's nearly four o'clock. Counsel for the defense has made a number of allegations about some of the evidence in this case, allegations which are not themselves evidence and which at this point are entirely unsubstantiated. With the court's permission, we would like a recess until tomorrow morning to give us a chance to look into it."

The judge nodded. "Looks like some sloppy police work." It was something he shouldn't have said in front of the jury, and Biggs reddened, but he didn't say anything. "Very well," Cheatham said. "Court recessed until nine-thirty tomorrow morning." He banged his gavel and stood.

"You did good," I told Natalie Stevens as the jury filed out. "You were paying attention, and it helped us score some points."

"You did a good job with it."

I made a face. "I'm embarrassed I didn't notice they had the wrong model number, but I don't know cars."

"And you tend to assume the police know their business." The deputy sheriff came up beside her and laid a hand on her arm.

"Yes, and I shouldn't. I'll try to do better."

Chapter 27

My cell phone rang as I was pulling out of the parking lot. I punched the button, held the phone to my ear. "Robin Starling."

"Oh. You're out of court. I was going to leave a message." It was Rodney Burns.

"What's up?"

"I think I've got something. Could you stop by, or do you want me to give it to you over the phone?"

"You got fresh coffee?" I wasn't totally zonked, as I had been the day before, but I was fatigued.

"I can have."

"Be there in fifteen minutes."

Fifteen minutes was optimistic, but I was leaving downtown ahead of rush hour, and I made it on the nose. The coffee pot was giving a last snort as I came in, and Rodney was standing by with his hand on the handle of the carafe.

"I've got it almost ready for you. You drink it black, don't you?"

"Sure," I said. Rodney was moving his head around and his shoulders were jerking. "Either you're on one heck of a caffeine high, or you've got something good."

"Oh, I've got something all right. I don't know if it's good, but it's something." He handed me my VCU Ram mug and took a sip from Edgar Allan Poe.

"You know how you asked me to track Mark Stevens for you, see if he flew somewhere other than China and then back to the United States?"

"Yes?" I said hopefully.

"Well, he didn't. Not that I could find."

"Oh."

"But look at this." He handed me a sheet of names. There were Chinese characters at the top, interspersed with English—Cathay Airlines, Hong Kong-Los Angeles. The date was December 9.

"What am I looking at?"

"The manifest for a flight from Hong Kong to LAX that departed 5:35 a.m., December 9. Mark Stevens arrived in Hong Kong about 10 p.m. the night before."

I scanned down the list looking for Stevens. What I saw instead was… "Larry Smith," I said.

"Bingo."

Larry Smith was the man whose identification David Stevens had given me, presumably the identification of the man Natalie was accused of killing. "There are a lot of Smiths in the world," I said. This one had been in seat 29B.

"Yes, there are."

"Any of these hieroglyphics next to the name tell us anything about him?"

"Not really. This tells us something." He gave me two more passenger lists, one of a flight from LAX to Washington-Dulles, and one of a flight from Dulles to Richmond International. I put down my coffee mug to shuffle between them.

"How do you get these things? I thought it took a court order."

"Well, sometimes."

There was a Larry Smith on both manifests. "So Mark Stevens flew from Richmond to Hong Kong, and just a few hours after he arrived, Larry Smith left Hong Kong for Richmond," I said. "And you're thinking it's the same person." I looked up.

Rodney eyed me owlishly over the rim of his mug as he slurped coffee.

I didn't see Paul that night, or Brooke. Dr. McDermott brought over Deeks, two bottles of Lowenbrau Dark, and homemade sandwiches with dill-pickle spears.

"I don't know what kind of beer you drink," he said. "This was my favorite back in the day, but it's been in the fridge awhile."

"Hopefully not since back in the day."

"No, not that long. A few months maybe."

I didn't really drink beer, but I wasn't going to tell him that. "Thank you."

Deeks barked and jumped up to brace his paws on my thigh. He was growing. I picked him up to give him a hug and got a faceful of dog slobber.

"Yes, I love you, too," I said. I put him back down.

"I try not to reward him when he jumps," Dr. McDermott said. "He's your dog, of course. I just don't want to be the one to mess him up for you."

He was right, of course. Deeks might hit a hundred pounds, and that was a lot of dog to be jumping up on people. "I'll try to do better," I said.

"Oh, I'm not criticizing."

We had our sandwiches and beer. If I ever did become a beer drinker, Lowenbrau Dark was going to be at the top of my list. "This is just what I need," I said, examining the bottle. "Another high-calorie item to become attached to."

"On the positive side, it's fat free," Dr. McDermott said.

"Isn't that true of all alcohol?"

"One of God's gifts to humanity."

After he left, Deeks and I walked about a mile-and-a-half through the neighborhood. Since it was full dark and Deeks always came when I called, I walked him off-leash. He disappeared once, I suspect to do his business up against somebody's house. I told myself I should feel guilty about it. On the other hand, if a brown dog poops in the dark, does it leave a turd in your yard? Well, maybe. I suspected that a tree falling in the woods made a sound, too, even when there was no one to hear.

On Wednesday Aubrey Biggs did not call Tom McClane back to the stand for redirect examination. He called his next witness with no mention of what he had called my unsubstantiated allegations, which suggested to me that they had now been substantiated. I might have to call McClane as my own witness just to clarify the point when it came time to put on the defense case.

The bailiff ushered Devon Matthews into the courtroom. She was wearing a sweater set and a wool skirt, and her blonde hair hung halfway down her back. The outfit and the hair gave her a sixties' coed look that was likely to play well with the jury.

She gave her name and address and said she worked at the Best Western on the Chippenham Parkway.

"In Richmond?" Biggs asked her.

"Yes, on the Southside."

"What are your duties at the Best Western, Ms. Matthews?"

"I'm a desk clerk."

"Were you on duty on Sunday night, December 6?"

She was.

"Did you see the defendant Natalie Stevens that night?"

Devon looked at Natalie, then her eyes darted to meet mine before her gaze returned to Mr. Biggs at the lectern. "I don't know."

"Didn't Natalie Stevens check into the motel that night?"

"A Natalie Stevens checked into the motel, but a lot of people come and go. I don't remember the face."

"But it was someone who gave the name of Natalie Stevens."

"Yes, that's right."

"And the person who gave the name of Natalie Stevens was a young woman."

"A woman anyway. I would have noticed if Natalie had been a man."

She got a few laughs off that, which Biggs ignored. "And it could have been the young woman sitting beside Ms. Starling at the defense table?" He was leading his own witness, but I liked the way it was going, so I didn't object.

"It could have been," Devon said. "I don't know."

Biggs really didn't like it when witnesses didn't testify the way they were supposed to. "Didn't the police show you a photograph of the defendant just a few days after the murder, and didn't you identify that photograph as that of the woman who checked in that night?"

"Not positively."

"But you did tell the police that it could be the woman, didn't you?"

"I think I said it might be."

She had made her point. I stood. "Mr. Biggs seems to be cross-examining his own witness, your honor."

"He does," Judge Cheatham agreed. "Mr. Biggs?"

"If I could ask just a couple more questions, your honor, I think you'll see where all this is going."

The judge looked at me, then nodded. "All right. Let's see."

"Why are you so tentative in your identification now, Ms. Matthews? What happened after the police showed you that photograph of Natalie Stevens?"

"Robin Starling also showed me a photograph."

"Robin Starling showed you a photograph? Robin Starling, the attorney for the defendant in this case?" His tone made it sound tantamount to altering the crime scene.

"Yes. She was there the day after the police."

"Whose photograph was this?"

"I don't know. I think it may have been the defendant's stepmother, but at the time I identified it as Natalie Stevens."

"She showed you a picture of the defendant's stepmother and told you it was Natalie Stevens?" His voice rose incredulously.

"I think she asked me if it was Natalie Stevens."

"Even though she knew it wasn't."

"I actually don't know whose picture it was. There's a woman who's been in the witness room with me who looks familiar."

"Subsequently, you came in for a police line-up, didn't you?"

"Yes."

"Were you able to pick out from that line up the young woman who registered in your hotel as Natalie Stevens?"

"No."

"Didn't you say you thought it was number four, the woman you now know to be Natalie Stevens, the defendant in this case?"

I stood again. "He's browbeating his witness, your honor."

Biggs jabbed a finger at me. "You should be careful."

"Your honor, opposing counsel is threatening me." I said it in the whiney voice of a schoolroom tattletale, and it drew some laughter.

Judge Cheatham banged his gavel to silence it. "Mr. Biggs," he said mildly, "don't threaten defense counsel."

It drew another titter of laughter, but the judge only smiled faintly. "It's time to move on, Mr. Biggs," he said.

Biggs was glaring at me, but he took a breath and consciously relaxed the muscles in his face. "You say that a Natalie Stevens checked in that night. She used a credit card with Natalie Stevens' name on it, didn't she?"

"Yes, she did."

"You assigned her a room?"

"Yes. Room 238. Second floor in the back."

"She took her cardkey and left?"

"Yes, two cardkeys."

"Two cardkeys? Was someone with her?"

"I don't know. I usually give out two cardkeys."

"But she didn't hand one of them back and say she was by herself."

"No. At least, not that I remember."

"Not that I remember," Biggs repeated.

"Sorry."

He shook his head. "No further questions," he said.

I went to the lectern. "Whoever registered for that room must have filled out some paperwork—and signed a credit slip?"

"Yes."

"Did the police take possession of that paperwork?"

Devon nodded. "I don't know if it will do them any good."

"Oh? Why is that?"

"It was all filled out in block letters."

"Even the signature?"

"That was just a line with a loop on the end."

"Did that match the signature that was on the credit card?"

"I don't know. I always make a point of comparing signatures, but I'm not a handwriting expert, and it's not the kind of thing you want to make an issue of."

"Do you ask for photo ID?"

"I do most times. I know I should. I just don't remember if I did in this particular instance."

Devon Matthews was my new best friend. "Thank you, Ms. Matthews," I said sincerely. "Just a couple more topics. I assume the district attorney went over your testimony with you before trial?"

"Yes, he did."

"He can't have been happy with your inability to identify the defendant in this case. Did he press you to make an identification?"

"Well, he asked me if I was sure I couldn't identify her."

"Did he ask you more than once?"

"Yes."

"More than twice?"

"I think so."

"As many as five times?"

She shrugged. "It could have been. He kept asking me to study her mug shot."

I looked at Biggs with raised eyebrows, then turned back to Devon. "You rented a room to more than one person named Stevens that night, didn't you?"

"I wondered if you were going to ask me about that."

"It was me or no one. A second Stevens doesn't fit the prosecution's theory of the case."

"Your honor!" Biggs objected, standing.

"Ms. Starling," the judge said.

"I'm sorry. I'll withdraw the jibe." Before Biggs could react to that bit of smartassery, I said to Devon, "So tell us about the other Stevens."

"Someone who gave the name of Mark Stevens rented room 240." At the edge of my peripheral vision, Aubrey Biggs dropped into his chair in evident disgust.

"Is that right next to the room rented by Natalie Stevens?"

"Yes. Right on the corner."

"It's quite a coincidence that a man with the same name as Natalie's father rented the room next door. Did the two come in together?"

"No. Mark Stevens came in not quite an hour later."

"Did he ask for the room next door?"

"I'm sure he didn't. I would have remembered. He might have asked for second floor at the back. People make those kinds of requests all the time."

"Is there a connecting door between the two rooms?"

"You know there is. You went up and saw it."

It was too much for Biggs, who slapped his hand on the table.

"Mr. Biggs," Judge Cheatham said. He tapped his gavel. "I'm the only one who gets to make noise pounding the table."

There was some laughter. Biggs opened his mouth to say something, but evidently thought better of it.

"You may continue with your cross-examination," the judge told me.

"I'm done," I said. I sat, and Biggs went to the lectern.

"Ms. Matthews, until asked specifically about it just last week, you said nothing to the police about this room rented to Mark Stevens, did you?"

I half-stood. "Your honor, he's leading his witness."

"She's evidently a hostile witness," Biggs said. "She's hardly been forthcoming with the police."

"Now he's trying to intimidate the witness," I said.

Judge Cheatham said, "At this point I'm going to allow a few leading questions."

Biggs said, "Did you or did you not withhold information from the police about Mark Stevens renting a room at your hotel that night?"

"I did not. I answered every question they asked me. I took them up to Room 238, I gave them documents. I cooperated in every way." Her voice was rising along with her color. She clearly didn't like Biggs, and I knew from experience that she could be nasty with people she didn't like.

"But you did share information with Ms. Starling that you didn't share with the police."

"I answered her questions. If the police had ever contacted me again after she uncovered the bit about Mark Stevens, I probably would have mentioned it to them, but they didn't. Nobody with the police or the prosecution talked to me again until last week."

Biggs' breathing was audible in the otherwise silent courtroom. "Did this Mark Stevens pay with a credit card?"

"No, he paid with cash."

"Did he show ID?"

"I don't know."

"You don't know. So really this could have been anybody."

"It couldn't have been a woman."

"What?"

"I would have noticed a woman trying to pass herself off as Mark Stevens."

Chapter 28

"What happened to Devon Matthews?" Brooke asked me over lunch. "Last time we saw her, she hated your guts."

"I told you she'd begun to thaw a little."

"She's done more than thaw. She was in there fighting for your client as hard as you were."

"Tell me," Paul said. Once again he had been unable to be there.

"The gist of it is that Devon refused to identify Natalie Stevens," Brooke said.

"And she stuck it up Biggs' backside every chance she got," I added. I put a forkful of salad in my mouth. Brooke sipped her water.

"Well, come on. Specifics, girls, specifics!"

So we gave him some specifics, as much as we could remember.

"I understand it perfectly," Paul told us.

"You do," I said.

"Since we last saw her, that young woman has been questioned extensively by Aubrey Biggs."

"Uh huh."

"Extensively and repetitively, and possibly with a bit of nastiness thrown in here and there."

"That'd cheese me off," Brooke said.

"When I first saw her, she seemed to think I was going to make a move on her boyfriend," I said. "That worry may have eased over time."

"Especially after you showed up at the motel with your sweetheart," Paul said.

"I am not her sweetheart," Brooke said. "We are just good friends."

"I meant me. You know that don't you?"

I patted his cheek. "You're cute when you're insecure." I went back to my salad. Lunch recesses don't last forever.

That afternoon Biggs called someone from the department of forensic science who ran us through the blood work. DNA tests showed that the blood on the bumper of Natalie's car, the blood on the fatal bullet, and the blood in Room 238, rented under Natalie's name, all came from John Doe, the decedent in the case. I asked a few questions on cross just to show I was alive, but I didn't get anything helpful out of it. Then Biggs called Chloe Stevens to the stand.

A bailiff brought Chloe in from the witness room, and she walked down the aisle in four-inch heels and a silk dress that stopped just short of mid-thigh. If the rail of the witness box hadn't had solid panels, nobody would have been able to focus on anything she said once she sat down and crossed her legs.

She identified herself as Chloe Stevens, the mother of the defendant Natalie Stevens. "Well, stepmother," she said. "I've been married to her father for just over thirteen months. We're so close, though. I love her like my very own."

I didn't glance in Natalie's direction, but I hoped she wasn't rolling her eyes or, worse, poking her finger into her open mouth in a gagging gesture.

"Were you at home the night of Sunday, December 6?" Biggs asked her.

"Yes. I was home all evening."

"Was your stepdaughter there with you?"

"She left to go to a party about six o'clock."

"When did she get back?"

"I don't know. I went to bed about eleven."

"And the defendant had not come home by that time?"

"Not that I heard. Of course, I was watching TV in my bedroom, so I might not have if she came in quietly."

When I glanced at Natalie, she leaned toward me. "Her car wasn't in the garage when I got home," she whispered. "I don't think."

I don't think. Natalie had been impaired when she got home that evening, now over a month ago, but I considered the possibility that Chloe hadn't been home at all.

"Did you hear her come in during the night?" Biggs asked.

"I don't know. A noise awakened me just before three. I supposed it could have been the garage door." Her tone was pleasant and conversational as if she had no idea she was digging Natalie a hole it would be difficult to crawl out of.

"Your witness," Biggs said.

It was a short testimony, a nice ending punctuation to an afternoon in which the prosecution had regained some of its momentum. I went to the lectern, determined not to let it end on that note.

"Hello, Chloe," I said.

She gave me a nod.

"You seem very much at peace in giving your testimony. Are you too simpleminded to realize that, if the jury believes you, they may sentence Natalie to life in prison? This stepdaughter whom you love as your very own?"

Biggs, predictably, objected. Loudly. Judge Cheatham sustained the objection. Chloe, who had for a moment looked startled and defensive, regained her composure.

"I'm sorry. That was outrageous, wasn't it?" I held up a hand, forestalling her answer. "Actually, I owe you, don't I? It was you who selected me out of all the lawyers in Richmond to defend your stepdaughter."

"Her father insisted we get the best."

"Mark Stevens played a part in my selection? Is he here in Richmond then?"

Biggs said, "Your honor, this doesn't have anything to do with what this witness testified to on direct. It's not proper cross-examination."

"It goes to show the bias of the witness," I said.

"How?" Judge Cheatham asked.

"Give me just a few questions, your honor. I think it will be clear."

He nodded. "I'll allow it."

To Chloe I repeated, "Is Mark Stevens here in Richmond?"

"No. He's been in China since shortly before…all this happened."

276

"But you talked to him about who should represent his daughter?"

"Yes. We talked by phone. He said he was going to talk to you directly. Didn't he call you?"

I of course wasn't there to answer questions. "He didn't give you my name, did he? He just told you to hire the best in Richmond. Money was no object."

"That's right."

"So you went into an executive suites and hired me."

"Certainly."

"A lawyer who had opened her own practice just two weeks previously."

"I didn't know that at the time. I think you've performed very well, though."

"Thank you. Why didn't you hire the lawyer who had worked in the office of the commonwealth's attorney, who also had an office in that executive suites?"

"I thought Natalie would be more comfortable with a woman representing her."

"Even an inexperienced, incompetent woman?"

She hesitated a beat, which was just want I wanted.

"You don't need to answer that," I said. "I think we've heard enough."

I went and sat down. Natalie's eyes flicked toward me. Probably describing oneself as inexperienced and incompetent wasn't the best way to inspire confidence.

When I exited the courthouse shortly before five o'clock, Detective Jordan and his partner Ray Hernandez were sitting on the low brick wall facing the revolving door. They stopped talking and stood, and my pace slowed. "You look like you're here for me," I said.

"We are," Ray said.

"What have I done now?"

"What haven't you done?"

I looked from one of their grinning faces to the other.

Jordan said, "The truth is, Robin, we're hoping to take you to dinner."

My phone dinged, and I dug it out. It was Rodney Burns: "I have something for you." I looked back at Ray and Jordan.

"Can't tonight," I said. "Why the charitable gesture?"

Jordan jerked his head, and we walked together along the sidewalk, the two detectives flanking me. When we turned the corner, Hernandez said, "We hear Aubrey Biggs ripped Tom McClane a new one last night."

"After you made him look like an idiot on the stand yesterday and tore a big hole in the prosecution's case," Jordan added.

I flinched. "It wasn't personal," I said.

"Oh, it is," Hernandez said. "For us it is."

Jordan said, "We were hoping you could kind of walk us through it, let us savor McClane's time on the stand a little."

"I was able to gain a little traction over some switched license plates. I don't think it made him especially uncomfortable."

"McClane's probably not bright enough to be uncomfortable," Hernandez said.

"Did he testify about how much he could bench press?" Jordan said. "That's the kind of thing he really likes to talk about."

"Not on the stand. Over coffee once." We were waiting for the light so we could cross to the parking lot that held my car. "Then his wife came to my office to ask what my intentions were with her husband. I think he'd come clean with her about some stuff that included whatever thoughts he'd been having about me."

Hernandez hooted.

"What have you guys got against McClane?" I asked.

"It's not that we have anything against him," Jordan said. Hernandez snorted. "It's just that he knows how everybody in the police department should be doing their jobs, but he doesn't take care of his own."

"Back in Texas," Hernandez said, "we would have said he was all hat and no cattle."

The light changed, and we started across. "I didn't know you were from Texas," I said.

"Midland. But I got out before the oil boom."

"Shrewd move." We had arrived at my car. I opened the door and swung my briefcase and purse across into the passenger seat.

"Are you sure we can't take you to dinner?" Jordan asked.

"Sorry."

They let me go.

My phone rang on the way out West Broad. It was Carly. "Hi, Robin, are you still in court?" Her voice had that hushed quality it took on when she was about to dish some dirt.

"Just got out."

"The police were here." She paused dramatically. "With a warrant."

"For me?"

"To search your office."

"What did they take? They should have left you a receipt."

"I don't think they found what they were looking for. The detective asked me if you had any personal spaces in the suites outside of your office."

"Was the detective a short guy with a flattop haircut?"

"Do you know him?"

"Better than I'd like."

"I was just closing up, but is there anything you need me to do?"

"No. Go on home."

I punched off as I stopped for a light. Tom McClane strikes back, I thought.

Rodney Burns was pacing the floor. The light on the coffeemaker was off, though there was a little coffee at the bottom of the carafe.

"What? No coffee?" I said.

He blinked. "Sorry. I was distracted."

I held up a hand to arrest his movement toward the Cuisinart. "It's all right. I don't need coffee."

"Look at the paper on the desk."

"What is it?" I picked it up and saw immediately what it was—a photocopy of the birth certificate for Larry Gholson Smith, born in Portsmouth, Virginia on March 26, 1979."

"You found him."

"I think so."

I shuffled to the next page and found myself looking at a driver's license for Larry Gholson Smith. The picture looked familiar, but it was a grainy photocopy of a tiny picture that probably hadn't been that representative to begin with.

"Is it Mark Stevens?" he asked me. "Natalie Stevens' father?"

"I've only seen his picture. It might be his brother David. They look something alike."

I flipped to the third page. It took me a few seconds to realize I was looking at a death certificate for Larry Gholson Smith. "August 7, 1991," I read. "So it can't be the same Larry Smith."

"A bit of a coincidence that the date of birth on the driver's license is the same," Rodney said.

"Yes, it is."

"And that he looks like Mark Stevens."

"Where did you get these?"

"State Registrar faxed them to me. You'll need a subpoena to get certified copies."

"So what does it mean?"

He sat and laced his fingers around one knee. "I think it means someone came across a certified copy of that birth certificate issued before Larry's death. He noticed that the date of birth was within a few years of his own and used it to create a false identity. You got a birth certificate, you can get a Social Security card, a driver's license, anything you want. If this person also knew that Larry Smith was dead, then it was all the better."

"Wouldn't the Social Security card have been issued at birth, or at least before the parents filed the first tax return listing Larry as a dependent?"

"Not until after 1986."

I sat in the chair across from him, laying the papers on the table. "Wow," I said.

"What do you think?"

"Portsmouth is in the tidewater area," I said. "David Stevens used to practice law there."

"And this could be him?" He leaned forward to push the papers toward me.

I looked again. "Him or his brother. I think they're about ten years apart in age. It really depends on when the picture was taken. Can you get me a certified copy of the driver's license?"

"Sure. When do you want it?"

"Tomorrow morning. Bring it to court as soon as you can get it."

He looked surprised. "Okay," he said.

I took the photocopies with me—birth certificate, death certificate, driver's license. I also took the wallet and keys that David had given me, still in the plastic grocery sack. They might be what McClane had been looking for in my office, and I didn't want to get Rodney Burns into trouble.

I'd been home fifteen or twenty minutes before I thought to get the mail. Dr. McDermott was sitting on my front stoop. He turned as I pulled open the door, and Deeks raced toward me from the middle of the lawn. I rubbed Deeks' head, picked him up and hugged him, put him back down. As Dr. McDermott had pointed out, it wasn't a good way to get him to greet people calmly, but I had my own emotional needs. I patted Dr. McDermott's shoulder as he rose creakily to his feet.

"Is our joint custody of Deeks still working okay?" I asked. "Your house weekdays, mine nights and weekends?"

"It works for me."

Deeks gave me a yap and ran back into the yard.

"He doesn't run off," Dr. McDermott said. "That's good."

"It's common enough in a puppy." It was one of the tidbits I'd picked up working in my father's veterinary clinic. "I just hope the trait stays with him as he grows older."

"Look at your front door."

I looked. An official-looking document was taped to it.

"The police were here a couple of hours ago. It's why I was waiting for you."

I felt goose bumps break out on my arms. "Was one of them a short man with a flat-top haircut?"

"I think so."

"They're after me."

"Are they going to get you?"

"I can hope not. Did they take anything? Do you know?"

He shook his head. I pried the search warrant loose from the door and took a look at it. It was directed to any peace officer in the Commonwealth of Virginia: "Proof by affidavit having been made to me by one David Stevens, I am satisfied that there is probably cause to believe that on the premises described as 4541 Beechnut Street"—my home address—"in the City of Richmond, Commonwealth of Virginia, there is now being possessed or concealed certain property, persons or things described as: A wallet and key ring with an assortment of keys belonging to one Larry Smith, which constitutes evidence that a public offense has been committed. Such public offense being ACCESSORY AFTER THE FACT IN THE CRIME OF MURDER IN THE FIRST DEGREE."

Dr. McDermott wasn't trying to read over my shoulder, but he was watching my face anxiously.

"On the positive side, I don't think they found what they were looking for," I said.

"And on the negative side?"

"On the negative side, everything's going to hit the fan tomorrow morning."

David Stevens had turned on me, and he was going for the kill.

Chapter 29

I dreamed about the photograph on the driver's license. The grainy faced man was reflected in the dark glass of my repaired French doors, in my bathroom mirror, on the blank screen of my TV. He followed me down the hall, then down an endless alley, never moving very fast, but always moving, always coming for me.

My eyes blinked open, and I lay in the dark, my heart pounding. I put out a hand and felt Deeks' fur. He gave my hand a quick lick, then nestled back down into sleep. My breathing slowed.

"No great mystery," I whispered. Larry Smith, contrary to what David Stevens had led me to believe, wasn't the dead man Natalie was accused of killing. He was either Mark or David Stevens, and David would be on the witness stand in the morning. We'd have our face-off then.

I slipped into sleep again, but in my dreams it was the grainy faced man on the witness stand, his features indistinct, his voice an incomprehensible croak.

A deputy sheriff brought Natalie into the courtroom ahead of the jury, uncuffed her, and retreated to stand against the wall.

"Who's your dentist, Natalie?" I asked.

She looked surprised.

"Do you have a family dentist? You and your father go to the same one?"

"Yes, we do. Dr. Davis."

I might have hoped for a less common name. "Do you know his first name?"

"Kevin, I think. Kevin R. Davis, DDS."

"Thank you. I'll be right back."

I went out into the hallway with my cell phone. Somebody needed to charm Dr. Davis's socks off. It was the sort of job I'd prefer to do myself—I know how that sounds—but I was in court. I called Brooke Marshall.

"Hey, Robin."

"Hey, Brooke, I need a favor."

"Shoot." But the voice came not from my phone, but from the air in front of me. Brooke was there, and the rest of the crowd from the elevator was streaming past us.

I punched *End* on my cell phone and told her what I wanted.

"When do you need this?"

"Thirty minutes. Say an hour, hour-and-a-half."

"Why don't I just make the sun stand still for you?"

"Could you do that? That would be especially helpful, but I didn't like to ask."

She got back on the elevator.

"If you need help, call Rodney Burns," I said as the doors started to close between us.

"You're sending me after a man, and you think I need Rodney Burns?"

The doors closed, and she was gone. I looked at my phone and hesitated. She was right. There was no point in calling Rodney, who was supposed to be getting me a certified copy of a driver's license anyway. Brooke could either do it, or she couldn't. I went back into the courtroom.

The gallery was about half-full. Chloe Stevens, who had been in the witness room until she had testified, was sitting in the front row, directly behind Natalie. Natalie wasn't looking at her, and her shoulders were stiff. I imagined that Chloe had reached across the rail to touch her, perhaps to offer a few words of synthetic encouragement. The jury was filing in.

"What was that with the dentist about?" Natalie murmured to me.

"Wild hair. We'll see if it comes to anything."

Aubrey Biggs pushed through the bar and went to his table without a glance in my direction. The bailiff called the court to order, and everyone stood as the judge came in. We all sat.

"Mr. Biggs, do you have another witness?"

"Yes, your honor. Call David Stevens to the stand." Aubrey was wasting no time in springing his trap.

David Stevens came into the courtroom wearing a medium gray suit, a white shirt, and a striped tie. Lawyer clothes. His thick black hair was perfect. He was sworn in and took his seat.

Biggs, at the lectern, buttoned his suit coat and straightened the pocket flaps. I felt like I should go hold a mirror for him.

"Could you give us your name and address, please?" Biggs said to David Stevens.

David could. He did.

"What is your relationship to the defendant, Natalie Stevens?"

"I'm her uncle. Her father's brother."

"What is your brother's name?"

"Mark Stevens."

"Have you ever had occasion to visit the home on Magnolia, where your brother lives with his wife and daughter?"

"Yes, many times."

"Have you been there since the arrest of Natalie Stevens on December 7?"

"Once."

"What was the occasion of that visit?"

David cleared his throat. "I searched her room. Her room and her bathroom and a living area, actually, which are all together in the loft that overlooks the kitchen and family room." Incidentally he was drawing a picture of Natalie as a little rich girl.

"You searched her rooms," Biggs said, summarizing. "What were you looking for?"

"Evidence that might link her to the man that was killed. At the time, you understand, we all thought it was a hit-and-run."

"What did you intend to do with this evidence?"

"I wasn't sure. Natalie had been arrested. Her stepmother and I, her father and I, wanted to know more about that. My brother especially was concerned that there might be something incriminating."

"And you intended to remove it."

"I don't know what I intended to do. The fact is, I did remove it. I love my niece." He made eye-contact with her and smiled, then returned his gaze to Biggs. "I always want to do what's right, but I love my niece."

"What was this evidence you removed?"

David Stevens took a breath. He had the attention of everyone in the jury, everyone in the court room. "A plastic grocery sack with a man's wallet in it. A man's wallet and a set of keys."

"Who did this wallet belong to?"

"The credit cards in it belonged to a Larry Smith."

"Was there a driver's license?"

"No, nothing with a picture. If the wallet ever had contained a driver's license, it had been removed."

"Where exactly did you find this grocery sack?"

"Tucked behind the rolls of toilet paper in the cabinet in Natalie's bathroom."

"And you took possession of this grocery sack and its contents."

"I did. I may have done wrong—I probably did do wrong—but I took it. I knew I couldn't keep it. It's weighed on my conscious something awful. But I did it."

"What did you ultimately do with it?"

"Gave it to Robin Starling, the young woman who is representing Natalie."

"You gave it to whom?" Biggs sounded as if he must surely have been hallucinating when he heard me being implicated, but of course this moment had been well rehearsed.

"To Robin Starling," David repeated, driving in the nail.

"The attorney representing the defendant," Biggs said.

"Yes. I assumed she would handle it appropriately. I guess I assumed she would turn it over to the police."

"Did she turn it over to the police?"

"Not to my knowledge. She never spoke of it again. My conscience continued to bother me, like I've said, so finally I came to you."

"Yesterday, over the lunch recess."

"Yes."

"And you made an affidavit."

"I did."

I stood. "Your honor, counsel is leading this witness by his nose."

Biggs jabbed a finger at me. "You. Should know when to keep quiet. If you know what's good for you."

"Are you suggesting that if I remain silent and allow you to railroad my client with a carload of irrelevant claptrap, I personally will come out of this all right?"

"Oh, I'm not suggesting that at all."

"Then perhaps you could keep your advice to yourself," I said.

The judge banged his gavel. Personal exchanges between counsel are a big no-no: We're supposed to address our remarks to the court. "Ms. Starling, do you have this wallet and keys in your possession?"

"Yes, your honor."

The answer seemed to surprise him. He stared at me a long moment. "Counselor. You can't withhold evidence like that."

"Evidence of what?"

"Evidence of the identity of the decedent in this case, the identity of the man your client is charged with killing."

"Is that what this is?"

Biggs said, "You know it is."

"Where are the wallet and keys now?" Judge Cheatham asked me.

"In my briefcase."

"Here in this courtroom?"

"Yes, your honor."

"Well, let's have them."

I lifted my briefcase to the table and pulled out the grocery bag, then carried it to the bench. As I walked back past the lectern, Biggs said, "You're going to lose your license over this." He spoke loudly enough to be heard all over the courtroom.

I gave him a big smile. "Eat me," I said.

It sparked a buzz of conversation in the courtroom, and the judge banged his gavel. Biggs raised his voice: "Your honor, I move that this, this lawyer be held in contempt of court. This behavior is outrageous. It's totally outside the bounds of…"

I overrode him: "But trying to intimidate the representative of a young woman on trial for her freedom is just peachy?" I don't like to shout, but I had to if I was going to be heard over the courtroom talk and the pounding of the judge's gavel. When the head came off the gavel and bounced into the middle of the courtroom, it occurred to me that maybe I had gone too far. In the sudden silence, the bailiff picked up the head of the gavel and put it on the bench in front of the judge.

"Ms. Starling," the judge said, his voice trembling. "I will hold you in contempt. I sentence you to a day in jail, and the deputy sheriff will be directed to take you into custody at the end of today's proceedings. Other consequences will surely follow, but they are unfortunately beyond the jurisdiction of this court."

David Stevens smirked at me from the witness stand.

I sat down at my table and placed my folded hands in front of me.

"Do we understand each other?" Judge Cheatham asked.

"We do," I said.

Judge Cheatham, looking from me to Biggs, seemed momentarily disoriented. "You were questioning this witness," he said finally.

"I'd like to show the wallet to the witness," Biggs said.

"Don't you think someone should check it for fingerprints or whatever else might be on it?"

"Oh, I'm quite sure no worthwhile prints remain on the wallet." Biggs tone was prim.

With a frown and another glance at me, the judge said, "You may show the witness the wallet."

Biggs got the wallet from the bench and took it to David Stevens. "Please tell us what's in the wallet."

David named the items as he took them out and laid them on the rail in front of him. "Two credit cards, a Visa and an American Express. A SunTrust cash flow card. A Starbucks gift card. Four twenty-dollar bills. And two business cards."

"Is that all that was in the wallet when you turned it over to defense counsel?"

"I think so, but I didn't make an inventory."

"What name is on the credit cards?"

"Larry Smith."

"And on the business cards?"

"Larry Smith."

"So your best guess as to the name of John Doe, the decedent in this case, would be…"

"Objection," I said. The questions called for a conclusion, and Biggs hadn't established David Stevens as an expert in determining the identities of dead men.

The judge glared at me, but he sustained the objection. Biggs turned to me and said with exaggerated sweetness. "You may inquire."

Standing at my table, I said, "I assume that the prosecution has granted you immunity in exchange for your testimony?"

"We, ah, discussed it."

"You didn't get it in writing?"

"Well, yes. Actually we did exchange some paperwork."

"So you lied just now when you said you merely discussed it."

"I didn't say merely."

"So you were merely misleading the court through omission," I said. "Very good. You mentioned that your brother Mark was concerned that something incriminating might be found in his daughter's bedroom. Did he express these concerns to you?"

"Yes, he did."

"In person?"

"No. Over the telephone."

"Never in person?"

"No. Mark is in China on business."

"Text messages? Email?"

"No, just the phone, I think."

"But you've kept in touch."

"Sporadically."

"Only sporadically? Even after he learned that his daughter had been arrested and charged with murder?"

"He's moving around all over China. It's all we've been able to work out."

"Really," I said. "He couldn't break away and come home to be with his only daughter when she's on trial for murder."

"He's putting together the biggest deal our company has ever had, and there's not much he could do here, is there?"

"Isn't there? There's been some testimony that a Mark Stevens rented a motel room right next to the room rented to Natalie on that fateful Sunday night. I don't believe you were in the courtroom. Have you heard anything about that testimony?"

"Yes, something about it."

"Could you tell us on what day your brother Mark left Richmond for China?"

David's glance slid to Aubrey Biggs and returned to me. "The morning of December 7."

I'd expected to have to use documentary evidence to prove the flight out, but of course David Stevens knew I could do it. Given the district attorney's lack of a reaction, I assumed he had briefed Aubrey Biggs. "That would be Monday morning," I said, "the day after this man the prosecutor wants us to call Larry Smith met his death. The very day that Natalie Stevens was arrested for murder."

David coughed, cleared his throat. "Actually, I think she was originally charged with manslaughter."

"Could you tell us when Mark Stevens returned from China?"

"He hasn't returned."

"The Cathay Airlines flight Mark Stevens took from LAX to Hong Kong was scheduled to arrive at 9:55 p.m. on Tuesday, December eighth. Did it arrive at that time, as far as you know?"

"I don't know anything about it."

"Another Cathay Airlines flight left Hong Kong for LAX at 5:35 a.m. on December ninth," I said.

"If you say so."

"I have the flight manifest here." I took some stapled pages from a folder, and looked up at the judge. "May I approach the witness?" He nodded, and I took one copy of the manifest to the judge, handed another to the witness, and took a third copy to Aubrey Biggs.

Biggs, looking at it, said, "Where did you get this? It hasn't been authenticated."

"I'm not asking for admission into evidence at this time. Mr. Stevens, do you see the name of Mark Stevens on that manifest?"

David turned the pages. "No, I don't. Is it supposed to be here?"

"Do you see any other name of interest? The name of Larry Smith perhaps?"

He flapped back through the pages.

"Page three," I said. "About halfway down." While I waited for him to answer, I got another set of stapled pages from the folder on my table, and I delivered copies all around. "Perhaps you can find the name on this manifest. It's an American Airlines flight from LAX to Dulles Airport that left LAX two-and-a-half hours after the flight from Hong Kong arrived. Look at the second page near the bottom."

"Larry Smith," Stevens read softly. There was some whispering going on at the prosecutor's table.

"Quite a coincidence, isn't it?"

"Larry Smith is a common name."

"Yes, isn't it? It is surprising, though, to find it on yet another manifest, this one for a flight from Dulles to Richmond International that left Dulles after a fifty-five minute layover." I handed around yet another set of stapled pages. "Mark Stevens had a motel room right next door to the room where murder was committed Sunday night, and the next morning he left for Hong Kong. Mere hours after he arrived there, one Larry Smith left Hong Kong and returned to Richmond, Virginia, arriving late Wednesday evening. On Thursday you gave me Larry Smith's wallet, minus the driver's license and passport, minus any identification at all that included a photograph."

David Stevens didn't say anything. At the prosecution table Aubrey Biggs was sitting stiffly upright, and his left leg jigged up and down beneath the table.

I said, "Which of those credit cards on the rail there in front of you paid for Larry Smith's flight? Was it the Visa or the American Express?"

David Stevens seemed to have been struck dumb.

I turned to the jury. "Murder was committed. Mark Stevens left, and no one has seen him since, though two people have testified to speaking to him on the phone. That would be his trophy wife Chloe Stevens and his brother, the man sitting on the stand in front of us."

Ralph Waldo, glancing at his boss, said, "Objection. That's not a question."

Rodney Burns came into the courtroom carrying a file folder.

"Could I have just a moment?" I asked the judge.

Judge Cheatham drew in a breath, but let it out again without speaking. I took it for assent and went to the rail to take the folder from Rodney.

"Question," I said, turning to the witness. "You and your brother look quite a bit alike, don't you, Mr. Stevens? A desk clerk who had seen you at a Best Western, say, might subsequently identify a picture of your brother as the man she had seen."

David shook his head. "No. We don't look so much alike."

"You don't look alike?"

"No, I don't think so."

"Not so much alike that if you came into possession of a plane ticket issued to your brother, you would be able to take the flight in his place using his identification as if it were your own?"

"Of course not."

"You flew to Hong Kong as Mark Stevens that Monday, didn't you? That way, when he turned up missing, he would have disappeared in China, not right here in Richmond, Virginia. You flew back as Larry Smith."

He had a sneer on this face, but there were beads of sweat on his cheeks and forehead. "That's a complete fabrication, and you know it."

There were three copies of Larry Smith's driver's license in the folder. Bestowing a silent blessing on Rodney Burns, I delivered one to the judge, one to Aubrey Biggs, and one to the witness stand. David Stevens' hand shook as he took it.

"What I have handed you is a certified copy of a driver's license made out to one Larry Gholson Smith. Could you tell us whose picture is on that driver's license?"

"No."

"It's not familiar to you? Not at all?" I retrieved the copy of the driver's license from him and walked in front of the jury box with it, taking my time as they craned their necks, making sure they all got a good look at it. I took it back to the witness.

"To me it looks like you."

David shrugged. "It's not. It can't be." His face, though, was now gleaming with perspiration.

"It was Chloe Stevens who checked into the Best Western that Sunday night, wasn't it? She used a credit card she had applied for in the name of Natalie Stevens. She was there to meet you."

"No."

Brooke Marshall entered at the back of the courtroom. With her was a broad-shouldered man wearing a sports jacket over a shirt with an open collar. He carried a white Tyvek envelope—and Brooke's hair was mussed.

"I'm sorry. If I could have just one more moment." I went back to my table, got a copy of the autopsy report and took it into the gallery to give to the man with Brooke. "Second page," I told him. As I walked back to the lectern, I said, "That's your brother's dentist. He's going to be comparing your

298

brother's dental records to the dental record in the autopsy report of John Doe. You were having an affair with your brother's wife, weren't you?"

David was shaking his head, but he looked punch drunk.

I said, "Mark Stevens had become suspicious of his wife. He was supposed to be on a business trip somewhere, and he told everyone he would be leaving the country without coming home. He did that in hopes that Chloe would become careless. He did come home, of course. Mark Stevens followed his wife to the Best Western, and he managed to rent the motel room right next to hers. When you and Chloe were in her room together, he forced his way in or got you to open the door somehow. You panicked. Or Chloe panicked. Which of you was it who shot him with the gun that had been taken from his house, the Glock 32 that was registered in his name? Was it you?"

David's lips moved, but no sound came out. He might have been mouthing the name *Chloe*.

Natalie was suddenly on her feet, turning toward the gallery. "You," she said to Chloe. Chloe started up, and Natalie stepped toward the rail and reached across it to grab her by the front of her dress and drag her half across. Chloe's eyes were round and staring. "You killed my daddy, you bitch." Natalie slammed her forehead down into Chloe's exposed face, then twisted, dragging Chloe over the rail and throwing her onto the defense table, which she slid across, taking my legal pads and folders and papers with her. Even as she landed on the floor, blood spattering from her nose onto the industrial carpet, the deputy sheriff was seizing Natalie and forcing her face down over the table, pulling one wrist behind her and then the other to cuff her.

In the confusion David Stevens left the witness stand and strode head down toward the gallery. I moved to block him, but my heel turned on me as I stepped around the lectern, and I staggered. When his hand shot out, I failed to dodge it, and it caught me in the shoulder. I spun and fell, landing on my butt with my legs splayed out in front of me. David Stevens was through the bar, striding down the center aisle, when Paul Soldano appeared in the aisle just beyond him.

"Move, fat man," Stevens lowered his shoulder and drove into him.

Paul's stance shifted subtly, his arms reaching out, his hands clutching as he fell backward, pulling Stevens with him, twisting at the last instant so that Stevens landed on his back with Paul's forearm across his chest. All the spectators, even the jurors, were standing, some moving and calling out, and Judge Cheatham, on his feet, was waving the stick of his headless gavel and pounding on the bench with his open hand in a vain effort to restore order to his courtroom.

Chapter 30

Judge Cheatham dismissed the contempt charges against me. Though I had been indecorous in court, I hadn't withheld any documents belonging to the murder victim. Aubrey Biggs, much as he might like to, couldn't charge me as Natalie's accessory-after-the-fact because he couldn't prove Natalie herself to be guilty of any crime. The motions and the arguments and the paperwork took most of the afternoon, but at the end of it, Natalie was free, and David and Chloe Stevens were in custody.

With some difficulty, I talked Natalie into joining Brooke, Paul, and me for dinner. "I really just want to sleep," she said.

"I know. You need to mourn your father."

"I just feel drugged."

"You've lost weight in jail. Come with us, we won't drag it out."

Before six, we were back at Enrique's, a couple of bowls of chips and a pitcher of margaritas in front of us along with four frosted mugs.

"At least there's one good thing about going out to eat with old people," Natalie said.

Brooke and Paul and I exchanged glances.

"You don't get carded," Natalie said. She poured herself a margarita, then lifted her mug to us and took a long swallow.

"Good?" Paul said, watching her.

She wiped her mouth with the back of her wrist. "The best thing I've felt since Chloe's nose splattered against my forehead."

"I bet."

"I knew something was wrong. Daddy would have come home if he could."

Paul made a face, nodding sympathetically.

I said, "Dragging Chloe across the rail and throwing her across the defense table was an amazing bit of athleticism."

Natalie was blinking, but she held up a hand. "Don't worry. I'll cry later. Tonight I'm going to eat, and I'm going to drink a little too much, and I'm going to think about how much pain and money it's going to cost Chloe to get her nose set straight again."

"If it can be done at all," I said.

Brooke raised her mug. "If it can be done at all," she said. We clinked mugs and drank, Natalie managing a smile despite her watery eyes.

"How did you come to show up in the nick of time?" Brooke said to Paul. "I thought you were in meetings all day."

"All morning. I walked over when I got out, thinking I might be in time to catch the fireworks. Who'd have thought I'd get to participate?"

"Good thing, too," I said. "David Stevens had a wallet in his jacket with credit cards and a driver's license in the name of Robert Ingalsbe. If he'd made it through that door, he might have disappeared forever."

"It was a pretty impressive move," Brooke said to Paul. "His feet actually flew up over his head."

Paul sat back, his chest expanding. "I was on the wrestling team in high school," he said, wagging his head in mock solemnity. Then he shrugged. "Briefly. You got to witness my signature move. Actually, if I'd known then that he was the one who shot Robin, I wouldn't have been so gentle."

"You paralyzed his diaphragm," I protested. "He couldn't breathe."

"But he did eventually."

"Fat man beats pretty boy," Brooke said. She popped a tortilla chip in her mouth.

"Hey, let's go easy on the labels."

"At least it let him know that sleeping with his brother's wife and fratricide are big no-noes," I said. "He told me once that dog law is the only kind of law he understands."

"What's dog law?" Brooke asked.

"It's beating or hanging people for bad behavior to let them know they've done wrong—like a dog-owner might train his pet. What I want to know is what happened to your hair. It was perfectly arranged when I first saw you this morning, but when you showed up in court with that dentist, it was all over the place. You didn't..."

"No, I did not." She jerked her chin at me and took a sip of her margarita.

"Well?"

"Well I may have rubbed my head against his chest a little when I was persuading him." She giggled.

"It turns out that Dr. Davis is single. Forty years old and never been married. I think he's a little shy."

"You don't think he just seemed shy because a woman he'd never met before came in and started rubbing her head against his chest?"

The waiter came with a huge round tray loaded with food, and Natalie put her mug down, empty.

"You want to spend the night with Deeks and me again?" I asked her as the waiter placed a sizzling pan of fajitas in front of her.

"I don't know yet. We'll see."

"Fair enough."

"What are you going to be doing now that you're not busy saving me?" she asked me.

"Tomorrow I'm going to stay home with my dog," I said. "Take some time to recuperate."

"How about Monday?"

I shrugged. "Go back to playing solitaire until another case walks through the door."

"After today, you should be getting a pile of business," Paul said. "A pile."

"I don't know what property Chloe has her name on and what she's going to inherit," Natalie said to me.

"She won't inherit anything, not if Aubrey Biggs does his job right," I said.

"I'd have more confidence in you doing your job right."

"Here, here," Paul said, and we all had another slug of lime juice, triple sec, and tequila.

"And something's got to happen with Steven's Imports. It's set up as a partnership between Daddy and Uncle David. Last year Daddy told me his share was worth five or six million dollars."

"You might be able to afford me," I said. "Two hundred dollars an hour won't put a dent in that fortune."

"So you'll help me?"

It was a job offer. I nodded. "You bet."

Her phone dinged, and she bent her head over it.

"What about you? What are you going to do?" I asked her.

She looked up. "Go back to school. I've only missed four days."

"Can I help?"

She shook her head. "Austin's on her way. My roommate at Longwood? She's going to spend the night with me, and we'll drive back to Farmville tomorrow."

"Here, here," Paul said again, picking up the pitcher and refilling our glasses.

"What is this?" Brooke said. "Some kind of drinking game?"

"This is how a fat man goes about getting his girlfriend tipsy to lower her inhibitions." He raised his mug and smiled at me hopefully.

"Oh, what the heck." I picked up my own mug and clinked it against his.